SONG OF THE HEART

Medieval Runaway Wives
Book 1

Alexa Aston

Dragonblade Publishing, Inc. is an imprint of Kathryn Le Veque Novels, Inc.
P.O. Box 7968
La Verne CA 91750
ceo@dragonbladepublishing.com

Produced in the United States of America

First Edition July 2020
Mass Market Paperback Edition

Dearest Reader;

Thank you for your support of a small press. At Dragonblade Publishing, we strive to bring you the highest quality Historical Romance from the some of the best authors in the business. Without your support, there is no 'us', so we sincerely hope you adore these stories and find some new favorite authors along the way.

Happy Reading!

CEO, Dragonblade Publishing

Additional Dragonblade books by Author Alexa Aston

Medieval Runaway Wives
Song of the Heart

King's Cousins Series
The Pawn
The Heir
The Bastard

Knights of Honor Series
Word of Honor
Marked by Honor
Code of Honor
Journey to Honor
Heart of Honor
Bold in Honor
Love and Honor
Gift of Honor
Path to Honor
Return to Honor

The St. Clairs Series
Devoted to the Duke
Midnight with the Marquess
Embracing the Earl
Defending the Duke

Suddenly a St. Clair
Starlight Night

Soldiers & Soulmates Series
To Heal an Earl
To Tame a Rogue
To Trust a Duke
To Save a Love
To Win a Widow

The Lyon's Den Connected World
The Lyon's Lady Love

PROLOGUE

August 1327—Stanbury

GARRETT STANBRIDGE, EARL of Montayne, left the training yard and made his way toward the keep. The summer day had been sweltering and he was drenched in sweat from sparring with his men throughout the long afternoon. He wanted a cold bath and colder tankard of ale, not necessarily in that order. Racing up the staircase that led to the keep, he pushed open the heavy door and entered, the cool washing over him. He spied Annie, his daughter's nurse, carrying Lyssa down the stairs and went to them.

Leaning forward, he pressed a kiss to Lyssa's brow.

"How are you, my sweet girl?" he asked and

she smiled, reaching her chubby arms toward him.

"I am much too dirty to hold you, Lyssa. Once I've cleaned up, you may sit on my knee and I'll tell you a story or two." He turned to Annie. "Would you have water sent up for a cool bath if Lady Lynnette has not already done so?"

"Yes, my lord."

He left and hurried up the stairs to the solar, ready to tell his wife about his day. It surprised him that she was not already waiting there for him. Usually, Lynnette made a special effort to be present when he returned to the keep each day. Though very shy—and very young when they'd wed—she tried her best to please him in small ways. He was hoping she would soon have good news for him. He'd noticed her belly seemed slightly rounded two nights ago when he'd made love to her and prayed that she was with child again. They'd lost their firstborn, a son, last June, shortly after Lyssa's birth. While Garrett doted on his daughter, he knew he needed sons to keep Stanbury strong.

He set aside his sword and stripped off his clothes, leaving them in a pile on the floor. Several servants brought in buckets of water and poured them into the copper tub. Once they left, he eased into it and lathered well before rinsing and drying off. Feeling refreshed as he dressed again, Garrett wondered what might be keeping

Lynnette. Mayhap she had gotten distracted in her garden, which she loved to tend. More likely, she and Edith, his mother, sat in the great hall and played with Lyssa, encouraging her as she toddled about. The girl was just learning to walk, despite being almost sixteen months old. Richard had begun moving upright at nine months, delighting his parents with every step. Still, Garrett understood why Lyssa lagged behind her brother's progress. Her mother was reluctant to put her down. Ever since the fever took Richard from them, Lynnette clung to their remaining child. It was only thanks to his mother's encouragement that Lynnette had finally begun allowing Lyssa to explore more on her own two feet.

His belly grumbled noisily and Garrett returned downstairs. The great hall was filled with people ready to partake in the evening meal. He moved toward the dais and greeted his mother with a kiss to her cheek.

"Where is Lynnette?" he asked, beginning to be concerned.

"I haven't seen her in several hours. Do you think she's lost track of the time?"

"It's not like her to do so," he replied as he gazed across the great hall, hoping to spy her in conversation with someone.

They took their places as servants brought them trenchers and cups of wine. Garrett ate, uneasiness filling him. Lynnette was predictable, doing the same tasks every day. To miss greeting him in the solar and helping with his bath was surprising. To miss the evening meal was unthinkable.

"I'm going to look for her," he told his mother, leaving most of his food untouched.

Leaving the dais, he spoke to several servants. None had seen the countess for hours. Garrett returned to the solar and found it empty. He wandered the corridors, calling her name, even opening various doors to no avail. Finally, he went to Lyssa's bedchamber, where Annie rocked the girl to sleep.

Quietly, he asked, "When was the last time you saw Lady Lynnette?"

"She decided to go riding after the midday meal," the servant replied. "She wishes to gain more confidence upon a horse."

Garrett turned abruptly and headed for the stables. Concern filled him. Lynnette was a poor rider, too timid to manage a horse who knew when its rider was unsure. It had aggravated him when she arrived as his bride. He'd given her lessons but none seemed to take. She tried sporadically to master the skill but had never kept with it for long. He felt guilty because he knew she always tried to please him. This latest effort at attempting to master riding was most likely due to her wanting to achieve a sense of ease upon a horse to make him proud of her.

He reached the stables and found Barth, his head groom. The man looked nervous when he spied his liege lord and Garrett guessed why. He could smell the alcohol on Barth's breath from several feet away.

"Were you here when Lady Lynnette went out to ride?" he demanded, overlooking Barth's drunkenness for now because of his growing concern regarding Lynnette.

"I saddled her horse myself, my lord. And Stephen's. He was to accompany her. But he didn't."

"Why not?"

Though the grounds surrounding Stanbury were thought to be safe, Garrett always cautioned Lynnette to take someone with her on her rides. She'd become too nervous to ride with him, feeling he judged her with every mistake she made, and so she'd taken to asking their reeve to ride with her on the few occasions she went out.

The groom shrugged. "You'll have to ask him, my lord."

"What time did she return?"

"I . . . I don't know." Barth swallowed, his eyes cast to the ground. "I've been busy."

Garrett strode down the row of stalls and came to a stop where Lynnette's horse was.

The stall was empty.

A sick feeling washed over him. She'd ridden

out by herself and hadn't returned. She could be hurt, thrown from the saddle, unable to walk. Or worse. He pushed that thought aside and hurried back to the keep. Entering the great hall, he spied his reeve and motioned to him. Stephen excused himself from the men he conversed with and came toward him.

"Yes, my lord? You have need of me?"

"I do. Why did you not accompany Lady Lynnette on her ride today? She is missing. Her horse isn't in its stall. I need to organize a search party to find her." He glared at the reeve. "None of this would have been necessary if you would have gone with her."

The reeve's solemn look as he gazed at Garrett made him go cold inside.

"Could you come with me, my lord?" Stephen asked and hurried from the boisterous noise of the great hall.

He followed but as soon as they reached the entryway, he called for the reeve to stop.

"I have no time for nonsense. I need to organize the search."

Stephen shook his head. "I fear . . . you will not find the countess, my lord."

Garrett seized the reeve's shoulders. "Why do you say that? What has become of her?"

"She is mostly like gone."

"Gone? Gone where?"

Sadness filled Stephen's face. "Gone from

Stanbury. With another."

He tightened his hold. "What do you mean? You're talking in circles."

"She's left with another man," the reeve ground out.

Garrett's hands fell away. "Another man?" he asked, not comprehending what he was being told.

"My lord, I should have told you," Stephen began. "I . . . I did not know how to do so." He swallowed. "Twice, Lady Lynnette went riding recently. She wouldn't allow me to accompany her either time. I worried about her. She is still a novice in the saddle after all this time. I decided to follow her at a distance. And that's when I saw them. In the woods."

"Saw who?" His belly tightened.

"A knight, my lord. One I did not recognize. Tall with dark hair. They . . . spoke at some length."

"And?" he demanded, nausea filling him.

Stephen looked miserable as he said, "They appeared to be quite close, my lord. They were familiar with one another."

Garrett didn't have to ask what the reeve meant. He understood that Stephen had witnessed Lynnette kissing this stranger. Or something even more intimate between them.

"I left my lady in the forest with this knight," Stephen said, shaking his head. "I thought she would return. Now, I'm not so sure. I fear there were more of these clandestine meetings that I knew nothing of. And that this knight convinced the countess to run away with him."

The words were like a physical blow. Garrett reeled from what he'd learned.

"No. It couldn't be," he said, dumbfounded. "She wouldn't leave me. Leave Lyssa."

Yet how much did he really know about his shy wife? Had she been in love with another man before she arrived for her arranged marriage at Stanbury? Had this man from her past come for her? Convinced her to flee with him? Were Garrett and Lyssa merely reminders of the babe they'd lost and she'd needed to get away?

The answers might drive him mad.

"We must look for her," he said with determination. "Find my captain of the guard and have him bring every soldier to the inner bailey at once."

Stephen hurried away as Garrett paced restlessly. His mother emerged from the great hall and came toward him.

"What troubles you, my son? Did you find Lynnette?"

"No."

Briefly, he recounted what the reeve had revealed. Shock filled his mother's face.

"Do you truly believe Lynnette would abandon her husband and child?" she asked. "It seems so unlike her. She is as timid as a mouse, Garrett."

"Mayhap I never knew her."

He thought back and realized how little his wife had spoken during their conversations. How he'd always talked about Stanbury and his soldiers. Their tenants. The harvests. Other than knowing his wife enjoyed time in her herb garden, Garrett was hard pressed to think of anything else about her—other than she had been a good mother. Had Richard's untimely death caused something to break within her?

He might never know—unless they found her.

Venturing into the inner bailey, he addressed the gathered soldiers. Garrett did not mention the unnamed knight or Stephen's suspicions. He merely explained how Lynnette had gone riding and never returned and he feared she lay hurt somewhere nearby.

"We must find her," he said firmly, believing they would.

The search that night proved fruitless. Garrett rode out many nights after that in all directions, asking others if they'd seen Lynnette. He described her appearance in detail, mentioning the necklace that she always wore, which he knew would stand out. The emerald stones had been his wedding gift to her, its clasp made up of a lion holding a sword. Each time, he returned home emptyhanded—and bitter.

Gradually, he ceased hunting for the woman who never sent word as to her whereabouts.

And never came home.

CHAPTER ONE

April 1331—Frothmore—home of Lord Ancil

MADELEINE PERCHED ON the edge of the enormous bed, her mouth dry, her heart beating wildly. Every night for the last three years had led to this moment. She hadn't known when the time to flee would arrive, but she knew she would recognize when the time was right. Tonight felt right, despite the obstacles to overcome. For one, she was in a foreign country. Even though she spoke English as well as a native, her journey would still be treacherous. She might make a mistake, one that would label her an outsider. Or even get her killed. She couldn't afford a misstep.

She flinched as she heard heavy footsteps echoing along the stone corridor. For such a tall, gaunt man, Henri de Picassaret made too much noise when he was drunk. When sober, though, her husband could be as stealthy as a cat stalking a mouse. These days, Henri hounded his own wife.

Madeleine swallowed hard and tried to calm herself. He must not suspect anything. She forced a serene smile onto her lips as the door crashed open.

Henri staggered in, his valet, Bertrand, scurrying after his master. Madeleine glanced quickly at the portly, balding servant. He wore a pained expression upon his sallow face and merely shook his head.

Bertrand steadied Henri and guided him toward the bed. Madeleine automatically rose and took Henri's other arm. Together, they managed to get the older man to the bed.

"My head aches," Henri complained, his words deeply slurred. "My stomach pains me."

Madeleine caught a whiff of alcohol on his breath. Usually, Henri drank only the finest French champagne, turning his nose up at other brews. When in England, though, he tried to accommodate his host's wish. Lord Ancil must have been serving a particularly strong mead. She grimaced at the sour smell that rose from her husband.

Madeleine nodded at Bertrand, signaling him to leave. "You know English food rarely agrees with you, Henri," she said lightly. "I have prepared one of my mother's soothing drinks to calm you."

Henri snorted. "Nothing could soothe my stomach now, Wife. Not even one of Cadena's mystical remedies."

Fear rushed through Madeleine's veins. He *must* drink from the cup tonight. Somehow, she must convince him—or she'd never escape her nightmare.

"Henri, be reasonable. You want to feel well enough to attend mass, do you not?"

Her husband never missed daily mass. Not that he was a particularly religious man. In fact, he went strictly to pray for his own good health. He bragged that he'd made a pact with God—his attendance at mass in exchange for his physical well-being. Henri was fanatical when it came to his health. Madeleine hoped her words would persuade him. She waited anxiously for his response.

"Ah, *Mon Dieu.* Give me the cup," he snarled.

Thank you, Sweet Jesu. Madeleine sent her own grateful prayer to God. She reached for the drink sitting on the bedside table and placed the pewter cup into her husband's hands.

"I was able to mix your medicine with a little wine. Hopefully, that will hide the medicinal taste. I'm sure the wine, too, will help settle your stomach."

Henri took a swig of the brew, his mouth creasing with disgust. He did, however, finish the contents of the cup. Escape would have been impossible otherwise.

"Disrobe me," he ordered.

Madeleine complied, glad it would be the last time she saw his pasty flesh. Though her husband was extremely thin from eating sparsely, his belly, round and bloated, protruded from his almost skeletal frame. She credited that to all the champagne he drank. If she never tasted the frothy wine again, it would be too soon, for it would always remind her of Henri.

She helped him into the bed and quickly covered his pale skin with the linen sheets then walked quietly to the other side and slipped under the covers. She was thankful Henri did not speak. She was too tense, her nerves too raw. Soon, his breathing slowed and deep snores filled the chamber.

It was time.

She crept from the bed and quietly dressed. Her fingers trembled as she slipped on her smock, kirtle, and cotehardie. Thanks to the number of jewels she had sewn into her garments' hems, the clothing was quite heavy. Henri had always lamented that she was useless at any of the womanly arts—sewing tapestries, supervising the household, or having babies.

That thought brought her pain. When she

married Henri three years earlier, she'd longed for babies and knew her husband was eager to have a son who would inherit the de Picassaret vineyards one day. She had imagined filling the chateau with many sons and daughters, hearing their laughter, teaching and loving them as her own devoted parents had done for her and her brother.

After she saw what life with Henri would be like, she hungered for babies even more. Though it might seem selfish on her part to want to bring a child into the world whose father was a monster, Madeleine had abundant love in her heart to give to little ones—but it was not to be. Just like her husband's two previous wives, she was barren. But throughout the last year she had harbored wicked thoughts concerning this and had foolishly voiced them to Henri one night. She accused *him* of being the barren one, his seed worthless in her womb.

She had paid dearly for those rash words. Henri had beaten her many times before, for even the smallest infraction, but that night was different. Usually, he only abused her back or legs, not wanting to mar what the world saw. This time, he struck her face repeatedly until her eyes had swollen shut. She also now carried a small scar at the top of her cheekbone, courtesy of his signet ring—and uncontrollable rage. Worst of all, he'd broken her knee in the vicious attack. As a result, she now walked with a slight limp.

Madeleine pushed aside the painful memories. It was obvious Henri grew tired of her. She wasn't the young, malleable girl and hadn't produced an heir. Instinct told her that her life was in danger. She didn't believe his previous wives' deaths were accidents. The opportunity to escape her nightmarish existence might never present itself again.

She crossed the chamber and reached for her lute, the one possession she valued above all others. She refused to leave the beloved instrument behind. Retrieving the rope from its hiding place under the bed, she stood and took one last look at her sleeping husband. No love filled her heart, no honor, nor loyalty. Henri had beaten any feeling she'd ever had for him out of her long ago.

She made her way hastily through the dim corridor and down the staircase. Fortunately, the layout of Frothmore was simple. In this time of peace, the sally port outside remained unguarded. Reaching it, though, would take every bit of courage she possessed. She couldn't leave using the entrance to the keep, knowing Lord Ancil had a handful of men guarding the door on the outside. Instead, she would escape from a small window she'd located upon their arrival and head toward the sally port—and freedom.

Reaching it, the chill of the night air struck her. She realized she'd left her cloak in the bedchamber and regretted her carelessness. Still, she'd rather catch her death of cold than remain with Henri one more night. Escape must occur now, in this moment.

She placed her lute on the ground and first wrapped the rope around and then knotted one end of it to the heavy, ornamental wall sconce nearby, praying it would hold her weight. She lowered the rest of the length through the window. It disappeared into the darkness. For a moment, Madeleine clasped the rope but didn't move. Heights terrified her but she must conquer her fear. She quelled the rising nausea as her stomach roiled and prayed for God to keep her safe.

She released the rope and, looping a scarf through her girdle, she swept it under the strings of her lute, tying the instrument securely to her waist. Once again, she gripped the rope and climbed up and through the window, grateful she was slender since it was so narrow. She only had a short distance to go and squeezed her eyes shut as she lowered herself. When her feet touched the ground, she expelled the breath she'd held. Only then did she dare open her eyes.

"Thank the Christ," she murmured, trying to calm her racing heart.

Skirting buildings and staying in the shadows

as much as she could, Madeleine finally reached the wall that surrounded Frothmore and moved close against it so she wouldn't be spotted, knowing the posted sentries watched for activity outside the walls and not from within. She made her way to the north side, toward London. Once she arrived in the city, she'd pawn enough jewels to purchase passage back to France. She would return to Bordeaux and her parents, if only for a short while.

Henri had allowed no contact with her parents since their marriage. He said she was immature and too dependent upon them and that she must learn to rely only upon him. Madeleine later learned he'd told her parents the break was at her request. She could only guess at the heartbreak his cruel words caused.

She was determined to see her *Maman* and *Papa* once more and tell them how very much she loved them before she took refuge in a convent. She was sure Pierre could arrange sanctuary for her. Her brother was ten years older and though they'd never been close, Madeleine knew she could count on him to help her in a time of crisis. Let Henri have the marriage annulled or, better yet, let him divorce her. She did not care to give herself to any man ever again. The marriage act only brought terror. Pain and degradation. She could no longer tolerate it. She'd seek refuge and peace with the good sisters. Her jewels would assure her of a place in the convent until her death.

Madeleine found the almost hidden door she was searching for and slipped through it. A sally port could be overlooked during a siege due to its size. Messengers used it in times of trouble. Many a sally port had been the saving grace for a castle's people during times of attack.

It would be her saving grace tonight.

As she cautiously crept away from the wall surrounding Frothmore, she watched over her shoulder for any sentry that might raise the alarm. With each step, fear enveloped her, causing her heart to pound, its loud drumming ringing in her ears.

Madeleine saw a guard move along the wall walk and gaze in her direction. She froze. Panic poured through her at being out in the open. Every muscle screamed for her to flee yet she pushed her fear aside. Movement would attract his attention. She remained stock still, holding her breath. The brisk wind favored her. The clouds blew constantly across the light from the moon, causing many shadows to dance upon the earth. She watched the sentry turn, his back now to her. Without hesitation, Madeleine made for the nearest trees at a steady gait. She reached the copse and entered without hearing a shout to halt.

Safe. She was safe.

She sank to her knees. A thrill rushed through her. She touched the ground almost reverently, brushing her fingers along the cool grass.

Freedom!

She could not remember the last time she'd been outside alone. Henri had a guard follow her wherever she went. He rarely allowed her outside the walls of his isolated chateau in the north. Madeleine breathed in the crisp air, reveling in the sounds of the night. She was practical, though, and knew her sojourn would be a long one. She must put distance between her and Frothmore before the sun rose and she was discovered to be missing.

Keeping to the edge of the woods, she finally reached the road north and began walking as swiftly as her knee would allow. After a mile or so, she began humming, softly at first, but with each step the volume grew. Madeleine relished her newfound liberty on the dark road to London. She thought it best to travel at night since almost all travelers would move during the day. She also would need to steal food along the way, and this would be better accomplished under cover of darkness. She didn't know how far London lay ahead but surely she could manage for a few days in this manner.

As Madeleine continued, she began to sing. Music had always been a large part of her life. She had been thankful that Henri allowed her to play.

It was the one thing she did in which he'd found no fault. While she sang, Madeleine thought of Yves, the troubadour that had showed up at her parents' home long ago to entertain guests. He sang for his supper that night and had never left Chateau Branais. Through the years, Yves become part of their family, teaching Madeleine all she knew about music. He'd told her she was the most gifted songbird in all of France.

She smiled, remembering Yves' praise, knowing she was fortunate to hear a song but once and the melody became engraved on her heart. It allowed thousands of songs to be locked into her memory. Yves regretted that she could not go out as a troubadour but everyone knew that the troubadours of France were always men.

Still, Madeleine used to entertain her parents and visitors that had come to the Bordeaux vineyard they managed for the wealthy English Stanbridge family. Henri had been one of the many visitors who came to discuss the grape. Obsession with the grape was a national pastime in France. Her father, Robert, thought Henri had good business sense and admired the wines the older man produced. When Henri asked for Madeleine's hand in marriage, her father had acquiesced.

Her mother was not as certain. It had been a love match for Cadena from the first time she'd seen Robert. She had wanted that for her only daughter, as well. She'd tried to persuade her husband to let Madeleine marry someone closer to her own age, even an Englishman. Cadena herself had been an English bride come to France and she raised Madeleine so that she was fluent in both languages of her parents.

Robert refused, knowing Madeleine would never have the opportunity to marry as wealthy a man as Henri de Picassaret. Yes, the man had bad luck with wives—one had died of a fever and the other was rumored to have taken her own life—but his daughter was young and strong and could give Henri many sons.

As her trek continued, Madeleine untied her lute, which continued to bump against her. She didn't mind carrying the instrument. After an hour, she began to experience some discomfort. She shifted her boot and forced herself onward. After a few steps, the problem returned. She halted and held her foot out in front of her, rotating her ankle. Feeling better, she started down the road again. Whatever it was began bothering her immediately.

Frustrated, she sat down in the middle of the road, her lute next to her, and removed the leather boot. She stuck a finger inside, feeling around for what irritated her foot, and grasped a tiny rock. She clucked her tongue at the culprit of her distress, holding the pebble up in the moonlight for further inspection.

"I think I shall call you *Henri*, little pebble, for being the source of all my discomfort." She tucked the smooth stone into her pocket, determined to let it be a reminder to her in the future of the troubles she'd escaped.

Madeleine started to sing a tender ballad that reminded her of her parents as she slipped her boot back on. When she'd married Henri, she assumed love would grow quickly between her and her wedded husband, just as it had for her parents. The song died on her lips at the thought.

Oh, how she had been proven wrong.

CHAPTER TWO

Stanbury

GARRETT PACED RESTLESSLY as Lyssa opened a gift from her grandmother. His daughter was five years of age today. It was the fourth birthday his wife had missed.

The thought of Lynnette brought a quick sting to his eyes. Aggravated, he turned away from the assembled group in the great hall and took a long pull of the mulled wine, draining the cup in one swallow.

Lynnette.

His insides ached just thinking her name. He still could not guess, even after so long a time, why she left with another man. Theirs had been an arranged marriage, like most of his class and rank, but a genuine affection existed between them. Or so he'd thought. They laughed at the good times and had cried together when their son, Richard, succumbed to a fever shortly before his second birthday.

Still, they had little Lyssa, barely six weeks old at the time of her brother's death. Garrett assumed they would have many more children but he'd been proven wrong. Lynnette's unexpected disappearance put an abrupt end to that. Though he'd ridden out for weeks on his own in search of his wife, she seemed to have vanished without a trace. Finally, he could no longer hide from the truth. His wife had deserted him and their daughter for her lover.

Garrett spat upon the floor in disgust, angry at himself for still caring about her. At times, his marriage didn't seem real. He could barely remember what Lynnette looked like, and then he would catch a glimpse of her in Lyssa and memories of Lynnette would come flooding back.

Ashby rose from the party of merrymakers, a thoughtful look upon his face. Garrett knew his childhood friend worried about him. It was true Garrett had lost his sense of humor these past few years and was in a black mood more often than not. His fits of depression could last for days, even weeks, and it was becoming harder and harder to rouse himself from his gloom.

Garrett poured another glass of wine and

drank the contents in a single swallow, his eyes daring Ashby to say anything. Before, his drinking had been of little consequence. In fact, he usually became quite lighthearted when he partook in a few cups of wine. Now, the more he drank, his mood turned ugly to hateful.

Lyssa squealed in delight, drawing her father's attention. "Oh, Papa, Papa! Come here, Papa!"

Garrett set his cup down and went to her, a smile upon his face. Despite everything, he always tried to be a good father to his only child. He was a family man at heart and relished the times when he pulled Lyssa into his lap and listened to her prattle on in the engaging way she had about her.

"What is it, Lyssa?"

"Look at what Aga made me," she said excitedly.

Garrett took the doll Lyssa handed him and glanced toward his mother. Edith gave him a tentative smile, wary of her son's mood. He'd been curt to her—to all women—since Lynnette abandoned her family. Part of it was not knowing where his wife had gone. Part came from knowing he could not marry again and beget an heir for Stanbury. He had soured on all women, not understanding how a wife could desert her husband and babe. The bitterness threatened to swallow him up at times.

Yet he knew his mother could not be blamed for Lynnette's transgressions. He studied the doll his mother had thoughtfully made for his daughter. He decided he must show his mother more kindness in the future. She had suffered far too much in the past for him to add to her misery.

Garrett asked Lyssa, "Did you thank your grandmother properly?"

His daughter shrugged, her characteristic shyness taking over. Garrett swept her into his arms and swung her around, then tossed her in the air several times. Lyssa laughed until she had trouble catching her breath.

He set her back down on the ground and whispered into her ear, "Go on, Lyssa, and thank Aga."

Lyssa skipped to her grandmother, pecked her on the cheek, and then threw her arms around the old woman, bringing tears to Edith's eyes.

"Off to bed with you," Garrett told his daughter. He motioned for Annie, her nurse.

Protesting, Lyssa informed him, "I'm five now, Papa. I don't want to go to bed so early."

He kissed her brow. "When you are a score and five, I'll still tell you when it's time for bed." He gently nudged her in Annie's direction.

Lyssa left reluctantly, dragging her feet, as Garrett turned to Ashby. "I have some papers to look over. It will take me no more than an hour or so to do them justice. Will you ride with me to London afterward?"

Ashby nodded. "I'm happy to do so. You are to meet with Henri de Picassaret tomorrow?"

"Nay, not until the day after, but I've business to see to before that. I don't look forward to the meeting with de Picassaret, though."

"Why?" Ashby asked.

"I've dealt with the man before. He's very astute and drives a hard bargain. He's offered for some of my properties in Bordeaux in exchange for some of his land near Reims."

Ashby was perplexed. "You are interested in champagne vineyards?"

"No, but we've done some business in the past. It's more a courtesy to see him and hear him out. I've learned in business it's never good to alienate someone."

"Then see to your papers, Garrett. I'll make sure our horses are ready."

IT WAS CLOSER to two hours before the two men got on the road. Garrett inhaled the April night air, chilly and fresh, his head bothering him again. The headaches had started shortly after Lynnette's disappearance and came upon him with no warning. Sometimes lasting a few hours, sometimes a few days, they were becoming more frequent in their arrival and duration. The pain was so great at times that he wondered if he was going mad.

He and Ashby rode in companionable silence. Garrett often marveled at what Ashby put up with, such as leaving for London in the middle of the night, but he would not trade his friend for all the silk in Italy. Ashby was the brother of his heart, the one person he could talk to and bare his soul.

They passed several manors and castles along their ride, even stopping at Frothmore briefly to leave a letter for Lady Ancil with the gatekeeper. She and Edith had been friends in childhood, and any time Garrett made one of his frequent trips to London, he dropped off correspondence from his mother for Lady Ancil.

Back on the road again, they rode for an hour until Ashby pulled up. Garrett slowed his mount and turned to his friend.

"What ails you, Ash?"

Ashby frowned, a puzzled expression crossing his features. "I could have sworn I saw a woman in the road ahead."

Garrett peered into the distance and saw nothing. "You're going blind, my friend, or mayhap you need more sleep. Or," he said in a sly tone, "you simply have need of a woman and wished her here."

For a moment, Garrett knew he sounded like the Garrett of old, and Ashby grinned at him.

"A soft bed and an even softer woman sound good to me." Ashby spurred on his horse and they continued on their way.

Ahead of them, a woman suddenly darted out into the road. She bent swiftly and picked up a large object and went scurrying back to the nearby trees. They reined in their horses and stared at each other in surprise.

"I told you, Garrett. I knew I saw someone."

"You were right. Shall we investigate?"

They guided their horses toward the spot where the woman had disappeared then dismounted. Both men stared into the trees, searching. Neither spoke.

The cloud cover broke at that moment. Strong rays of moonlight poured over the area.

Heart pounding, Garrett spotted someone crouched behind a tree. As he and Ashby dismounted, he called out, "We mean you no harm. Are you hurt?"

MADELEINE GROANED INWARDLY. She instantly blamed Henri-the-Pebble for her current situation. To remove Henri, she'd placed her lute down beside her. The sound of horses as she slipped her boot back on had caused her to head for a hiding place. Only when the riders came closer did she remember her beloved lute. She couldn't chance the oncoming horses crushing her beloved possession, so she'd ventured from safety to rescue the instrument.

"*Merde*," she swore softly. She looked down at the smooth stone in her hand. "You bloody pebble."

The two gentlemen must have heard her voice and now approached. Madeleine knew she must take control of the situation in a direct fashion. She bravely stood, her lute in hand, and swung the instrument high above her. Storming toward the pair, she scowled.

"If you dare come closer, I'll bring my lute crashing down upon your heads," she warned. "'Tis the only valuable I have. If I destroy it, you'll have nothing." She tried to appear as menacing as possible as she studied the men before her.

The one on her left was tall and fair, his blond hair a bit unruly, his frame lean and athletic. He had a nice smile and he was no more a highwayman than her Uncle Raymond. He was dressed as a knight and carried himself with confidence.

The other one was quite different.

He was taller and broader than his companion, with short, dark hair and brooding eyes. He moved with a natural grace and wore his clothes with casual ease. His dark eyes seemed to pierce her soul with a ruthlessness unlike she'd ever known. This man frightened her—and yet at the same time, she felt drawn to him in some inexplicable way. Mayhap it was the sadness he wore, draped about him like a cloak that drew her to him.

The dark one held his hands out, palms up, no weapon in sight. "We wish you no harm, my lady. We would but render you aid. What brings you to the middle of nowhere at night with only a lute for protection?"

Madeleine detected a hint of sarcasm in his voice. Mayhap these weren't noblemen after all but highway swine who'd stolen the very clothes they wore. No, she was certain they must be nobility, simply by the arrogant air of the dark-haired man. No ruffian could mimic that.

She thought quickly. Henri was to meet a Lord Montayne while they were in London. He'd carried on about what a ruthless reputation the man had in business and how he planned to get the upper hand with the English nobleman in a bargain he hoped to strike with the man. Madeleine prayed that these men before her might know of Lord Montayne's unforgiving nature and launched into her lie.

"I am lady to Lord Montayne, good sirs.

Mayhap you have heard of him."

The two men exchanged a glance and then continued to stare at her without speaking.

"Yes, I know my husband's very name can bring even the bravest of men to utter silence." She paused. "That's how I frightened our attackers."

"Your attackers?" the dark stranger asked.

"Yes, the men who waylaid us on our way to London." She sighed audibly and then teared up, getting more into her performance now.

"Poor Simon. Lord Montayne's valet, you know. He was escorting me to our London residence when we were attacked. Oh, 'tis all my fault," she told them as a single tear cascaded down her cheek. She wiped it away briskly. "I took far too long to finish my tasks at hand. We should never have started out so late."

"And when was this, my lady?"

Always the dark-haired devil, she thought, never a word from his companion. She shot a look at the fair-haired gentleman, her eyebrows raised. Ignoring the dominant one, Madeleine asked, "Would you like to know how we fared, my lord?" she asked the silent man.

He flushed slightly, but managed to reply, "And then what happened, Lady Montayne?"

Madeleine placed a palm over her heart as if to still it. "'Twas horrible. Three men rushed into the road, daggers raised. Simon's horse reared and he fell from it. He struck his head and did not move."

At this, her eyes widened. "I think it frightened the robbers badly. They ordered me to remove the few jewels I wore, but they were all shaking. Then I told them who my husband was and that put the fear of our Lord in them." She smiled and leaned forward as if sharing a confidence. "It does help sometimes to be married to such a man known for his terrible temper and black moods."

"I'm sure," both men muttered at the same time.

She stamped her foot suddenly, allowing her fury to shine. "They will pay, I tell you. My husband will see to it."

"And you were unharmed, my lady?" Again the darker man spoke, his tone conveying an insolence while his face remained a mask of propriety.

"I'm a bit shaken," Madeleine admitted. "The brutes tossed Simon's body off to the side of the road and took my jewels and our horses. All they left me was my lute." She had lowered the instrument by this time and stroked it fondly.

The stranger asked, "Why did you leave the scene, my lady? Surely you must have feared the men who robbed you. Why would you push forward and possibly have to confront them again?"

Why indeed? Madeleine had gotten so worked up over poor Simon and her missing jewels that she hadn't quite decided that part of her story yet.

"Mayhap I was more upset by the event than I imagined, my lord," she ventured weakly. Let them think her a silly, simple woman without a brain in her head.

"Then," the menacing stranger said, "my friend and I must escort you to safety."

He held his hand out to the fair-haired man. "May I present Sir Ashby? And I," said the dark-haired devil, "am Sir Garrett."

He bowed low, as did Ashby, and continued. "We also were on our way to London, Lady Montayne, despite the late hour. I know Sir Ashby and I could not leave you stranded here on such a dark and desolate road. It's too far a distance to take you all the way back to Stanbury but we're happy to bring you to London with us."

"Oh, then you know of my home?" Madeleine asked breathlessly. Trying to maintain her composure, she added, "Of course, you would, Sir Garrett. If I'm not mistaken, you have been entertained there by Lord Montayne."

His smile gleamed at her in the moonlight. "As a matter of fact, I have, my lady. Although I don't recall seeing you there."

Madeleine cocked her head to one side. "No, I've been away often the past few years. My mother has been quite ill and I've spent much time with her."

"I am sorry to hear of her illness," he answered. "But, come, let us mount our horses and ride to London."

Madeleine watched Sir Ashby turn his head and discreetly cough into his hand, hiding his mirth. She wondered what he found so humorous about the situation.

Sir Garrett started toward his horse and then stopped, turning to her. "Coming, my lady?"

Madeleine felt her feet moving as if they had a will of their own. "Of course, Sir Garrett. I thank you for your kind offer. I'll reach London much faster on horse than by foot."

She was reluctant to ride with them but didn't want to seem churlish and arouse their suspicions. Surely there must be plenty of time between here and London. She was resourceful and could create an opportunity to slip away. Besides, her feet already hurt enough, thanks to little Henri-the-Pebble.

Sir Ashby quickly mounted his horse as Madeleine moved toward them. He reached his hand out to her. "May I help you up, my lady?"

She had almost placed her hand in his when the devil himself spoke. "You must be jesting, Ash. Your nag was tired before we left for London. Lady Montayne is welcomed to ride with me."

Ashby withdrew his hand, and Madeleine looked at Sir Garrett.

"My lady?" he said, his hand extended to her.

"Thank you, my lord," she answered as she placed her hand in his.

CHAPTER THREE

GARRETT EASILY HELPED the woman onto his horse, settling her in front of him. Although she was very tall, she was slim, as light as the rushes covering the floors of the great hall. She shifted, obviously uncomfortable at first, until he moved her back, closer to his chest. He felt her stiffen at the contact, her back ramrod straight, holding her lute out to her side.

"My lady, I fear you think me forward, but I must know that you are secure," he assured her. Gently, he added, "I would like to hold you in place. The road is bumpy at times and you have had enough mishaps this night. I would not want you to take a sudden spill."

She turned and eyed him with suspicion for a moment. Then she seemed to come to a decision about him. Her posture, though still erect, seemed to relax a bit, as did her facial features.

For a moment, Garrett thought he caught a glimpse of a smile tugging at one corner of her mouth.

"I've no interest in flying off and landing in a ditch, Sir Garrett. How would you have me sit?"

He hesitated, finding her an enigma. One minute she was shy and unsure of herself, the next haughty and arrogant. Just like a Montayne, he thought wryly.

"More like this, my lady," he answered, and he moved her slightly to one side, bringing his arm about her waist lightly to hold her in place.

She became as still as a stone. He could not even detect a breath coming from her.

Concerned, he asked, "Can you ride thus, my lady?"

She remained motionless for a long moment. Finally, he felt her exhale. "Of course, Sir Garrett. Shall we start?"

"We need to secure your lute," he told her. "Obviously, it means a great deal to you. May I allow Sir Ashby to attach it to his saddle? I don't think I can manage it and you, Lady Montayne."

She shook her head and tightened her grip on the instrument. "I'll vouch for my friend, my lady. He'll take good care of it."

With a sigh, she nodded curtly and allowed him to slip the lute from her hands. He handed the instrument over to Ashby. "Attach this to your saddle, Ash. And guard it with your life."

His friend nodded agreeably, a ghost of a smile still hovering about his mouth. Both men spurred their horses and set off.

Although headed toward a popular city such as London, the road was neither large nor smooth. Thick, green foliage lined the pathway, with an occasional tree limb having blown across the way. Boulders littered the thoroughfare and were difficult to see in the moonlight that came and went in odd snatches.

Garrett found it hard to keep Ebony at a canter with so many bumps along the way. The woman sat as straight as a board in front of him. When holes in the road forced him to tighten his hold on his passenger's narrow waist, he found her slender build deceptive. She had soft curves that melted into him as Ebony sidestepped a piece of debris or tried to avoid a rut.

Garrett found the contact pleasurable yet it filled him with guilt. Though he'd not led the life of a monk since Lynnette had left, having such sweet temptation literally in his lap caused his mind to race in directions he knew it shouldn't go. He willed himself to concentrate on the road and not the woman in his arms, though it seemed an impossible task.

The night wind grew cooler as they rode, and as she shivered, Garrett noticed for the first time that she was without a cloak. Rather than listen to another outrageous tale of how she'd lost it, he simply drew his own cloak from where it whipped in the wind behind him and wrapped it around them both. She went rigid at his touch but he tucked the cape securely about her, nonetheless. Immediately, her chills ceased, and he sensed the tension draining from her.

A faint, "Thank you, my lord," swept back to him, so soft that he wasn't sure if she had spoken or if it was the whistle of the wind.

After an hour of silence, the road smoothed once again. Gradually, Garrett felt her become limp in his arms. Instinctively, he cradled her until she fit snuggly against his chest as he, too, let himself be lulled by the horses' hooves beating a constant rhythm in the dark night.

Her scent was intoxicating. It was light, something floral that he couldn't quite place. She leaned back fully into him now, her head braced against his jaw. He moved slightly and inhaled, her wavy hair tickling his cheek as it came out of its braid. He reached up and took a strand, the color of wheat, soft and inviting, and rubbed it between his fingers. He suddenly longed to see all of her hair unbound, to be able to run his fingers through the strands slowly, sensually.

Startled, Garrett came out of his reverie. *Holy Christ!* What had come over him? He looked quickly over at Ashby. His friend gave him a lazy smile before returning his gaze to the road ahead.

Garrett tried to think rationally. Who was the

young woman seated in front of him, the one who'd had him thinking lustful thoughts for the first time in ages? More important, why did she claim to be his *wife*?

Of course, she'd told them how her husband's name frightened off the robbers. Garrett knew some called him *Satan Himself*—although never to his face.

He knew he was feared by many and loathed by a few more. Yet Lynnette had brought a softness to him for a short while. When she fled, the softness became harder than stone. Now, it was only in sweet Lyssa's company that he became human.

So if this chit had heard tell of him, then she was wise to use his name to cower the thieves.

But had there been any thieves? Her tale seemed implausible. So why was a lady—for surely she was a lady, her clothing and regal bearing, as well as her cultured tone, testified to that much—in the middle of nowhere? She had no obvious jewels, no money, no protector. Her story was full of holes.

And then there was the faint scar, high on her cheekbone, another intriguing mystery. What lady of breeding carried a scar across such perfect features?

Why did he feel the urgent need to protect her? Especially when he didn't even know her name.

His thoughts raced as they rode. Yet as dawn broke over the horizon and they came within sight of the gates of London, he was no nearer an answer than when this unusual journey began.

Suddenly, Ebony stumbled. The horse quickly lifted his hoof, only to falter again. Garrett's heart thundered as he realized it was his own carelessness that had caused this mishap. His horse started whinnying and bucking erratically, tossing Garrett off in the process. He landed painfully on his hip and a roar of anger escaped his lips as Ebony galloped past him.

Garrett saw that the woman had somehow managed to stay on the horse. Her fingers grasped the thick mane, clinging to it. She grabbed Ebony's reins and brought him to a halt. She walked him back toward where Garrett lay sprawled on the ground, stroking Ebony's neck and murmuring soothing words into the horse's ear.

A string of curses burst from Garrett as Ashby's rich, deep laughter disturbed the quiet, misty morning. Ashby reached down a hand to Garrett, who scowled up at him, but took it nonetheless.

Once on his feet, Garrett limped slowly over to Ebony, his anger cooling since he knew the accident was his fault. "If horses could wear sheepish grins, I'd say you could teach them, you silly steed." He stroked Ebony's muzzle fondly, shaking his head. He looked up. "Are you all right, Lady Montayne?"

She frowned for a moment before answering. He could guess as to her confusion. He saw the moment that she realized that *she* was Lady Montayne and instantly willed herself back into her chosen role.

"Quite fine, thank you, Sir Garrett. But are you?"

Garrett rubbed his right hip, tender to the touch. "Nothing a little rest cannot cure, my lady. But Ebony has thrown a shoe."

He lifted his horse's hoof, studying it for a long moment, then he stared off into the distance. "London's gates won't be open to travelers for another half-hour or so. I wouldn't want Ebony going that far at any rate."

"We passed a small row of cottages not three minutes ago, Garrett," Ashby pointed out. "I believe there was a smith's stand."

"Then we will make our way back slowly." Garrett motioned to their fellow traveler. "Lady Montayne, might you be so gracious as to ride with Sir Ashby? I'd like to keep any weight off Ebony's back until he's been properly attended."

Her face brightened. "I would be happy to comply, my lord, but I would rather enjoy the chance to stretch my own legs, as well."

Before she slid from the saddle, Garrett was there. His hands closed about her slender waist, lifting her easily.

Her feet touched the ground and she met his eyes. "Thank you," she said meekly.

His hands rested around her waist a moment longer than necessary before he dropped them to his sides and turned to take Ebony's reins.

Ashby dismounted, too, and the party walked slowly, stiff from their many hours in the saddle. Light was beginning to ease upward, erasing the stars that had been scattered across the sky. A few birds began calling to one another, singing in the new day.

A BRISK WIND rose as they continued onward. It surprised Madeleine when Sir Garrett removed his heavy cloak in order to drape the heavy fabric around her shoulders. He even tightened the laces around her neck to secure the welcomed warmth.

She'd become unaccustomed to kindness and lowered her eyes to avoid his gaze. "'Tis thoughtful of you, Sir Garrett," she managed to say quietly and turned her head away to wipe a tear before it fell. She knew he studied her intently and refused to meet his eyes, focusing instead on the road ahead.

They walked in companionable silence for a short while, soon reaching a small gathering of cottages. As Sir Ashby had said, a blacksmith shed sat directly next to a shabby cottage.

"I'll awaken the smith," Ashby told them and sauntered off to knock at the door.

Within minutes, he roused the smith from his sleep. The man appeared quite agreeable to be able to service well-dressed gentlemen at such an early hour. As they led their horses toward the shed, Madeleine touched Sir Garrett's arm lightly.

"I fear at any moment my stomach will grumble fiercely, my lord," she whispered. "Mayhap we could break our fast? This smith's wife might be persuaded to prepare us something."

"A fine idea, Lady Montayne." Garrett fished out two coins and handed them to her. "Offer these to the good woman and I'll wager she can accommodate us in no time."

"Yes, my lord. I shall take care of personal matters and then speak to her straight away." Madeleine scanned the area, plotting for a way to get out of this impossible situation.

She could not accompany these men into London. With no idea where the Montaynes lived, she could not direct them to her supposed residence. Even if she pointed out a random house and tried to shake them off, good manners would insist that these gentlemen see her safely inside the abode.

Madeleine hobbled toward the cottage as

Garrett made his way to the shed. She didn't take time to rap on the wooden door. Instead, she opened it and quickly slipped inside. She needed as much time as possible to put her scheme into action.

The smith's wife was bent over, stirring the fire on the opposite side of the compact room. She started when she caught sight of Madeleine.

Before the older woman could address her, Madeleine crossed the distance between them and took the woman's gnarled hand in her own. Her eyes met those of the peasant and she blurted out, "You must help me. Please," she begged. "I have been taken from my father's house." Madeleine burst into tears as she began to spin a new set of lies.

Uneasily, the woman gave her a cautious pat.

Madeleine did her best to look distraught. "My father refused to give me in marriage to one of the men outside," she told the wife. "He is desperate to marry a fortune, having gambled his own away. He is mean and cruel, and he has taken me from my home."

She glanced over her shoulder and turned back to the woman. "It's the dark-haired one who's a devil. He wouldn't take no for an answer and stole me from my very bed. We ride to London as soon as his horse has been shod. Will you help me? I beg you."

The woman studied Madeleine carefully. Her

eyes lit up as Madeleine slid the coins Sir Garrett had given her from her pocket and offered them to her.

"Help me hide and these are yours. After they leave, I can find my way to my brother. He lives just inside the southern gates of London. He will protect me."

Madeleine's lips trembled as she felt the desperation she tried to portray.

After a moment, the older woman finally spoke. "I will help you," she agreed, taking both coins and placing them under a pot. They spoke briefly and hatched a quick plan.

Opening the door, Madeleine saw the blacksmith hard at work, Ebony's hoof in his hand as he attached a new shoe. The two knights appeared deep in conversation, both men facing the smith, watching him. Madeleine nodded and stepped back as the smith's wife approached her rescuers, two cups in her hand.

"Welcome, my fine gentlemen. I have brought you some refreshment. You are parched, I am sure, from a long ride. Come, have a bit of ale." She circled around them so that both men turned away from the smith to face her.

"Many thanks," Sir Garrett said.

"We are most obliged," Sir Ashby told her.

As they held the cups up and tilted the cool contents to their dry mouths, Madeleine sneaked quietly from the doorway and went to the back of the shed. As promised, she found the loose board. She lifted it and slipped through the tight space, hearing the woman's noisy conversation in the distance.

Mother of God. She is loud enough to awaken the king in London. Gratefully, though, Madeleine found herself at the far end of the shed, where the hay was plentiful. She remained low to the ground, covering herself with the dry stalks until she was hidden from view.

GARRETT COULD FEEL the slight tinge of a headache as the woman prattled on.

"'Tis a great day when two such fine lords visit our humble establishment. Many ride on to London but my husband does a better job than any smith around. May I get such important gentlemen some bread? More ale, perhaps?"

Garrett replied, "Bread and more ale would be nice. And I know our traveling companion would like some, too."

The woman stared blankly at him. "My lord?" she asked, her brown face wrinkled in puzzlement.

"The lady with us," Garrett insisted. "She went to ask if you would provide us a small meal."

The smith's wife shook her head. "I spoke to no one."

Garrett instantly knew that the unknown woman had fled their company. He might never discover her identity. Despite her lies, something about her spoke to him. Touched him. He needed to find her now. Learn her name. Learn why she pretended to be his wife.

He broke out into a full run toward the cottage then slowed to an awkward trot as his sore body protested the sudden movement. He rounded the back of the cottage, searching in both directions.

She wasn't there.

Quickly, he raced back to the front, slamming straight into Ashby as he came around the corner.

"What's the matter, Garrett? Lose something? Or someone?"

Garrett brushed him aside and burst into the thatched bungalow. He growled low in his throat, storming about the tiny space, lifting a stool and tossing it aside, pushing the straw mattress around with his foot, then picking up a dish and catching himself before he sent it slamming to the ground.

Ashby entered and watched his antics.

Garrett shook his head. "Not a trace of her, Ash. She's gone."

By now, both the smith and his wife had followed them inside. The couple exchanged frightened looks.

Garrett could only imagine how he must appear as he tried to control his rage. He felt the familiar pounding at his temples and could feel heat rise to his face. "There was a lady with us," he said evenly, through gritted teeth.

"I spoke to no lady, my lord," the wife insisted, shaking her head slowly.

"Then where has she disappeared to?" he mused aloud. He paused and then suddenly chuckled, in spite of the situation. "And with my favorite cloak!"

CHAPTER FOUR

ASHBY WATCHED GARRETT leave the small confines of the cottage to restlessly pace the yard in front of the barn, his hands behind his back. Ashby knew well enough to leave his friend alone for the time being. Garrett always needed solitude when he mulled over issues that troubled him.

The beautiful stranger was definitely something that troubled his friend.

The entire adventure had brought Ashby a powerful thirst. "About that ale, madam?" he asked the smith's wife, his usual smile doing the trick.

"Coming right up, my lord," she responded quickly.

Soon, he'd inhaled several pieces of bread and cheese and drunk more than a good share of ale. Ashby peered out the doorway of the cottage.

Garrett still wore a deep frown but his pacing had slowed. It was safe to approach him once again.

Taking a fresh mug and a plate of food toward the barn, he approached his friend. "Need a respite from your pacing, my lord?" he inquired. "You've worn a trench into the ground."

Garrett turned to him. Seeing the mug, he reached for it and quaffed its contents. Ashby took it from him and had it refilled. When he returned again, Garrett had moved near the horses, seating himself on a bale of hay just inside the barn. Ashby went to him and handed him the second cup of ale and the plate.

Seating himself beside Garrett, he asked, "Do you really think she was a lady?"

Garrett exhaled loudly and sipped on the ale before replying. "Yes, Ash, I'm certain of that. She held herself as one and had the demeanor of one highborn. No common thief or whore could ever match her bearing. It's in the blood and can't be imitated."

Garrett drank again from the cup. "Her speech, too, was refined. She spoke the King's English very precisely, even better than you or I, as if she'd spent time at court. Her dress was well-cut, her hands soft, except for calluses on the tips. I noticed that when she grabbed at my hand a time or two when the road became rough."

Ashby nodded. "Possibly because she plays her lute often."

His friend roared with satisfied laughter. "Yes, her lute," Garrett said, a smug smile upon his face.

Ashby looked over at the horses. Still tied to his mount was the lady-in-question's instrument. He smiled, too. "You both have something the other desires."

Garrett nodded. "I would have that cloak back. It's the warmest one I own. I almost didn't bring it since spring is upon us but I changed my mind at the last moment. A lute for a cloak? If I catch the chit, I'll return her lute—after I smack her bottom with it—and take pleasure in doing so."

Ashby grinned at the image Garrett painted. "Would you dare hurt your own wife?" he asked, not masking his amusement.

"Egads! Could you believe the audacity of that creature, Ash? Claiming to be married *to me*?"

Ashby chuckled. "It was a smart ploy on her part, Garrett. Since Ryker's death, you do own the blackest reputation in these parts, even if I know it's all for show. The woman was clever enough to throw out a name that would stop most men in their tracks. Do you think she is from this area?"

"I doubt it. It's just a feeling I have, but if she were, I'm sure we would have heard of her beauty. Why, if I'd met her, I might never . . ." His voice trailed off.

"... have married Lynnette," Ashby finished.

A scowl darkened Garrett's face. Ashby wished he could take back his words as Garrett threw his cup to the ground, banging his toe in the process. An oath escaped his lips.

"Let us be off, Ash. I tire of this place." Garrett stalked to the cottage, likely to pay the smith for his work and their meal.

"And look what damage your marriage to Lynnette did you, my friend," Ashby said sadly to himself. "You are no longer the carefree Garrett of old."

He sighed and mounted his horse. Garrett strode from the cottage and threw himself into the saddle. Spurring on their horses, they quickly shot out of the yard and toward London.

MADELEINE FINALLY RELEASED her sneeze, blowing hay upward with great force. Her nose had burned and itched since she had shoveled the mounds of hay on top of her. Several times, she feared she would sneeze and reveal her position to her rescuers. Fortunately, they left without guessing she'd hid under their very noses as they discussed her. The thought made her groan aloud.

Why, of all the people she could have met on

the road to London, did it have to be Lord Montayne? She could have met thieves or murderers, loners or secret lovers, even a wild animal or two. No, she had to come across the one man, other than Henri, that could jeopardize her plans, ruining them before she'd even had a chance at escaping England.

Lady Montayne, indeed! Why had the man allowed her to continue her charade? Oh, yes, he was *Sir Garrett*, simply a knight ready to aid a lady in distress. She wished that Henri had never mentioned doing business with the man. It would have been better if she'd simply pulled a name from the air, rather than a potential business associate of Henri's.

She sat up abruptly, brushing hay from her hair, and sneezed again. She tried to stand but became entangled in the cloak—his favorite cloak—and promptly fell back into the pile again. The sweet rush from the hay filled her nostrils, causing them to tingle. Another loud sneeze escaped.

Madeleine attempted to stand again. She succeeded this time and exited the shed.

The smith's wife rushed up to her. "Oh, my lady, he was an angry one, that dark devil!"

"Yes," Madeleine agreed. "I owe you my life, good woman." She took the older woman's hands in hers and squeezed them gently. "You are a brave woman for standing up to him as you did."

She relaxed for the first time since she'd left Henri. "He's mad that his heiress fled his clutches," she continued. "Now I hope that he will drown in his debts and have to marry an ugly second cousin."

She and the smith's wife giggled companionably and headed for the cottage. The woman tied a handkerchief filled with a wedge of sharp cheese, an apple, and a generous slice of bread.

"Best be on your way, my lady. I'd hate for you to run into the likes of that one again."

Madeleine nodded in agreement. "I would like to avoid the two gentlemen. I'm sure you understand. I thought first about going to my brother in London but I'm afraid they might spot me before I reach him." She paused and then added, "I have an uncle who lives just southeast of London. Mayhap you could tell me which road to take to seek him out?"

The smith's wife gladly explained to Madeleine the best passage to take then she headed north again, waving goodbye. Best to take her time and avoid both London and Lord Montayne for now. He was the last person she wanted to see. She would take a day or two and enjoy her newfound freedom and then make her way to the famous city and its waterfront. Her only trip there with Henri had been short and far from pleasurable. Perhaps this time would be different.

The sun had now fully risen. Warm sunshine melted into her, and she slipped the cloak off, draping the heavy fabric over her arm. The loss of her beloved lute saddened her. Mayhap she could trade the cloak for another instrument. She stopped to go through the pockets and found several loose gold coins within.

She smiled, slightly mollified that Lord Montayne had lost both his cloak and coins. His trick canceled any regret she might have about appropriating his property. He knew she was a liar but he had played along, taking her almost all the way to London. What would have happened when they arrived?

Yet she remembered his small acts of kindness. He had generously wrapped the cloak about her on both the cool ride of last night and again this morning as they walked after dismounting the horses. And, for a brief while, she felt so safe and secure in his arms as she rode atop Ebony.

Madeleine closed her eyes, imagining for the moment being enclosed again within Lord Montayne's embrace. She could feel the hard muscles of his chest against her back, his arm tight about her, holding her near him. He smelled of soap and horses, his breath light and fresh in her ear. She had an immense longing to be back on Ebony with him, the sweet ache filling her.

Then Ashby's voice popped into her head. *Married to Lynnette* rang in her ears, and Madeleine's eyes flew open. That black-hearted lord was married, she thought bitterly. A sigh escaped her lips, breaking the morning quiet.

"As if I were not," she mused aloud. It was interesting that the Earl of Montayne's wife apparently made him as unhappy as Henri made her. "Could never be," she murmured, fingering the pebble in her pocket, and continued down the road. Her heart, though, still ached at the waning memories of the dark, handsome devil.

HENRI DE PICASSARET pushed the matted hair off his brow. He finally dared to open his eyes. Harsh light streamed through the dull windowpane. As often was the case upon awakening, his head felt ready to burst, as did his bladder. He struggled to sit up, the pounding in his head almost unbearable. He was in a foul mood. He'd lost in cards to his host, Lord Ancil. Didn't the English have the decency to lose to a guest?

Henri massaged his temples lightly, hoping to still the roaring noise. He rose and shrieked for Bertrand. The man lurked behind every crack and cranny.

"You wish to dress, my lord?"

Henri let loose a stream of profanity, finally quieting when the thunder in his head became too loud to hear his own words. "Yes. Dress me, you fool. I must get to mass."

Once there, he would feel better. He always did. Henri knew he was one of God's chosen. By doing this daily duty to God, his Father honored him with riches beyond his dreams. Now if only God would see about finding him a wife that would give him children. It was his own cross to bear that none of his wives could get themselves with child, especially this latest one. She could do nothing but look pretty and speak well. Granted, his guests loved her singing and the games she invented. They even enjoyed the little sketches she did of them. A good time was promised at Henri de Picassaret's and he always delivered. Now, though, he'd grown tired of hearing her praised by his guests.

"How talented she is, Henri. How clever of you to find such a jewel."

But she was not the jewel for which he had hoped. She was barren, like his previous wives. He had already begun searching for a new wife. One more docile and more fertile than Madeleine Bouchard.

She had been a spoiled child and was now a spoiled woman. He'd had to discipline her much too often. He no longer thought it worth his trouble. He would ask God this morning how He wished Henri to handle the heavy burden placed upon him.

Henri held still as Bertrand finished. Dressed and perfumed, he headed for the chapel to lose himself in his reveries. Before he realized, mass was over and he hadn't heard a thing God might have told him. It was all that bitch's fault. If she and her unacceptable behavior hadn't weighed so heavily upon his mind, he could have heard what God wanted him to do with such an unruly wife. Now he would have to discipline her over it before they left for his business in London with Lord Montayne.

Henri walked carefully down the corridor to his room. Control was most important at these times, he had learned. He did not punish Madeleine when he was enraged. No, that was wrong, to hit in anger. He only did so to teach his wife a lesson.

Yet how he looked forward to this. A tremendous pressure built within him each time he disciplined a wife, Madeleine, in particular. It was as if God continued to test him by giving Henri such resistant wives time and again. God eased him, though, and brought him a sweet release of peace once the lesson had been taught to his headstrong wife of the moment. Other men might experience guilt over such lessons but serenity filled Henri after such a session.

Henri paused in front of the door, breathing deeply, regaining his poise before he entered. When ready, he slowly turned the knob and walked into the chamber, closing the door quietly behind him.

An empty room awaited him. Lord Ancil's servants had made the bed and tidied up while he was gone. He crossed to a chair and sat.

Henri waited for half an hour, then an hour. He tried to stay calm, knowing God must be testing his limits. He could not disappoint Him. He cracked his knuckles slowly, the loud crunch the only sound besides his slow, measured breathing. As the time passed, his anger grew. The unruly emotion started in his stomach and slowly rose through his chest until it boiled throughout him. The tic that pulled at the corner of his mouth when Madeleine tried him began twitching.

"Bertrand!"

His manservant opened the door at once.

"Find Lady de Picassaret," Henri said evenly then sat back to bide his time.

Bertrand returned a quarter of an hour later. "There's no sign of her ladyship, my lord. I have searched everywhere inside the castle. Mayhap she has gone for a walk or out for a ride?" he suggested hopefully.

Henri slowly shook his head. "She would not do so without asking my permission. Was she at mass, Bertrand?" Oftentimes, Madeleine attended mass, but Henri rarely saw her, so strong was his devotion to His Lord.

"I did not notice her ladyship there, my lord. In fact, I have not seen her all morning."

"Then find her," Henri ground out through clenched teeth and Bertrand left to search once again.

When he returned, Henri watched as his valet would not meet his eyes and shifted from foot to foot.

"I have asked everyone, my lord. No one has seen her. My lady did not leave the grounds to walk or ride. She is in no room in this castle." Bertrand paused a moment and Henri spotted the sweat that had broken out upon his servant's forehead and above his upper lip.

Suddenly, Henri's mouth twitched rapidly. He felt his anger building to a frenzy yet he remained in tight control. God would be proud that he held his temper.

He remained seated but eyed Bertrand carefully. "You have more to add?" he asked, his voice calm but deadly.

"Only that late last night one of the guards thought he spied a woman just outside the castle. There was little moonlight and the shadows can play tricks, you know."

Henri watched the sweat drip off Bertrand's lip and the servant visibly trembled now.

"And?" Henry prodded, his foot tapping on the stone floor.

"The guard thought he was mistaken, my

lord. The shadow was there one moment and gone the next. He decided there was no reason to be alarmed. That it was nothing."

"Nothing, you say?" Henri stood, his fists clenched, his voice rising. "Nothing? That my wife has left without permission? In the dead of night? In a strange land?"

His anger was white-hot, as if heat seared his flesh. "She has abandoned her husband and her vows?"

Henri rose from his chair, towering over his portly servant. He grabbed Bertrand by the shoulders and drew him close, his forehead resting next to his servant's.

"I will find her, Bertrand. *I will find her.* I will make her wish she never set her eyes upon me."

When Bertrand remained silent, Henri continued. "God wants a wife to submit to her husband," he explained. "I will have her yield. She will long for death. And then, only then, will I kill her slowly—and take pleasure in it. God would not ask me to remain faithful to a disloyal whore."

Henri released Bertrand, who staggered back from his master. Satisfied, Henri could see the great fear on his valet's features. Bertrand had witnessed Henri meting out punishment before and he knew his servant would do anything to keep his master's wrath from descending upon him.

MADELEINE ARRIVED ON the waterfront in the late afternoon after waiting two days before entering the city's gates. She had spent most of the day searching for news of ships departing for France. She had finally secured passage on one that would sail within hours. The high price surprised her but she would have sold all her jewels and paid all she had to reach home, if only for a little while.

She knew her parents would be shocked to see her but she would make them understand what she'd been through. She loved them more than anything on God's earth. She would explain how cruel Henri had been to keep her apart from them. Then her brother would help arrange for her to enter a convent.

Madeleine knew true liberation lay almost within her grasp. She had traveled many back roads to reach London. She wanted no more encounters with Lord Montayne. He'd mentioned having business in the city and she knew he would be meeting at some point with Henri. The thought chilled her. Lord Montayne seemed a very clever man. What if he figured out who she was? Would he tell Henri?

She took her small bundle and held it more tightly to her, even as she tugged the black cloak around her. She had remorse for having taken such a fine garment. She had not meant to but things had happened so quickly at the smith's house that she had not realized she still had it about her when she'd put her plan into motion.

She wondered idly if there was a way to return it to Lord Montayne, perhaps with a note thanking him for his kindness.

Suddenly she was rooted to the spot. *No, it couldn't be.* Dread filled her as she stared at the man not twenty paces in front of her, his back to her as he conversed with another man. The bald pate. The portly, barrel-shaped body. The all-black clothes that Henri insisted every one of his servants wear.

The man gestured as he spoke, and she caught a glimpse of his face in profile.

Madeleine's gut clinched in fear.

Bertrand. *Why was he on the wharf?* It was far too early for Henri to be returning to France.

It didn't matter, she told herself. If Bertrand was here, then Henri could be, too. What if they were taking the same ship as she? How could she steer clear of them?

Madeleine fought the growing sense of panic and the wild urge to run. Instead, she remained calm despite her pounding heart. Turning, she hastened in the opposite direction along the dock at a brisk pace, in spite of her limp, even as she heard Bertrand and the man he spoke with coming her way. She turned abruptly, ducking behind a stack of cartons placed haphazardly and waited, not daring to breathe or even look up.

The men paused directly in front of the boxes that concealed her.

Bertrand spoke, his English flawless, though colored with his native French accent. "So you see, Monsieur de Picassaret is anxious to find his wife. He will pay a great deal to have her returned to him safely."

The other man grunted. "I'm sure she's the one but she gave a different name. Your description is too close not to be the same woman."

Madeleine heard the shifting of papers. "Yes, here it is. She's listed as Bouchard. Madeleine Bouchard. Sailing on the evening tide tonight."

Merde! But there was no time to spout *Our Fathers* as penance. She must hear what else that snake said about her.

Bertrand snorted. "Her family's name. Nevertheless, she is my master's wife."

"What shall we do when she boards?"

"Let her suspect nothing. Simply post a man outside her cabin. Confine her there until I arrive with additional help."

"And if for some odd reason the woman is not whom you seek?"

"I have paid for several men to watch the harbor. If she seeks passage on any ship from

London, I will know of it."

"Very good," replied the other man.

Madeleine waited as the men shuffled off in the opposite direction. Her heart sank. Tears spilled silently down her cheeks. What was she to do? She could not board that ship, nor could she reclaim the vast sum the captain had charged to take her as a passenger.

She huddled on the ground, her growing despair clouding her mind. She tried to think of a new escape plan but fear drove all rational thought from her mind. The bitter taste of defeat began closing in.

She was startled when a young boy rounded the corner and ran smack into her. His eyes widened first with surprise and then they glowed with mischief.

"Evan! Evan, come out at once before I throttle yer bones, and ye know I will."

The boy put a finger to his lips, his eyes wide and playful.

Madeleine started to rise but he placed a hand upon her wrist and tugged her back down.

"Evan, 'tis the last time I take ye anywhere with me. Oh, go hop in the water and swim away with the mermaids, for all I care."

The boy burst out laughing at her words and, immediately, a petite woman leaped from around the corner. She took a step back when she saw Madeleine crouched there. Then she spotted her son.

"Evan, me boy, ye are the bane of me existence. If I could give ye back to God in His heavens, I would. I'd say to Him, 'Mister God, me Lord, sir, ye've made a dreadful mistake. Ye meant to give me a good boy, I'm sure, but somehow me good lad was replaced. Instead, I've got the silliest rascal, a tyke descended from elves, no doubt. Could ye please let me return this imp?' And Mister God will say to me, 'Now, Gwenith, I only give ye what ye deserve.' So of course, I'd say back to Him, 'Mister God, I . . .'"

The boy squealed, throwing himself into his mother's arms.

"There, now," she cooed to him. "Maybe God didn't make such a mistake after all."

Madeleine watched all this in bewilderment. She rose, wiping her tears, then blurted the first thought that entered her mind. "You've got the most gorgeous hair!"

The woman before her laughed heartily. "I'm delighted to find out ye like this red mop of mine. Gwenith's me name."

Madeleine smiled at her. "I am Madeleine Bouchard."

Gwenith grinned at her. "Pleased to meet ye, Madeleine Bouchard." She poked Evan in the ribs.

"Pleased to meet ye," the young boy echoed. "Mama, can we go now? Ye said 'twas a nasty place here."

"Then why'd ye run off from me, lad?" Gwenith scolded.

Evan considered this. "Why, to protect ye, of course. To keep all the bad 'un's away."

Gwenith's rich laughter tinkled musically. "Ye are a scamp, me little one. A charming one, but a scamp, nonetheless." She squeezed his shoulder affectionately as she glanced across at Madeleine.

"Well, we must be off." Gwenith began to turn as a tear slowly trickled down Madeleine's cheek.

Gwenith peered at her with concern. "Are ye lost, Maddie? Did ye fight with yer Mister Bouchard?"

"No," Madeleine said hastily. "Mister Bouchard is . . . well . . . he's . . ." Her voice trailed off and suddenly her tears began flowing freely.

"There, there, me girl," the young woman said, and placed an arm around Madeleine's waist as she balanced the squirming boy in the other. "Ye look like ye could use a friend, love." She gave Madeleine a squeeze.

"'Tis a long story." Madeleine sighed. "I find my plans have . . . changed. I'm not sure what to do, and I don't know London very well."

"Some things are not even worth discussing," Gwenith told her, looking Madeleine square in the eyes. She paused a moment, and Madeleine saw she was sizing her up.

"I'm a mummer," Gwenith shared. "Evan and me, we travel all around the south performing our little plays. Sometimes," she confided, "being on the road is the perfect way to forget yer troubles. Would ye care to join us? Can ye act or sing a bit?"

Madeleine's thoughts were in a swirl. She had nowhere to go, not a friend in all of England. She also had no way of escaping to France, at least not at the moment. Impulsively, she said, "I do sing and play the lute."

Gwenith looked about and frowned. "Have ye a lute?"

Madeleine shook her head, feeling a flare of anger heat her cheeks, knowing her lute was in Lord Montayne's hands.

"If ye've money to buy one, then let's do it and be off. We must meet up with Farley tonight, for we leave in the morning. Are ye game, Maddie Bouchard?"

Madeleine smiled at her wearily, then said a silent thank you to the Living Christ. Things were beginning to look up.

CHAPTER FIVE

GARRETT PULLED HIS new cloak about him as the wind suddenly gusted. The April day was gray and bleak, much like his mood. The overcast skies were threatening London with rain at any moment. He nudged Ebony lightly, spurring the horse on before the coming storm soaked them.

He guided the steed through the tight streets that already teemed with people, though it was but eight of the clock. As he continued, a fine mist began, slowly turning into a lazy drizzle. Garrett cursed under his breath. He had hoped to reach his destination before the rains began. Now he would arrive wet and miserable, feeling as black as his soul at this moment. He pondered on his mood, which had been dark since they'd reached London. Or rather, as Ashby had pointed out, since just before they'd come upon the city.

Thanks to Lady Montayne.

The vision of the woman calling herself thus invaded his private musings. He had tried to shake off her image over the last two days with no luck. She came to him at the oddest times, when he least expected it.

Why was he so taken with a stranger? Especially one whose true name he didn't even know. He closed his eyes briefly and the blond beauty appeared again. He could see those deep amethyst eyes that dominated her face. The flawless skin, the delicate bone structure, the generous mouth that wove her outlandish tales, were all too real.

And the feel of her. Garrett remembered how little she weighed, despite her height, which was taller than any woman he'd seen. She'd fit quite nicely against him once she'd fallen asleep in the saddle.

Garrett cursed again and opened his eyes. The picture of the mystery woman dissolved, leaving him to wonder again why she plagued him so. He thought back to his conversation with Ashby the previous day.

"You're coming out of your mourning for Lynnette, Garrett," Ashby reminded him. "It's simple to see. You're ready to live again. You've met an exceptionally attractive woman and you were drawn to her." Ashby shrugged nonchalantly, which infuriated Garrett.

"I've had plenty of women since Lynnette's leaving," he told his friend bluntly.

"Aye, Garrett, but you've not gotten close to any one of them. They were nothing more than a quick roll in the hay—sometimes literally." Ashby laughed, amused by his own clever reply.

Garrett suspected Ashby was right. He'd changed when his wife had disappeared. He did everything possible to keep busy, the better to have no time to think. To feel. Driven in all he did. He'd thrown himself into the management of his estate in England and the vineyards he owned in France, even taking his first trip to the Bordeaux area the previous year. He had learned more about wines during his month in France than he would have thought possible. Robert Bouchard, who oversaw the Montayne family estates in France, had proven to be reliable and knowledgeable. His son, Pierre, had even more expertise. By the time Garrett came home, he could list all the fine intricacies of a Cabernet Sauvignon and how it was distinguished from a Merlot.

Unfortunately, he had turned to his cups lately, drinking more heavily when the headaches came upon him, as much to numb the throbbing in his head as to ease the pain in his heart.

Now, some strange woman had come into his life and intrigued him with her beauty and her spinning of yarns and, suddenly, he felt alive again, wondering what new story she'd invent once they reached London and she didn't know where the Montayne family home lay. Then she'd cheated him by vanishing without a trace. Garrett suspected the smith's wife had known more than she'd let on, but short of beating the woman into a confession, he'd been helpless. Despite his reputation, he had never struck a woman, and so he and Ashby had pressed on to London without their female companion.

Garrett arrived at Lord Fenton's, the gentleman who'd introduced him to Henri de Picassaret. He dismounted and handed Ebony's reins to a young lad, who gazed at the steed with admiration.

Garrett ran his fingers through his damp hair and hurried up to the shelter of Fenton's home. A pretty blond maid answered his knock and led him down a long corridor. Normally, Garrett would have enjoyed the sway of her hips—but she wasn't the blond female who weighed on his mind. He was glad he'd left Ashby behind in the Montayne shipping offices, for this comely wench would have distracted his friend from the business at hand.

The servant showed him to a cozy room, complete with a roaring fire. He slipped his cloak off and tossed it aside, taking a seat near the fireplace. He stretched his legs out in front of him, crossing them at the ankles. The heat quickly warmed him, slowly moving from his booted feet up his chilled limbs.

A servant entered and Garrett recognized him from his previous dealings with de Picassaret, although he couldn't recall the retainer's name.

In stilted English, the stout man said, "Comte de Picassaret has been detained, my lord. He will arrive shortly. May I get anything for you?"

Garrett shook his head. "No, thank you."

The man nodded and left, leaving the door ajar. Garrett heard him pause in the hallway and begin speaking rapidly in French. Though he could hear two voices, he couldn't make out everything said. The words came rapidly, spoken more as the French did in the north. Still, he was able to ascertain that the comte was terribly angry. Something about plans being ruined and responsibility being questioned.

Frustrated at his lack of understanding, Garrett closed his eyes and imagined himself back in Bordeaux, the lazy sunshine of the south permeating him. Speech there was more melodic and slow. Garrett had picked up much more of the language while there than he ever had from his tutors. Unfortunately, he had rare opportunities to use it since he despised any time spent at court, so he'd lost his command of the nuances of the language since he'd returned to England.

Eventually, he heard sharp steps approaching and sat up quickly. Henri de Picassaret strode in.

Garrett was shocked by the Frenchman's appearance.

The man had aged half a score since they'd met the previous year in France. Henri's skin was even paler than before. Deep wrinkles lined his face. His ice blue eyes were bloodshot, as though he hadn't slept for several nights. His iron gray hair had a dull cast to it. Always lean despite his ample belly, the comte now seemed gaunt. As usual, his thin mouth was set in a tight line.

Garrett rose and offered his hand. Henri shook it perfunctorily. Both men took seats across from one another.

Henri spoke first. "I hear that your wife ran off, Montayne." His eyes flicked rapidly over Garrett, who sat stunned by the Frenchman's opening remark.

Garrett stood abruptly, his fists clenched. He fought to keep his anger from erupting at the older man's cruel words. "That topic, de Picassaret, is not open for discussion. Good day."

He moved to leave but Henri stood and clutched his arm tightly. For such a frail-looking man, his strength was surprising.

"No, my apologies, *monsieur*. I was thought-less. I am sure that you grieve for your lost wife."

Garrett was slightly mollified but did not take his chair.

"Come," Henri said, his tone now conciliatory. "Let us not talk of wives when there is business to conduct." He paused. "I merely heard that an acquaintance's wife had recently run off. The man is beside himself and has no idea where to begin looking." He offered Garrett an apologetic smile. "I thought you might advise me, for my friend, since you have experienced something similar."

Garrett glared at Henri. "Some things are best left private," he said, his mouth set. They stared at each other for several moments before taking their seats.

Henri opened the discussion again. "I am ready to offer you an unusual business proposal, Lord Montayne." Henri's eyes glittered. "It is one that you must accept immediately, however, for I am to return to my home shortly."

"What do you propose?"

Henri smiled. "I would like to go into a partnership with you, *mon ami*. You have a good head for the business and you know wine. Your vineyards in Bordeaux regularly bring in a substantial profit."

"My family has been in the wine business for many years now. What kind of partnership do you seek, *Monsieur le Comte*?"

"I know you trade your wines not only in England but also ship to the Hanseatic ports and the Low Countries. I would like my champagnes to also go to these places."

Garrett arched his brows. "On *my* ships?"

Henri nodded. "In exchange for our wines traveling to their destinations together, I would give you control of one-fifth of my vineyards outside Reims for a period of ten years."

Garrett considered the proposition, which differed greatly from the Frenchman's previous offer. "I would own part of your vineyard in exchange for your champagne accompanying my wines. Do I understand you correctly?"

"Yes, you have grasped the essence of my offer. We can work out the details, of course, at a later time."

Henri waited for Garrett's reply but Garrett rose and began to pace around the room, his hands locked behind him.

He stopped abruptly. "I know little to nothing about champagne and really have no inclination to begin now. I rarely travel to Bordeaux as it is. Reims is far away from my home. Why do you suggest this?"

Henri shrugged in the typical Gallic manner, a shrug that could encompass many things. "It would open up new markets for my champagnes, of course. You have a large, swift fleet and it is well protected." He grinned. "You also have a reputation for getting the best prices available, my lord. You seem to squeeze more gold from the traders than anyone in all of England."

Garrett nodded. He knew that to be correct. He drove a hard bargain, as did his managers. His family was much better off in the years since he had been in charge of their finances.

Henri shifted in his chair. "Naturally, I would not expect you to care for the vines. I would look out for your portion of the champagne vineyards as if they were still my own. You'd simply have to transport the wine, along with my own stock, and collect the profits."

He looked expectantly at Garrett. "Then we are in agreement?"

Something kept him from committing. The offer appeared simple on the surface. In regard to business, though, he was a patient man. He'd never leaped into any transaction without more information. He would not start now, especially with a man he barely knew.

"Your proposition is intriguing, my lord," he said as he returned to his chair. "I could be interested in entering the champagne trade. But I hesitate."

Henri appeared startled, as if he'd assumed Garrett would immediately accept his idea without question.

Before he could speak, Garrett added, "I have never undertaken something so vast quite so suddenly. I would first have to see your vineyards."

Henri appeared taken aback. "But why, *monsieur*? They are impeccably kept. My secret recipe for adding the cultured yeasts and sugar yield the finest champagnes in all of France! You have drunk of my champagne. You know it to be the best."

"'Tis quite fine, de Picassaret, I'll agree with you. I simply need more time to study the situation and learn more about champagne."

"Impossible!" Henri sputtered. "I want an answer from you today, this minute!" His voice rose as his complexion mottled bright scarlet. "You must give me an answer now. I insist!"

Henri reached over and grasped the arms of Garrett's chair in his hands. He leaned close, spittle flying, and demanded, "Now! I want you as my partner *now*! I want this settled before I sail for France."

Garrett remained composed as Henri hovered inches from him. His voice was low when he responded, his tone deadly. "Remove your hands from this chair, *monsieur*, or they will be removed from your wrists."

Henri stared at him blankly for a moment. Slowly, he released the chair and stepped back. He seemed uncertain of where he was. Garrett was afraid the man had gone mad before his very eyes. What else could explain such bizarre behavior?

The manservant rushed into the room. He wondered how much of their conversation had been overheard.

"I am sorry, my lord," he addressed Garrett,

even as he went to Henri and put an arm about him. "My master has been under much strain lately."

Henri looked at Garrett with clearer eyes now. "Lord Montayne, consider my offer. If you wish to come to Chateau Maraine to inspect my vineyards, you would be most welcome. I sail for France the day after tomorrow."

He turned to his servant. "Come, Bertrand, we must go to mass again. There is much I wish to discuss with God."

The pair left the room, leaving Garrett puzzled by such odd behavior.

He retraced his steps and exited Lord Fenton's home, reclaiming Ebony from the stable boy. As he mounted, Garrett wondered about the state of Henri de Picassaret's mind. Had he witnessed a spell of madness? Why had de Picassaret become so unhinged when Garrett had refused to act immediately? He had noticed the Frenchman was a bit high-strung in the past but today he had been truly unbalanced for a few minutes.

Garrett pondered over their meeting as he headed for his London home, deciding being in business with Henri de Picassaret would be unwise, especially after seeing the Frenchman's volatile temper and odd behavior, which hinted at the possibility of madness. Though he would merely transport de Picassaret's champagne to new ports, Garrett was thorough and always liked to learn as much as he could about the cargo he moved. While drinking champagne was most pleasurable, he knew how long it had taken him to acquire knowledge of the wines grown on his own lands. He also must consider his reputation. He was known for being fair and reliable. De Picassaret's questionable behavior would make him undependable and possibly untrustworthy. Garrett wasn't willing to risk his reputation on a venture he didn't really need to be involved with. It would take a far more enticing deal before he would even consider linking himself with Henri de Picassaret.

As he rode, a steady rain fell and showed no sign of letting up. Soon, he was soaked to the skin, cold and irritable. The pounding in his head began a constant beat. He couldn't wait to arrive home. A drink would do him wonders.

He spotted her a few short blocks from his destination. He could not be mistaken. She wore a simple tunic of brown cloth, but her head was uncovered. A long braid of golden hair trailed down her back. Carrying a heavy basket balanced on one hip, she trudged along the uneven street. He wondered briefly if she'd sold his cloak.

"Lady Montayne!" he called out as he leaped off Ebony. "Wait!" He rushed to her, grabbing her elbow.

The woman started and her basket fell from

her grasp. Apples rolled all along the muddy street. Garrett stared into brown eyes filled with fear, not the amethyst ones that had haunted his dreams.

"My mistake," he quickly apologized. "I thought you were someone else." He released the stranger's arm. The woman backed away. She then looked out over all the apples spilled from her basket, most likely bruised. Her lip quivered.

Garrett realized how precious the fruit must have been to her. He bent and quickly placed the apples back into her basket, waving her away when she tried to help. Removing a few coins from his purse, he said, "My fault entirely, madam. Will you accept payment for the damage I have done?"

He took her hand and placed the coins into her palm. Surprise flooded her face and she looked at him in wonder.

"Thank you, my lord." Her voice quivered as she spoke.

He bowed and remounted Ebony.

Was he going as crazy as Henri de Picassaret? *Or had he been bewitched?*

CHAPTER SIX

MADELEINE COULDN'T HAVE spent a happier two months. She genuinely liked all the members in the troupe of mummers she had fallen in with. Being with this large group gave her a taste of a different life that was carefree and yet full of hard work. She said a quick *Hail Mary* to thank her Dear Lord for sending Gwenith into her path.

The June heat was oppressive, though, and it wasn't even noon yet as she rested in the shade from her duties. She reached around, lifting her long braid high, and used it to fan the back of her neck. The slight breeze gave her momentary relief. She dropped the braid and started to turn but was stopped in her tracks when her braid remained aloft. For a moment, icy fear swept through her. Images of Henri crowded her head. Blinding panic filled her.

She only relaxed when a familiar laugh floated on the air behind her. Whirling, her braid now freed, she caught a glimpse of Royce, a fellow member of the mummers' troupe, ducking behind the mature oak tree that had provided her shade for the past ten minutes. Silently, she crept toward the huge, gnarled trunk and melted into its side.

She moved quietly around the tree, stretched across the far side, then reached out and goosed him in the ribcage. He let out a yelp and wheeled around.

"You don't play fair, Madeleine," he said, his eyes teasing her.

"And you do, Royce? Shame on you." She shook her finger at him comically, much as she remembered from her childhood how Cook had done when a scullery maid displeased her.

The thought of home and her youth gave her pause and the smile fell from her face. She fell silent, an aching lump lodged in her throat.

Royce must have noticed the change in her. He took her elbow. "Come, wench, we have need of sustenance. I can smell the hot chewets floating along the breeze."

Madeleine stopped. "Now I know you jest. There's been no breeze all day." He looked at her imploringly. "But I seem to have caught a whiff of those meat pies all the same. Lead the way, Master Royce," she commanded in a noble tone.

They strolled along a row of booths and purchased two steaming chewets, their meat savory and hot. They passed stalls filled with salt, soap, honey, and cheese, the pungent smells intermingling with the sweat of crowded human flesh.

Royce had them settled against an ancient oak at the far end of the meadow, where they ate in amiable silence.

Madeleine counted her blessings, starting first with sweet Gwenith, already as close as a sister could possibly be. They'd spent practically every waking moment together since joining up on the London docks, with never a cross word between them. Madeleine loved her friend's head of wild, red curls and her impish smile, but Gwenith's outer beauty only scratched the surface. Her sunny nature had a way of keeping Madeleine's spirits up, no matter how much work needed to be done. These past two months had flown by in the presence of Gwenith's optimism and good cheer.

Her second blessing was time spent with Gwenith's boy, even if young Master Evan was a scamp of the first degree. Madeleine often wondered how Gwenith managed to keep up with her son's antics. Her friend had far more energy than most to be able to stay abreast of Evan's roguish ways. Still, she counted the boy as a treasure close to her heart.

Maybe she could turn Evan loose on Henri. With that thought, she stroked the smooth pebble in her pocket. A girlish giggle popped out at the thought of Henri running in fright from the small boy.

"What are you thinking about, Madeleine?" Royce asked. His voice was gentle and his eyes had lost their usual playfulness. Royce reached out and took her hand.

The depth of emotion in Royce's gaze startled her. These past few weeks traveling with the troupe had been a means of escape for her before she made her way to France. Though she enjoyed everyone's company, she did not want any lasting attachments—especially not those of a romantic nature. She was a married woman, despite having fled her abusive husband. She would keep those vows.

How could she let Royce down gently? He'd been a good friend to her, never asking about her past. When others had done so, Royce had always stepped in and helped change the subject or asked a favor from her, leading her away from prying questions.

Theirs had been an easy friendship. That was why his look of tenderness and soft words caught her by surprise. His hand held hers easily yet firmly. Madeleine slowly withdrew from his grasp. She crossed her arms and sighed.

"Oh, Royce, so it's come to this," she whispered softly.

The gleam of interest in his eyes was unmistakable. Royce looked at her as a man looked at a woman for whom he had tender feelings. He moved in to kiss her.

Madeleine's heart lurched. Fear prickled within her but she shrugged it off. This was just Royce. Not all men beat a woman for the slightest infraction, she told herself. Not all men forced relations.

"Madeleine!"

She bolted to her feet as Osbert came toward them. The jovial mummer fairly galloped across the green meadow, his round face red from the exertion.

Osbert laid his hand upon her shoulder. "'Tis Gwenith, I'm afraid. She calls for you."

Fear beating rapidly in her chest, Madeleine picked up her skirts and ran across the field to where their tents were pitched away from the stalls filled with goods. Gwenith had been sick for almost three weeks. She couldn't have taken a turn for the worse. She couldn't have.

Stomach knotted, Madeleine hurried into their tent. Gwenith, her face ashen and haggard, managed a weak smile upon seeing her.

Madeleine dropped to her knees next to Gwenith's pallet, noting how thin she'd grown. Taking her friend's hand, she squeezed it gently and pushed aside the curls that had fallen across

Gwenith's face.

"'Tis a real mess I'm in, Maddie, that's for sure," Gwenith managed to get out before being seized by a fit of coughing.

She held tightly on to Gwenith's hand until the spasm passed and then poured her a cup of cool water from the nearby pitcher.

"Sip on this, Gwenith," she said in soothing tones, helping her friend to sit up. A trickle dribbled down Gwenith's chin and Madeleine wiped it away with her sleeve.

"I'm fine now, Maddie. I promise." Gwenith's eyes were huge in her pale face, even more wan than usual. "I just wanted to visit with ye a minute, that's all." Another fit of coughing erupted.

Madeleine ached with every cough.

Finally, Gwenith calmed again. "Ye've been with Royce?" her friend asked, the corners of her mouth turning up slightly.

"Yes, I have," Madeleine begin. "I'm afraid Royce has more than friendship on his mind. If Osbert hadn't come to fetch me, I fear Royce might have said something he later regretted. Or kissed me."

Gwenith searched Madeleine's face. "Ye just now discovered his interest in ye, Maddie?" she asked in disbelief.

She stared at her in surprise. "You knew his intentions were romantic?"

Gwenith chuckled. "Only me and a dozen other mummers, me sweet." She bit her lip to hold back her laughter. "'Twas obvious from the time I brought ye back with us, Maddie. He's smitten hard. The only wonder is it took him so long to speak his mind—and for ye to realize he had feelings for ye."

Madeleine eased from her knees and sat on the floor. "I never saw this coming, Gwenith. And to keep the gossip straight, Royce has made no such declaration to me."

Gwenith pursed her lips. "As if I'd gossip about ye, Maddie." She stroked her friend's hand. "But I'm sure Royce spoke with his eyes and his heart if not his lips."

She sighed. Not wanting to discuss it further, she busied herself fussing with Gwenith's pillows and adjusting the blanket.

"Ye're so good to me," Gwenith whispered and fell into a deep sleep.

Madeleine remained by her side for several minutes. Gwenith had become the sister she'd never had. When she'd run into Gwenith and Evan after glimpsing Bertrand on the waterfront, it had been an answered prayer. Gwenith had realized Madeleine was in trouble without having to be told and that day Gwenith had returned to the mummers with her in tow. Madeleine had become an integral part of the group in a short time. When she'd first played the lute and sang for them, her fate became sealed. Now, she played for audiences before the mummers performed and provided entertainment between acts, as well. Sometimes she was pressed into service by narrating the short dramas. She had even composed a few original songs. It had been a happy few weeks.

Once a month had passed and Madeleine was sure Henri was safely on his way back to Chateau Maraine, she began preparations to leave the troupe. They had been on the circuit since early April and a few other talented people had joined in their progress. Madeleine was sure she could be replaced without much fuss.

She had gone to Farley, the head of the mummers and told him of her intentions to leave.

The hefty, bearded man boomed at her, "No, my girl, I can't let you go. You have the most wonderful voice I've heard in my two score of years. Our audiences will not be half what they are if you desert us. Would you see all of my people starve? I think not."

He crossed his arms over his rotund belly and thrust his chin in the air as if that had settled the matter.

Madeleine turned to Elspeth, his wife. "Surely you understand that I am ready to return to my home?"

Elspeth nodded solemnly. "Sure 'n I do, me sweet. Pay no mind to that barrel-chested oaf.

He'll dance to what'er tune I decide. Now be gone, child!" and she swatted Madeleine's rump.

Madeleine glanced over her shoulder as she left to witness Elspeth light into Farley, and him defend himself. "But, dearest, I was merely jesting with the girl. I would never . . ."

Farley's voice faded as Madeleine hurried back to pack her meager belongings. Besides the clothes she wore, she had few personal items. She had purchased a new lute. It had done well by her and helped her to earn her way until she was ready to see her parents again.

But Gwenith's sudden illness had put a stop to her plans. Not deliberately, of course, but Madeleine had remained all the same. Her friend looked so tired and as Madeleine heard the hacking cough that Gwenith couldn't seem to rid herself of, she decided that she owed it to Gwenith to stay until she was completely well. She would help care for Evan, who would certainly keep anyone healthy running ragged, and she could now take part in the summer solstice.

All the members of their entourage looked forward to this Midsummer's Eve festival. They would spend three days at Summerville, home to Lord Denton. Maybe by then, Gwenith would be in better health and Madeleine could cross the channel with peace of mind.

Solstice was less than a week away, though.

Instead of improving as Madeleine had hoped, Gwenith continued wasting away. Her clothing hung on her. She'd stopped performing entirely in the last few days. It troubled Madeleine and she was torn about what to do.

Royce, too, had upset her, more than she would admit to Gwenith. She hated to lose his friendship but she could not tolerate any type of flirtation. There was still a half-hour or so before the first show of the afternoon. Since Gwenith now slept, Madeleine decided to take a turn in the fresh air. Walking always seemed to clear her head.

She pushed aside the flap of the tent and stepped out into the bright June sunshine. The colors and sounds of the faire assaulted her senses at once. She moved among the crowds, familiar now with these sights and sounds. *Maman* would be appalled by this type of life but Madeleine rather enjoyed the freedom it gave her after being a prisoner within her own home.

Suddenly, she froze in her tracks. Hannah, a pert-nosed brunette with a squeaky voice who sewed most of the costumes for the troupe, moved in her direction. Escorting her was none other than Sir Ashby, one of the two noblemen who had aided her escape from Frothmore that night almost two months past.

Madeleine knew with certainty that the nobleman would recognize her. They'd spent too much time together in one another's company for him not to know her upon first sight. She groaned. Where Sir Ashby was, she was positive his friend, the brooding Lord Montayne, would soon appear. She did not care to see him face-to-face, especially since he had been so angry at her when they'd parted.

She decided to skirt around the crowd and make her way back to the performance area. She would plead a sore throat and have Farley allow her to take York's place in the play. York was a decent lute player, though not much of a singer. Still, he could perform before and between their scenes while she could be in plain sight of all, disguised by the heavy costume and mask York wore.

Moving stealthily, she hoped to avoid attention. Just as she thought she'd made her way unseen, she heard shouts headed her way.

"Stop, thief! Stop!"

The cutpurse ran by her swiftly, throwing a cursory glance over his shoulder. She despised people who preyed upon others and would see this shabby scoundrel caught. Madeleine stepped out, ready to give chase when something slammed into her, knocking her to the ground. She tried to draw a breath but the wind had been knocked from her.

Instinct caused her to roll into a ball, her arms wrapping around her in a protective cocoon. She had spent many a time lying on the floor after one of Henri's swift punches to her belly and knew she must guard her ribs at all costs. *Oh, God, it hurt so much when one broke. Please, not again. Not again.*

A hand, firm but reassuring, touched her shoulder. A voice came through the fog rolling through her brain. It wasn't Henri! She half-laughed, half-gasped, as she opened her limbs and came to lie on her back. She even reached into her pocket and stroked Henri-the-Pebble, validating that she was alive and unharmed.

Yet who had attacked her? She peered up into the blinding summer sun but could not see who stood above her. Then the shadow moved, covering her face from the harsh light.

"Why, if it isn't Lady Montayne," said the dreaded familiar voice. "Where the Hell is my favorite cloak?"

CHAPTER SEVEN

"I COULD ASK the same thing about my lute, my lord."

Garrett peered down into the angry face of the woman who had haunted his dreams by night and left him absentminded by day. Their encounter had been brief but he had never met a more remarkable woman. Not even his petite Lynnette had brought such a sweet longing to his loins as did the bewitching creature before him.

Her honeyed hair, loosened from its intricate braid, curled around her shoulders. Tiny beads of sweat graced her upper lip. Without thinking, he wiped it away with his thumb. She flinched slightly, her dark, amethyst eyes glowering up at him.

Garrett smiled in spite of himself, offering her a hand to help her to her feet. He had forgotten how very tall she was as she stared at him, her cheeks flushed with anger.

"Perhaps we could arrange a trade?" he suggested.

She eyed him suspiciously. "I'm not sure if I trust you, my lord," she countered.

"Trust *me*?" he sputtered. "This from the woman who traipsed about the countryside claiming to be *my wife*?" Garrett paused to let his words sink in. He wanted this woman to know exactly who he was and that her pretense had been discovered.

She shrugged nonchalantly, an almost Gallic air about her. She didn't sound French but there was an unmistakable manner to her movement. He'd spent enough time in France to recognize the gesture.

"I chose a bloody awful name to scare away anyone who accosted me on the road. How was I to know I'd run into *you*?" She snorted in an unladylike fashion. "I've heard tales of the wicked Lord Montayne, how he frightens old and young alike and gobbles up babes for his dinner. Why, the very mention of his name causes grown men to plead for their lives and their loved ones. Oh, no, my lord, I was an *honest* liar. *You* were the one who resorted to trickery and hid your true identity from me."

Her accusation so startled Garrett that his jaw flew open. She lifted her chin high and turned on her heel before he could make a retort. He grabbed her elbow and spun her around to face him. "Not so fast, my lady."

He studied her a second. Finally faced with her visage squarely in front of him, Garrett was at a loss of what to do. His emotions swirled out of control as he studied her narrowed eyes.

"I'm curious," he finally sputtered.

She looked puzzled. "Curious?" she echoed.

He nodded, his words spilling from him. "I know not who you are, nor where you come from. I've dreamed of you since that night, only to awaken to an emptiness." His voice became low and tinged with sadness. "I don't even know your name."

"What's this?" an angry voice exclaimed.

A man of about three and twenty strode toward them. He looked as Garrett imagined God's angels to look—tall, fair-haired, and blue-eyed. But this angel was muscular and had fisted hands. He appeared ready to deliver God's wrath upon Garrett.

He released the elbow of the still nameless woman and turned to face the man, who marched straight past him and put an arm about the mystery lady.

"Are you all right? He didn't hurt you?" The stranger turned and glared at Garrett.

The woman finally spoke. "No, Royce, things are fine," she said evenly. "Lord Montayne helped me when I was in a precarious position a few months ago. I am grateful for the aid he rendered to me." She flashed Garrett a look that he read to mean stay quiet so he did.

"You've got those dark eyes, my sweet. I fear you are angry with this lord, even if he did help you."

Her amethyst eyes now focused their fury on the one she had called Royce. "I'll thank you kindly not to interpret my glances," she said curtly.

Garrett noticed the man seemed hurt by her words, but kept his arm steady about her nonetheless.

She turned back to Garrett. "My thanks to you once more, my lord. It was a pleasure to see you again." She smiled brilliantly at him. "And give my best to Sir Ashby." With that, the couple turned, melting into the noisy crowd.

Garrett swore softly under his breath. He still had no clue who this mystery woman was. Why had he let her go so easily?

MADELEINE WAITED UNTIL they were well out of Garrett's earshot then turned to Royce. "Kindly remove your arm from me, Royce," she said icily.

He drew it away quickly. "I only meant to protect you, Madeleine. That gentleman looked quite put out with you and had hold of you. I only intervened because I feared for your safety."

She studied his contrite expression and softened. "I thank you then, Royce, but I could have done without your calling me *my sweet.*"

"It's how I feel, Madeleine. I tried telling you earlier, but we were interrupted by Osbert." His eyes reflected the hope she heard in his voice.

She placed her hand on his arm. "I—"

"There you are, Madeleine. About time you arrived. I sent Royce looking for you," Farley interrupted them. "Didn't want to start the performance late."

She dropped her hand. "Farley, may I have a quick word with you?" He nodded and she continued. "I would ask that York take my place today. I'm far too upset about Gwenith now to perform. I could easily play York's role."

Although this had been her original idea to avoid Lord Montayne and Sir Ashby, she still thought it a good one. The mighty lord had no idea she was a part of this troupe.

For all he could guess, she'd simply been enjoying the pleasures to be found at a country faire. She preferred to keep him in the dark, both to her identity and her traveling companions. When Gwenith became stronger, she still intended to leave and return home to France. The nobleman need never know who she was since, by now, he surely had finished his business with Henri.

Farley shook his head. "Impossible, my dear. That fool York just broke his leg minutes ago."

Madeleine gasped. "What happened?"

"'Twas a woman." Farley chuckled. "'Tis always a woman with York."

Madeleine frowned. "A woman broke his leg?"

"No, no, child. He broke it showing off for a woman." Farley nodded sagely. "York thought to impress her and got up on Eamon's stilts. He lost control of the blasted things and fell. Elspeth is fussing over him now, along with the pretty young thing who caused York to behave like an idiot. But York cannot play for an audience today."

She resigned herself to performing, hoping Lord Montayne wouldn't attend their show. He probably thought lowly mummers beneath him. She hurried to gather her lute from the tent.

Gwenith awakened when she entered. "Maddie? Ye look a mess. Whatever happened to yer hair?" she asked weakly.

Madeleine reached back to touch her braid. "Oh, it's nothing, Gwenith. I tried to help catch a cutpurse. No success, though, just a bit of rolling about on the ground, with the cutpurse long gone."

"I can see that. Ye must change yer tunic. 'Tis muddy on the back."

Exasperation filled her as she slipped quickly out of her clothes and into new ones, knowing how anxious Farley was to begin the next show. It didn't leave time to rebraid her abundant hair. She would have to wear it down. She pulled the sections apart until her hair was free and quickly brushed smooth. With a kiss to Gwenith, she hurried from the tent.

Passing Hannah, she noticed the glow of the younger girl's face. Usually, Hannah was churlish and fussy, never pleased with how the costumes looked on the mummers. Today, though, she radiated goodwill.

"Good luck to you, Madeleine," Hannah called sweetly.

Madeleine laughed softly to herself. If this was what a bit of time with Sir Ashby did for the girl, she wished Farley could hire the knight for an entire day. Thinking about Hannah's usual disposition, she thought a week might suffice nicely.

She approached the side of their makeshift stage. Already, the crowd was larger than any she'd seen so far. She scanned the mass nonchalantly, searching for a sign of Lord Montayne. When she saw none, she exhaled, not even realizing she'd held her breath. Part of her was relieved at his absence, while part of her longed to see him again.

He'd taken her by surprise earlier. He'd been

in her thoughts off and on for the several months since her escape. His image had appeared before her at the most unexpected moments. So many times, in fact, that it had begun to worry her. Now, he'd emerged when she'd least thought to see him.

And what of his words to her?

She recognized the anger that tinged his tone when he'd first come upon her. He not only missed his favorite cloak, but he was furious about her lies, pretending to be Lady Montayne. What struck her most, though, was his bold admission. *He'd dreamed of her, as she did him.* Madeleine shivered, though not from fear.

Nervously, she scanned the crowd again, hoping she'd missed him and that he really had come to the performance. She felt a tug on her arm. Looking down, she spotted Evan.

"Whenever are ye going to start the show, Maddie?" he asked in a stage whisper. "Farley's fit to be tied."

Madeleine realized she had been daydreaming. She squeezed Evan's shoulder. "Run along, young master, and get ready. You have a big role today."

Evan beamed. "Aye. I get to hand the sword to Rolf at the best moment. Mama says all eyes will be on me."

Madeleine gave him a slight push and settled herself. She strummed a few chords, calming the restless throng.

Soon, she was lost in the story.

"IT'S ABOUT TIME you showed your face," Garrett growled as Ashby strode toward him.

"You're in a pleasant mood, my friend," Ashby replied. "I have met the most wonderful girl, Garrett. Except for sounding like a creaky wheel needing to be oiled, she's picture perfect."

"I've no time for your conquests, Ash. *She's* here."

Ashby frowned. "And which lady would you be referring to, Garrett?"

"Lady Montayne."

Garrett regretted his choice of words as soon as he saw the look on his friend's face. Ashby thought he meant Lynnette.

"The imposter who called herself my wife," he amended. "The damned chit who made off with my cloak."

Ashby's features relaxed. He shrugged with an amused shake of his head. "Are you still bothered by that, Garrett?" A knowing smile lit his face. "You're smitten, my friend. I cannot believe I didn't see it before. That would explain why you've been so distracted. All because of a woman."

"Nonsense!" Garrett snarled at him. "I've had much on my mind. I simply want what's mine returned to me."

"As I think the lady herself would like her lute given over."

"Will you help me find her again or not?" he demanded.

"It's a big faire, Garrett," Ashby pointed out. "Besides, I only came back to find you for the play."

"Play?"

"Yes, the mummers' little drama. My new-found friend, Hannah, is the seamstress for this troupe. She says there's a remarkable woman who narrates and sings."

"So?"

"So I promised her we'd watch." He swung an arm around Garrett's shoulders and began leading him in the direction of the stage. "We'll look afterwards for the mysterious Lady Montayne."

Garrett knew better than to try to dissuade Ashby. The man had an eye for ladies, young and old alike. He fell into step with his friend, their long strides covering the distance in a short time. Perhaps he could scan the crowd for the mystery woman.

"Hannah promised to save us a place," Ashby said. "She'll be just off the stage."

As they pushed through the edge of the mass,

music could be heard. A sweet, lilting melody that touched Garrett in an indescribable way.

Then a voice entered into the song. He came to a halt, moved by the low, mellow tones.

Ashby tugged on his sleeve. "She's up there," he whispered.

Garrett followed as if in a dream. Ashby moved and stood by a pretty brunette and they both motioned him over. He walked toward them and turned to the far side of the stage but he instinctively knew who he would see.

His Lady Montayne.

She wore a tunic of rich plum. Her golden hair hung free past her waist. He longed to run his fingers through the unbound, silken tresses. No, he'd sit at her feet, a slave to her song, the most beautiful music he'd ever heard. Indeed, sung by the loveliest creature on earth.

She sang with her eyes closed and he studied her greedily. Despite her height, her bone structure was delicate. Her wrists were small. Her thin, elegant fingers strummed the lute as if they held magic in them. She wore a wistful smile and she had the most kissable mouth he'd ever laid eyes upon.

As she sang, Garrett wondered at the sadness that seemed to cloak her. She had to have suffered through great sorrows, else she couldn't bring such richness to the words. A lump gathered in his throat even as he wanted to wash away her pain.

The last note sounded and reverberated for a moment and then the crowd showed its enthusiasm for her talent. She smiled graciously and then began to weave new magic with her words. She told of a young king who sought honor and how he'd lost his heart to a beautiful maiden while on his quest.

Once her song ended, the audience settled back as the play began. His songstress remained perched at the far edge of the stage, her sad eyes watching the mummers. Garrett studied her profile—the high cheekbones, the pert, straight nose, and, again, that generous mouth that he longed to touch with his own.

At that moment, she raised her head. Their eyes locked. Her lush mouth trembled slightly. He smiled casually. Her chin went up as before, defiant as ever.

It didn't matter. The hunter had his prey within his grasp.

CHAPTER EIGHT

MADELEINE FROZE AS she caught sight of Lord Montayne's smile. He seemed so assured, so confident, as he beamed at her from across the crowd. Could he hear her heart pounding through her tunic, so loud it seemed to echo in her ears?

She licked her lips nervously but her eyes never left his. Their gazes remained locked together. She was distantly aware of the mummers taking their bows and the audience's cheers of approval but she continued to focus on Lord Montayne. All else faded from view.

His dark hair was cut close to his head. Although his skin, too, was dark, his eyes stood out in his handsome face. Even from this distance, Madeleine could see the long lashes that framed them. He stood with legs planted firmly in place, his muscular arms now crossed in front of his wide chest. Sir Ashby tugged at his sleeve but was ignored. Montayne's eyes never left hers, holding her captive in a silent battle of wills.

Slowly, the noise from the audience died down and the mass began dispersing toward the stalls. Madeleine knew she couldn't speak to him. Lord Montayne sent her emotions into chaos. She'd never before experienced this uncertainty and exhilaration. How could she possibly endure anything more? She stood, holding her lute close as she maneuvered into the throng, easing between groups of people as swiftly as she could without drawing attention. She had a plan. She would keep fast to it.

No handsome devil with dark eyes would alter her course.

THE MINUTE SHE broke the spell, Garrett began to follow her. His lips longed to call out to her but they held no name he could use.

Despite his swiftness, he lost her before a minute passed. Another cutpurse raced by, overturning a cage of white doves. The birds scattered amidst the crowd, causing shrieks and cries. A cart overturned in the ensuing excitement. By the time he leaped over it, she was gone. He cursed softly under his breath. How could she slip away again?

Ashby caught up to him. "So you misplaced the maiden again, Garrett?" His mouth twisted as he tried to prevent a smile and failed.

Garrett cursed again, this time much louder. "I haven't misplaced her," he snapped, causing Ashby to chuckle softly.

"She couldn't be that hard to find, my friend. She's bound to be the tallest woman here. With her height and that gorgeous mane of hair flowing behind her, I'd think every man at the faire would follow her."

Garrett stared hard at Ashby, his eyes narrowing into small slits. "We'll not leave until she's found, Ash. Mark my words."

"Then let's start with the mummers. Since she's part of their troupe, she's bound to turn up there sooner than later."

The two men headed back toward the makeshift stage. Hannah stood waiting for Ashby and ran to them as they approached.

"Where did you go, my lord?" she chastised Ashby with a flirting glance. "I was afraid I'd displeased you. You hurried away so quickly." Her full lips turned from a pout into a more inviting smile.

Ashby burst out laughing. "You are a treasure, little Hannah," he exclaimed. "But come, Lord Montayne and I shall enjoy your company while we find some refreshment. Let us try some of that mulled wine you spoke of."

Ashby took Hannah's arm and began leading her away. He glanced back over his shoulder and motioned Garrett to follow. Meeting his companion's glare with a lecherous grin, he gave Hannah's bottom a fond pinch. She swatted his hand away playfully and he slipped an arm around her waist.

They purchased their wine and some hot sticky buns and made their way across the crowd. Ashby picked out a soft patch of ground and they sat.

"So, my dear, you were telling me about life with the mummers." Ashby glanced back to Garrett. "We would love to hear all about your troupe."

Garrett thought he'd go mad. The chit was comely, but her voice grated on his nerves worse than rusted armor. Still, Ashby was good with the girl, both in listening and complimenting her at the right times. He had always admired his friend's easy charm when it came to women. Gradually, Ashby led Hannah around to the information they sought.

"You were right about the lute player, Hannah. Rarely have I heard so talented a minstrel—and never one that was a woman," Ashby proclaimed.

"You could've knocked me over with a feather the first time I heard her sing," said Hannah.

"Just like a songbird, she is, and right nice, too."

"Even one so beautiful?" interjected Garrett. "I find beautiful women to often be tiresome, so enchanted are they with their own looks."

Ashby groaned. "Sweet Hannah, listen not to my friend. He's had bad luck with beautiful women." He paused and then added, "And even worse luck with ugly ones."

Hannah cackled at his wit while Garrett waved a fist at Ashby. "See, dear Hannah, even now he mocks me, wishing he found you first," and he gave her a sweet smile. "But tell us more about the lady troubadour," Ashby continued. "Has she been with your group for long?"

"Nay, my lord. 'Tis been but two months now. She came back with Gwenith."

"Gwenith?"

"Oh, poor Gwenith didn't perform today. She's been much too sick. Madeleine has been caring for her and little Evan, Gwenith's naughty son."

Garrett interrupted. "The woman who sings, her name is Madeleine?"

"Aye, my lord," Hannah replied. "She's as kind as she is pretty and tells the most amusing stories. Half the men in the troupe swear they're in love with her, even fat, old Edgar."

Hannah frowned. "But she cannot even take a needle to thread properly. She's all thumbs, though she has tried to help me once or twice."

"Is she sweet on someone?" Garrett asked softly.

Hannah's eyes grew large. "Nay, my lord, she keeps to herself. Oh, she's close to Gwenith and Evan and treats everyone right nice, she does, but she goes all quiet when someone asks about her past. She's mighty mysterious about things, if you ask me." She sighed. "I think Royce is sweet on her."

"Royce?" Garrett asked. Even as he spoke the name, he remembered the muscular, blond man who possessively had taken his mystery woman in hand and led her away. No, he didn't like this Royce at all—but he'd found out what he needed to know.

Her name was Madeleine.

MADELEINE WOVE HER way through couples who were arm-in-arm, racing children, and happy families enjoying both the calm weather and goods to be had. She didn't stop until she reached the copse of trees and, even then, she continued until she had gone a distance she deemed safe.

Breathless, she finally collapsed upon the soft, mossy grass, cool against her overheated skin. She tried to breathe slowly and deeply and regain control of her racing pulse.

Why had she run? What did she have to fear from him? She'd done nothing wrong. Well, perhaps just a wee bit wrong. She remembered the cloak still in her possession, the rich, plush fabric and how it felt when wrapped around her. She had tried it on twice since that April night, inhaling the subtle masculine scent that lingered on it and feeling oddly safe within its folds. She wondered what it would be like to be in Lord Montayne's arms.

What was it about him that caused her to act this way? Oh, he was a handsome devil, with those dark, soulful eyes and brawny build, but could it be more than that? Surely not. His manners and his attitude were boorish. He might be her ideal man in looks but his personality wasn't attractive in the slightest. Besides, why should she think of him at all? Despite his dashing appearance, she was a married woman. Although Henri had broken every marriage vow made, she was still his faithful, lawful wife. Madeleine loved God far more than any mortal man. She would not be tempted, even if her husband was a cold and cruel man who gave no love to her.

Lord Montayne's words continued to echo in her mind, though.

I dream of you.

No married man should ever utter such thoughts aloud. She would do well enough to avoid him. Never be in his presence again. For a man who would admit something so raw and unguarded to a woman would seek to act upon those words. Lord Montayne was powerful and wealthy. He was the type of nobleman who would try to bend her to his will, wanting things from her that she couldn't possibly give.

Even if she yearned to do so.

That thought frightened her more than one of Henri's rages. Immediately, Madeleine uttered a swift *Hail Mary* for good measure, fearing her own wicked thoughts regarding this earl might lead her astray.

She eased back against a broad oak, its trunk firm behind her, and rested her lute upon the ground. She slipped Henri-the-Pebble from her pocket, fingering the surface absently as she considered the path her life had taken.

She closed her eyes to rest a bit and her mind began to drift.

THE CLOCK TICKED much too loudly. Madeleine found herself wanting to cover her ears. She crossed the crowded room, hearing bits of muffled conversation as she passed. She had the oddest sensation that people were talking about her.

She glanced over her shoulder. No one in the room would meet her eyes. She hurried from the crowd and entered the room that housed the buffet supper.

It was wrong, terribly wrong. The air was filled with a putrid scent. She gagged and swallowed hard. She walked over to the tables laden with rotting food. Maggots and flies covered the many dishes. All at once, the quail and dove sat up from their dressings and sauce, squawking and screeching. The birds tried to fly away, only to fall to the floor, flapping helplessly.

Feral dogs appeared from the open doorway and proceeded to trap the birds, inhaling them with grunts of pleasure. Madeleine watched in horror as they rapidly devoured the decaying meal. Within moments, the dogs had finished off the feast, looking for something more to whet their appetites. They seemed to catch Madeleine's scent and she began backing away from them, her mouth dry, her pulse pounding.

The pack rushed her and she screamed and ran to the doors. She passed through and slammed them shut, wincing as the dogs threw their massive bodies against the heavy panels.

She raced back to where the guests were, her limp much more pronounced now. She arrived disheveled, her hair streaming down her back. She must warn her guests of the rabid animals.

Suddenly, the strains of music within the hall ceased. The lights dimmed. Everyone turned their attention to the top of the staircase. Madeleine followed their stares.

A lone figure stood poised there, dressed in black from head to foot, his face in shadow. Madeleine sensed an innate evil emanating from the man. Slowly, *he began descending the stairs.*

She knew he was coming for her.

The throng buzzed now, their words indistinguishable. The man moved steadily down the steps but she was frozen in place, helpless to move. When he got to the bottom, he moved in her direction. The way parted until he reached her. Suddenly, the light was brilliant, almost blinding her, but she suddenly recognized him.

Henri.

She exclaimed, "Henri! The feast has been ruined. The food is not edible. The dogs. Oh, God, the dogs! Henri—"

"Silence!" He placed his hands on her shoulders, his fingers tightening against her tender flesh.

"Henri, not here," she begged. "Not in front of—"

"Our guests? Come now, Madeleine, they all realize that you must be disciplined." Henri smiled at the visitors. "Surely you see I must do something about her?"

Murmurs of assent echoed throughout the hall. Madeleine tried to tear free but Henri's grasp held firm, causing her to cringe.

"Lady de Picassaret is so perfect."

"Henri's wife is so clever, so amusing."

"De Picassaret has his hands full with that one."

Madeleine heard fragments of the comments. The voices in the room grew louder and louder, as did their laughter. She managed to break free from Henri's hold and stumble across the hall, watching as the faces of the guests changed. Gone were the placid features she had first seen. Instead, their countenances took on a macabre quality, twisting and melting.

She tried to open the door and escape but it was locked. She rattled the knob with all her strength, to no avail. Turning, she saw the strange creatures closing in on her, led by the dark, solemn figure of Henri.

"You must be disciplined, Madeleine. No good will come to you unless you are properly corrected. Come here, my dearest, and take your punishment with grace."

She screamed and screamed, but no one heard her.

MADELEINE AWOKE WITH a start, a cool sheen of sweat covering her brow. She had dreamed of Henri again. Her hands were clammy. Fear had left a sour taste on her tongue. Would it be like this forever? Would thoughts of Henri always haunt her dreams?

Pushing her tangled hair from her face, she sat up, having no idea of the time and knowing she must start back. There were still two more performances that day. She prayed she hadn't missed one. She hurried back through the forest and into the swarm of people, soon arriving at the stage, her lute in hand.

"Sweet Jesu, girl, it's about time you showed your face," grumbled Farley. "I thought you'd abandoned us."

"No, Farley, I'd not do that." She placed a kiss upon his brow. "You've been much too kind to me."

The burly man blushed hotly. "Then be kind to our audience and work your magic," he told her, muttering to himself as he walked away.

Madeleine scanned the crowd, but she caught no sight of Lord Montayne or his companion. With mixed feelings, she prepared to begin her song. Before she struck the first note, Evan pulled at her tunic.

"Maddie?" he whispered loudly. "Mama needs ye. She's awful bad, she is."

Before she could reply, Osbert slipped in next to her. "'Tis bad off she is, Madeleine. Elspeth's been with her. She sent me to fetch you."

Madeleine appeared torn. "But Farley—"

Osbert snorted. "Forget about Farley. Elspeth will deal with him. You're needed for more important things."

"But York—"

York appeared as she spoke. His leg was heavily bandaged and he used a makeshift crutch but he hobbled up to the edge of the stage nonetheless.

"I'm fine, Madeleine. Go to Gwenith."

She hesitated a moment.

"It's all right, Madeleine," York assured her. "My lady friend who helped put me in this"—he tapped his leg gently—"thinks I'm doing a brave thing by performing when I feel so poorly. I'm sure," he said, a wide grin breaking out on his handsome features, "she'll reward me properly for my efforts. Now off with you."

She needed no further urging, taking Evan's hand in her own and hurrying back to their tent.

Gwenith lay there, flushed and feverish. Madeleine ran to her, touching her cheeks, frightened by the scalding flesh.

She turned to Elspeth and said, "Please boil some more of the barley."

The woman began muttering in her thick Scottish brogue, mostly words Madeleine couldn't understand and had no time to try and decipher. She and Elspeth had disagreed heatedly about Gwenith's care from the beginning. The older woman had been in favor of sending immediately for a barber to bleed Gwenith, which Madeleine objected to vehemently. She had seen the practice used several times in her youth and had lost a favorite cousin in that manner. She was determined to try other methods to save Gwenith.

Instead, Madeleine implemented the practices of her gentle mother. Cadena had had a way with herbs and had freely passed along her knowledge to her only daughter.

As she waited for Elspeth, Madeleine nursed Gwenith patiently, wetting cloths with cool water and pressing them to her friend's hot skin.

Finally, a sullen Elspeth returned from the cookfire and passed the barley to her. After mixing in some honey, Madeleine coaxed Gwenith to sip it.

"Come on, love, just a bit more," she urged.

Her friend sighed. "Ye're a tyrant, Maddie, but I'm glad ye're my tyrant." She drank the last bit, falling back onto her pillow.

Her fever eased afterward but every cough stained her handkerchief with bits of blood, black and thick.

Despite her best efforts, Madeleine realized that Gwenith was growing worse. She brushed a strand of hair from her friend's face. "I'm off to fetch a physician, Gwenith, dear. Lie here and rest. I'll be back before you know it."

Gwenith protested, no louder than a weak kitten. "Oh, Maddie, there's none to be had 'round here, that's for sure. The best ye'll find is a barber. Savage beasts," she muttered.

"No, Gwenith," Madeleine assured her. "None of that foolish nonsense. I'll return as soon as I can, dearest, and I will find someone to help." She tenderly kissed Gwenith's brow. "Get some rest. That's a direct order from your very own tyrant."

She slipped to the far end of the tent and lifted the hem of her skirts, feeling carefully before placing her finger into a loose stitch. She broke a few of the threads, removing what she needed and putting the ring into her pocket with the pebble. She kept her hand there, afraid she'd lose the precious item.

Then she made her way toward a stall in the heart of the faire. Old Pascal traveled this circuit and had bought a piece of jewelry from Madeleine when she'd first arrived two months before. She'd been low on coin, having forfeited the money paid for her passage to France, and he'd been generous in the price they'd settled upon. She hoped he'd be decent again.

As she approached his booth, she removed the sapphire ring from her pocket, having left the matching bracelet within her hem. The pair had been a birthday present from Henri, who liked to keep up appearances with his friends. Otherwise, Madeleine doubted he'd have gifted her with even a hardened bread crust to mark that day of celebration.

Before she could address Pascal, she jumped when a low voice said in her ear, "So you've moved on from cloaks to jewels now. Where did you steal such a fine ring from, Madeleine?"

CHAPTER NINE

"YOU'VE JUDGED ME poorly, Lord Montayne," Madeleine huffed, pocketing the jewelry and stepping away from Pascal's ears. The tradesman might be charitable but he was a ferocious gossip. Madeleine had no intention of airing her affairs before him.

She managed several paces away from the booth when the nobleman roughly took her by the arm. "Prove it," he said as he swung her around to face him.

"I owe you no explanation, my lord," she curtly replied, shrugging off his hand. She turned and moved in the opposite direction.

He was immediately by her side, grabbing her wrist and dragging her across the faire grounds. She faltered as she attempted to keep up with him. He stopped and helped her to an upright position. She felt her cheeks burning brightly as she glowered at him.

"I'm sorry," he said gently, releasing his hold on her.

"I have a slight limp," she retorted. "Usually it's not noticeable unless it seems that I'm being dragged along by a madman at an unreasonable gait. That always brings it out." She smoothed her tunic and tucked stray wisps of hair away from her face.

"Where are we going?" she demanded of him.

He looked at her blankly. "I'm not sure."

"You're not sure?" She glared at him, mumbling under her breath. "You are *stupide*."

Madeleine noticed he raised a brow and seemed to assess her. She hoped he hadn't heard her remark. She must be sure everything she spoke was in English. It was hard, though, since the man riled her anger, making her want to lapse into French.

"Come, we'll sit over here." He indicated a large stump at the edge of the pasture. He motioned for her to follow him.

She knew it was useless to avoid him any longer. She only worried about getting back to Gwenith as soon as possible.

"What can I do for you, my lord?" she asked with forced bravado, hiding her inner fear.

"Just who are you, Madeleine?"

"Nothing but a poor mummer, my lord.

Practicing my skills whenever I meet new people. You know," she said, eyeing him up and down, "you were quite talented yourself, not letting on as to your true identity. Perhaps you'd care to join our little group?"

"Quit provoking me!" he snapped.

"Then don't provoke me," she answered sharply. "Leave me alone." She calmed herself and continued in a lower tone. "I will return your cloak. I'm no thief, my lord, and somehow I would have seen the garment returned to you. I appreciate the help you gave me that night. I regret I took the cloak by mistake."

"But why did you take off? As if you had something to hide? Are you running from the law?"

Madeleine sighed. "I had reasons, my lord, too complicated to share." She glanced around impatiently. "I must go now."

"And sell your stolen ring?"

She trembled, having reached her breaking point. "It's not stolen. I sell it for a friend. She's very ill." The tears welled in her eyes. "I must have money to buy medicines for her. I must find a physician, as well. She is depending upon me."

"Is this Gwenith of whom you speak?"

Madeleine started. "I see you've learned much about me, my lord." She wiped at her tears. "Yes, it's for my dear Gwenith. She means the world to me. Though we are not blood kin, we are closer than sisters." She rose and began walking away from him but stopped and said, "If you'll come to the master mummer's tent, I'll see that your cloak is there." Her features softened. "I thank you for its use. It was kind of you to lend it to me—and I'm not used to such kindness."

HER SMILE WAS tentative but beautiful all the same. Garrett let her leave to finish her transaction. He watched her until she was gone from his sight, noticing for the first time the slight hitch in her gait. He wondered what had caused such a young woman to have a limp, unless it was something she'd possessed since birth.

She'd said she was selling the jewel for a friend. Did that mean it belonged to Gwenith, and Madeleine pawned the ring for the sick woman? Or had she lifted the piece from an unsuspecting lady, ready to sell it to aid her friend?

Why would a common mummer possess so fine a piece? She had told him nothing but lies from the time they'd first met. Why should he believe her words now?

He had not gotten a good look but he had seen enough to recognize the gemstones as sapphires, and good quality at that.

His curiosity got the better of him. Eventually, the lies would have to end. He didn't know why he was so drawn to Madeleine and he didn't intend to let her disappear. Just as he had searched her out when she hadn't performed at the play that afternoon, he would find her again.

He returned to the old man's stall, where he watched Madeleine conduct the end of her transaction. She seemed a bit disappointed. Her mouth was tightly drawn, no trace of the smile she'd left him with evident now. She hurried away and he gave her a minute before approaching the vendor.

The man stood taller as Garrett approached.

"My fine lord, how might I help you today? I have many wares to be had." He waved a hand across his display. "You'll find none finer than Old Pascal's stall." The vendor flashed a toothless grin at Garrett.

"The woman. Did she sell a sapphire ring?"

Pascal nodded. "Yes, my lord." Suddenly, a look of panic entered Pascal's eyes and he sputtered, "'Twas not yours, my lord? I had no idea. I've dealt with the wench before and nothing seemed amiss."

"No," Garrett assured him. "I was merely interested in its purchase."

Pascal visibly relaxed. "Would you like to see it, my lord?"

Garrett nodded and the vendor reached

under his displayed wares. He brought out the ring and handed it to Garrett. As he'd suspected, the gems were of high quality, catching the sun's rays and sparkling in his hands.

"Name your price."

Pascal seemed taken aback but quickly recovered, giving Garrett a figure. Garrett narrowed his eyes. "Is that what you gave Madeleine for the ring?" he asked icily.

"Nay, my lord. I'm just a poor trader and must make a profit. I gave the girl the best she could get under the circumstances, this not being London. It's not just anywhere that you can sell a ring the likes of this one."

Garrett reached into the purse at his waist and withdrew a handful of coins. He casually tossed them upon the table, noting the gleam in Pascal's eyes. The old man lifted a gold coin and brought it to his mouth. Turning to the side, he bit into it. Satisfied, he scooped up the remaining coins and placed them under his table.

Pascal nodded to Garrett. "You've made a fine purchase, my lord. Your lady will be proud to wear such fine stones."

Garrett kept his remarks to himself and moved away. He wound his way through the intricate stall area, where everything from salt to weapons were being bartered and sold. The late afternoon sun was beginning to dip low in the sky, and many people were trying to conclude their transactions.

He found the last play of the day being performed. The troubadour narrating was talented but his song had none of the depth that Madeleine's voice had held. He wandered behind the stage, where the group was in a frenzy.

He spied a fat monk emerging from one of the many tents pitched in the area.

"Were you here to see Gwenith?" Garrett asked.

The monk looked surprised. He studied Garrett carefully before answering, his eyes disappearing into slits within the folds of his face. "Yes, my lord. You know the woman?"

Garrett nodded curtly. "How is she?"

The monk shook his head, the rolls of fat now jiggling. "Not good, my lord. She is rapidly fading. Her fever runs hot and there's blood brought forth with every cough." He crossed himself. "May God be merciful."

"What would she need to become well?"

The holy man took a step back then tapped a fat finger against his jowl. "I'm not sure she can be made whole again, my lord. It could be the sweating sickness. More than likely 'tis scrofula. She would need total bed rest, of course, and none of this moving about from place to place. Constant care, too."

The monk narrowed his eyes. "I'll pray for her, my lord. 'Twould be right to light a candle for her." He hesitated, eyeing Garrett hopefully.

When Garrett did not respond, the monk shrugged. "It was only a thought, my lord. A small donation and mayhap God will relieve her burden."

Garrett scowled, not believing a coin offered and a lit candle would make even a ghost of a chance. Yet for reasons he could not explain, he tossed the monk a gold coin. Ignoring the thanks lavished upon him, he dismissed the monk with a wave of his hand and quietly entered the tent he'd seen the man come from.

He hovered in the doorway, his eyes adjusting to the faint light inside. Propped up on a pallet was a woman who, although pretty, was obviously quite ill. Her eyes burned unnaturally bright in her wan face. Her pallor contrasted sharply with the vibrant red hair cascading around her shoulders.

Madeleine sat by her side, murmuring soothing words to her. She held Gwenith's hand in one of hers, the other pushing the hair from her brow. A young boy, his face stained with tears, huddled next to Madeleine, clutching her skirts tightly.

Garrett stepped back outside the tent, his emotions too close to the surface. He prided himself on his control but the scene he witnessed brought back too many painful memories. He had spent many hours at his beloved older brother's bedside before Luke expired from typhoid fever. His mother had begged Garrett to leave, afraid he would also fall ill. In a strange way, Garrett had secretly hoped he would. He had idolized Luke, following him around like a puppy his entire life. If Luke were gone, then life had not seemed worth living.

Garrett remembered the last time they'd spoken. It was late, the castle bedded down for the night. Most of the servants avoided Luke's chamber, their fears of the fever keeping both them and Luke's friends away.

A single candle burned next to the bedside, casting eerie shadows on the wall. Luke had been sleeping, his body restless, flinching and twitching. Suddenly, he'd opened his eyes, which burned with the typhus, making them shine brightly.

Grabbing Garrett's hand, he whispered, "I still have the scar, you know."

Confused, Garrett asked, "What scar?"

His brother grinned mischievously. "The one on my shoulder. The one you put there, you cretin."

Garrett chuckled. "I wanted to hunt, just as you and Father did."

"And I was your quarry?"

Garrett shrugged. "I was only four, Luke." He grinned at the memory. "I thought Father would flay me when I charged you with that spear."

Luke shuddered. "How you lifted the damned thing is beyond me."

"I know," Garrett said softly.

Luke slipped back into sleep as quickly as he'd awakened. Those were the last words he'd spoken. Garrett held his hand for an hour before he'd felt the warmth give way. He was still holding it when the morning rays cast their first light upon a new day. The first he'd faced without Luke. Unluckily for him, he never caught the fever. No hovering between life and death for Garrett. But he'd never been the same. With Luke's passing, something of him, too, had died. With Lynnette's abandoning him for another man, it seemed what little feeling he'd had left had gone, as well. Only at rare times did he feel anything, and that was when Lyssa brought a smile to his lips.

Mayhap that was what was different about Madeleine. She had caused him to feel again. How, he did not know, but in some inexplicable way, she made him want to live again. She had a spark of vitality about her, capturing his imagination as Luke had all those years ago. When she spoke, he had an interest in whatever came from her mouth. Most of it had been absolute nonsense, but it was entertaining, all the same. She had a wit about her. For a woman, she thought fast on her feet. He relished the thought of verbally sparring with her again, which brought a rare smile to his face. He was only five and twenty and had many more years left to him. It was time he shrugged off his complacency and enjoyed life.

He stopped a barrel-chested man. "Who is in charge of your troupe?"

The man scratched his head. "Farley is, though if the truth be told, his wife, Elspeth, runs things." He chuckled. "Farley included, that she does."

"Where might I find this Elspeth and Farley?"

He was directed to a tent that was much larger than the others. Not for luxury on the part of the owners, though. As he entered, he found he could barely move, so great was the clutter inside it. The tent must house every costume and prop used in their performances.

Garrett wove his way around to the voices he heard.

"York did an adequate job, dearest."

"But he's not Madeleine, Elspeth. The girl has something about her. I can't explain it. The crowds want to see her, hear her, not silly York crooning away."

"At one time, ye were happy to have York, Farley."

"Well, he's not enough anymore. You must insist Madeleine continue to perform, Elspeth."

Elspeth started to answer her husband but stopped and turned in Garrett's direction. "Who's skulking about there? Come forward," she commanded.

Garrett came to stand in front of her.

"I'm sorry to be so abrupt, my lord," she apologized nervously. "Ye must be Lord Montayne, come for yer cloak. Madeleine said ye'd be by for it." She fetched the garment and handed it to him.

"Where do you go from here?" Garrett asked.

Farley answered, "Why, we go to Lord Denton's. Summerville way."

Garrett nodded. "Yes, I know the estate. I'm from Stanbury myself."

Farley nodded. "Yes, we've been that way before, my lord. The properties are fairly close to one another."

"I have a proposition for you."

Garrett exited Farley's tent several minutes later. He returned to the tent Madeleine was in and slipped inside.

As before, she was next to Gwenith, the boy's head now in her lap. He was fast asleep. She stroked his hair fondly. As Garrett moved toward her, she raised her head. Surprise registered on her features.

He could tell she'd been crying. Her eyes were swollen and puffy. The front of her tunic was damp and rumpled. He knelt down beside her and placed a hand upon her shoulder.

"What are you doing here, my lord?" she

whispered. "Did you not find Farley's tent? I left your cloak there." Even as she said it, she glanced at the cloak draped over his arm.

"Yes, Madeleine, I've gotten it back." He cupped her chin with his hand and stroked her trembling bottom lip with his thumb. Then he leaned forward and gently kissed her.

"*Au revoir*, Madeleine."

Rising, he quickly left her.

CHAPTER TEN

MADELEINE WATCHED LORD Montayne disappear from the enclosed space. His presence had filled the small tent. Now the place seemed empty and forlorn.

She reached up, grazing her fingertips against her lips in quiet wonder. She could still feel his warm breath, the press of his mouth softly against hers.

What had possessed him to kiss her?

Madeleine would never regret that he had. Henri had kissed her on rare occasions and only in public when duty called for it, always on her brow or cheek. The only time he'd kissed her on her mouth was to seal their vows before the priest on their wedding day. When Madeleine questioned why he did not kiss her at other times, Henri informed her that kissing had nothing to do with making an heir and so he was uninterested in it.

Yet Madeleine longed for the intimacy of kissing a man she loved. She'd soon discovered that Henri would never be that man. She had relegated kissing far into a corner chamber of her mind. She'd stopped daydreaming about it and such foolish ideas as romantic love.

Until Lord Montayne.

She admitted to herself that she had often thought about kissing the nobleman these past two months. When she wrapped his cloak about her, she longed to be enveloped in his arms, as well. He would hold her firmly, yet tenderly, and then he would kiss her, over and over, until she was breathless.

She had not thought this fantasy could ever come true and, in truth, it had not. Garrett had barely touched her, his lips brushing hers softly but for a moment. It gave Madeleine a glimpse, though, of the magic that might have been if she hadn't been married to Henri. Maybe real love did exist after all.

She felt a deep longing within her but knew this ache could never be filled. Even if she imagined herself falling in love with an English lord, nothing could come of it. She was married. So was he, although there seemed to be a different standard among men who had taken their marriage vows and women who kept theirs. Madeleine resolved never to see him again. He had his cloak. That was all he'd come for.

Or was it?

GARRETT FOUND ASHBY still in Hannah's giggling company. The sun had now set and he was anxious to leave. He caught Ashby's eye and motioned him over.

"Are you ready to ride?"

Ashby raised his brows. "No," he said frankly. "And I thought you wouldn't be either. Or was the alluring Madeleine not taken in by your many charms?"

Garrett stared at him coldly. "She's not like that, Ash."

His friend laughed. "Oh, so now she's a lady?"

"That's not quite what I meant."

"Then what do you mean, Garrett? I rode off to London with you at the drop of a hat. Not that anyone's counting, but it was the third time we've done so in as many months. You promised me a little fun on our way back and I aim to have it." He frowned. "You could use a little of that fun yourself, Garrett."

"I need to get back to Stanbury. I've arrangements to make."

Ashby tilted his head. "Arrangements? What

are you preparing for?"

Garrett shrugged. "It seems we'll be holding a little faire at Stanbury, Ash."

Ashby grinned and slapped Garrett on the back. "When was this decided?"

"It's something I worked out with a Mister Farley, who's head of the mummers. They were to travel next to Summerville and quarter there for a few weeks."

"Yes, we've been to the summer solstice celebration there before, Garrett, don't you remember?"

"I've decided they need to spend their next sojourn at Stanbury instead." Garrett paused. "Of course, Lord Denton doesn't know this yet."

Ashby hooted with pleasure. "Serves the old bastard right. Imagine, him being passed over for Stanbury. What I wouldn't give to see the look on his face when he's informed of the change."

"Stop your gloating, Ash. He'll be told soon enough, I'm sure. It's also costing me plenty from my pocket to see that it occurs." For a moment he felt like the Garrett of old. He quickly sobered and clamped a hand on Ash's shoulder. "So I ride back to Stanbury tonight. You may come with me now or follow later. It's up to you."

Ashby glanced behind him to where Hannah stood a distance away, tapping her foot impatiently. "I might need just one night of rest before I continue on, Garrett. Too much travel at one time has never suited me."

Garrett shook his head. "You and your women, Ash."

Ashby shrugged. "What can I say?

MADELEINE LOOKED UP as Elspeth came into the tent. Disappointment washed over her, wishing it would have been Lord Montayne again. Despite her determination to keep away from him, she longed to see the man again.

"How's the little love?" Elspeth motioned down to Evan, who was curled around Madeleine.

"Good, for once. If we could keep him asleep at all times, some might mistake him for an angel."

Elspeth chuckled and bent to lift Evan. She placed him on a pallet of straw and then reached a hand down to Madeleine. Madeleine winced as her injured knee reminded her of the viciousness of her husband. Hating that she had to depend on others, she leaned heavily on Elspeth to get to her feet. She bit her lip, trying to ignore her knee's constant throbbing.

"I'm here to spell ye," Elspeth told her. "Ye haven't had a bite to eat nor a chance to rest." Elspeth waved her hand in front of her. "Don't push me off, child. Ye know I'm right. Now go and get some food in yer belly. I'll sit with Gwenith and the tyke."

Madeleine nodded and exited the tent. A slight breeze greeted her. She brushed her hair away from her face and moved slowly toward the campfire, wobbly on her stiff legs.

This time of day had turned out to be her favorite since she'd joined Farley's group. The day's performances were done and the troupe's spirits were lighthearted. There was food to be had, tales to be told, songs to be sung. The after-show celebrations all made Madeleine feel a part of a family, something she'd sorely missed.

Edgar pushed a plate into her hands. "Go fill it up, Madeleine, and then perhaps you'll tell us a story?" he asked hopefully, his bushy white eyebrows raised in expectation. Edgar was old enough to be her grandfather but he was very flirtatious with her.

"If I can think of one, Edgar, I shall," she promised.

"Of course you can, Madeleine. You'll never run out of tales," he cackled.

Madeleine caught a whiff of mutton and freshly baked bread at the same time and her mouth watered in response. Soon, her plate was loaded and she inhaled the meal, finding she was much hungrier than she'd thought possible.

The mutton was tender and she cleaned her

plate quickly. Edgar took it from her and refilled it despite her protests.

"I know you can do justice to it, Madeleine," he said and handed her a second helping with a wink.

She patted his hand in thanks and Edgar blushed until his bald pate glowed beet red. Those present laughed loudly. Madeleine realized then how much she had come to love her new life performing for the crowds, being with those who were richly blessed with love and laughter in their lives, feeling a part of a gathering. It brought tears to her eyes and she blinked rapidly several times before they spilled down her cheeks. She quickly wiped her eyes with her sleeve.

"Are you through eating, Madeleine?" Osbert asked, an expectant look on his face. "Edgar says you'll tell us a tale when you've had your fill."

Edgar poked Osbert in the ribs. "I said she *might* tell us a tale, you oaf. Only if she wants, of course."

The cries rose then, as several begged her to entertain them with a story.

"Come on, Madeleine, sing us but one song," said Osbert.

"Yes, indeed," added Ruth. "You've a much better voice than York," she proclaimed, casting a sideways glance at the troubadour.

York clutched his heart. "Crushed again," he said mockingly. "Will no one but God Almighty ever recognize my talents?"

Several grumbled at York's antics but even more tried to persuade her to stay a bit longer. Madeleine felt she couldn't let them down and before she knew it, an hour had passed.

"I must return to Gwenith," she finally told those gathered around her.

There were some good-natured grumbles but all understood why she retired early. As she began her way back to the tent, Royce fell into step with her.

"You tell a fine tale, Madeleine," he praised.

"Thank you, Royce. Your compliment is much appreciated."

They walked along in companionable silence. This was the Royce she had come to trust, she thought. She enjoyed being around him. She opened her mouth to tell him so and was shocked when he swung her into his arms and kissed her.

He held her close to him and surprised her by quickly pushing his tongue into her open mouth. He stroked her own tongue with his as he caressed her back with his large hands. Pushing her palms against his chest, Madeleine broke away from him.

"We mustn't, Royce," she sputtered, left breathless by the kiss. Her thoughts were whirling, realizing how different his kiss was from the one she'd received earlier from Garrett. Garrett's had spoken of hidden mysteries and promises to be fulfilled. Royce's seemed rough and cheap in comparison.

"Why not, Madeleine? I am a man. You are a woman. I am attracted to you and I know you are to me by how you responded to my kiss. What's wrong for two people to show how they care for one another?"

Madeleine wrapped her arms tightly around her body. Her head was swimming. "Because I'm married," she finally managed.

"Married?" he said in wonder. He cocked his head to one side and squinted, deep in thought. Finally, he met her gaze. "I don't care, Madeleine. I love you," he said desperately. "We'll run away if that's what you want. We can go across England into Wales for all I care. We'll change our names. I'll do anything to be with you."

For a few seconds, she was tempted. To become a new person, to leave her myriad of problems behind. The idea held promise.

But it was wrong. She was married to Henri, for better or for worse, and most of it had been worse. She would stay wed until she died. No, she must return to France and enter a convent. It was the honorable thing to do. God expected it of her. She refused to let the Almighty down.

Suddenly, Garrett's image came into her mind and she pondered his kiss, too. It had been a very different kind of kiss, full of sweetness and promise. No, if she had been given a choice to run from her problems, she would have fled with the enigmatic nobleman who seemed constantly in her thoughts. As it was, this married woman would only run to God's open arms.

She banished the picture of Garrett that danced in her head, knowing she must fight the attraction she felt for the moody lord of Stanbury. It would cause untold sorrows. She must be strong. She had handled far worse to this point and would manage this, too.

Looking at Royce, she wondered how she could crush the hope his eyes held. She could not bear to hurt him after all his kindness toward her. Maybe she could let him down gently. Her lies would ease him and she promised her Dear Lord she'd do ten *Our Fathers* for what she said now.

"Royce, your kiss was very nice, indeed, and I would be a liar if I said I did not enjoy it. But I have much on my mind now. I have a husband I've left, Gwenith to nurse, Evan to watch after. I can't leave now. Can you understand this?"

"No, Madeleine, I can't. I want you." He grabbed her elbows roughly and jerked her close to him, their eyes locking. Her heart raced with fear. Her eyes darted wildly about. Royce seemed to sense her alarm and slowly relaxed his grip. Instead, he folded his arms about her gently and gave her a reassuring hug.

"You ask too much of me." He sighed. "I know you have a heavy burden on your heart but once Gwenith's better, we will talk of this again."

She hadn't the heart to tell him she would be long gone by that time so she simply nodded.

"Goodnight, Royce," she said and walked alone the remaining way to the tent.

GWENITH HAD A fairly good night and Madeleine had spent a pleasant morning with her friend. She'd left Gwenith napping while she went to perform in the first show of the day.

Madeleine eagerly scanned the crowd but did not catch sight of Garrett. She did see Ashby, though, Hannah by his side. He waved gaily to her, even as his eyes wandered when a pretty girl passed in front of him. *Like a bee flying from flower to flower*, she thought.

When the play was completed, she was surprised when he made his way over to her.

"A lovely performance, Madeleine." He smiled at her. "May I call you Madeleine?" he asked impishly.

"Better than Lady Montayne, I suppose," she quipped.

He laughed heartily at her words. "Oh, I will enjoy having you around, Madeleine."

His words perplexed her. "What mean you, Sir Ashby?"

"I hope I haven't let the cat out of the bag." He rolled his eyes and began whistling.

"My lord?" she asked pointedly, her eyes narrowed, imploring him to answer.

He threw his hands in the air. "I give up, dear lady. I could never stand for a woman to look at me in anger." He sighed. "Your Mister Farley has agreed to have the mummers and the faire move to Stanbury next."

Madeleine frowned. "You must be mistaken, my lord. We are to leave in two days' time for Summerville. There we will spend at least two weeks and celebrate the summer solstice."

Ashby flicked a ladybug from his shoulder. "Not anymore, Madeleine. Garrett has arranged for you to bypass that stop. His home, Stanbury, is where you'll spend the next few weeks."

"But . . . but . . ."

"No buts, dear Madeleine. You'll be nearby to entertain us for many pleasant hours." He lifted her hand to his lips and kissed it tenderly. "Until we meet again."

Madeleine yanked her hand free and whirled, needing to find Farley. Surely he would not confirm such gibberish.

She spotted him and, lifting her skirts, hurried as fast as she could across the short distance between them.

"Farley! I must speak with you at once."

He turned. "Hello, Madeleine. How is

Gwenith today?" he asked pleasantly.

"Much better, Farley, but what's this about skipping Summerville?"

Farley lifted his shoulders. "We were made a better offer, Madeleine. I have many people who depend upon me. I chose to go where we'll earn more money."

"So Stanbury is our next stop?"

"Yes, indeed."

Madeleine turned and flounced off, passing by a laughing Ashby.

"*Zut!*" she swore under her breath as she stormed away. "And I don't intend on saying any *Hail Mary's*, either," she muttered to no one in particular.

CHAPTER ELEVEN

S TANBURY WAS, MADELEINE admitted to herself, one of the loveliest estates she'd ever seen. Although she loved her native France, and the wine country in particular, England in full bloom was spectacular. The lush, green hills rolled gently throughout the countryside, fading into forests filled with tall, strong trees that had stood for hundreds of years. She'd only been here two days but she felt she would never tire of this scenery.

As she stood admiring it yet again, Evan tugged on her tunic to get her attention. Madeleine lowered her gaze to the colorful bouquet of wildflowers he held in his hands. He smiled at her, a wiggling, tousle-haired imp.

"These are for Mama," he said, splitting the bouquet into two sections and indicating those in his left hand. "And these are for ye, Maddie."

"Thank you, Evan." Madeleine curtsied then swept the flowers up, inhaling their sweet scent. "I shall treasure them."

"Of course ye will. They're from me!" He squealed with delight and went running off to the tent area. He hollered over his shoulder. "And they're from *him,* too." Evan continued running, flying across the green grass as fast as a jackrabbit being pursued by dogs.

Madeleine cocked her head and frowned. "What did he mean by that?"

A voice that was all too familiar responded, "He meant that the flowers were from the both of us."

She spun around and inhaled sharply. "Lord Montayne," she managed to say calmly, although her heart beat as fast as the pursued jackrabbit's. She was glad to have the flowers in her hands, else she'd be wringing them to no end.

"Madeleine," he replied softly, a trace of a smile crossing his face. He nodded in Evan's direction. "I came across Master Evan nearly an hour ago. He's quite the fountain of knowledge."

She sighed. "Evan is much too nosy for his own good, my lord. He's a wicked little eavesdropper who then blabbers everything he thinks he knows." She eyed the nobleman warily and then turned to walk away, uneasy about what Evan might have told him about her. "What did you learn?" she asked lightly.

He fell into step beside her, and they strolled along the meadow. "Well, I did find out that Osbert is always in a good humor, even if he is the head mummer. Most head mummers have dreadful tempers, you know."

Madeleine stared at him in wonder. "What other information did Evan impart to our host?"

"Oh, only that Hannah and Ruth are terrible flirts and Elspeth and Farley fight all the time—but they don't mean a word they say. Derwyn does very good magic tricks when he isn't drinking too much, and Mary lets Evan sneak sweets when no one is looking."

She noticed the slight smile on his face as he continued.

"Also, Jack wants to ask for Mary's hand in marriage, but he's afraid Mary's father wouldn't approve." He shrugged. "I've forgotten Mary's father's name, it seems."

"'Tis Ellard," Madeleine told him.

"Yes, that's right. Ellard. And least I forget, Evan knows Edgar has a terrible crush on you but he'd never think to ask you to marry him."

Madeleine's brows shot up. "Why not, my lord? Am I not attractive enough for Edgar?" she asked playfully. "Or mayhap because he's so old?"

"Nay. Edgar would be pleased to have you as his wife but it would be disloyal to the memory of his sweet Rosamund. Edgar does not wish to trouble her soul since she watches his every move from heaven."

She burst out laughing. "You discovered all this in but one hour?"

"There was much more but I've forgotten the rest. Mostly, we picked flowers for his mother and you and the boy rambled on a bit. He seems to love you both very much."

Madeleine began nervously rearranging the bunch in her hands, not sure what to say. She finally remarked, "Are you glad there will be so many strangers trouncing upon the lawns of Stanbury for the summer solstice?"

Lord Montayne gave her an amused glance. "Better here than Lord Denton's."

"Why is that?"

"So you won't be so far away."

She quickened her pace, her braid bouncing against her back. Garrett sped up and caught her elbow.

"Did my declaration make you uncomfortable?"

Madeleine stopped and studied him. His dark hair fell across his brow, the slight breeze giving it a tousled look. His brown eyes glittered, framed by long lashes. Chiseled cheekbones and a firm mouth completed the picture. She found her own mouth had gone dry, so handsome was he to look upon.

She recovered quickly, however, and said, "Of course it did, my lord. I am nothing to you and I intend to remain nothing to you. I am not a woman of easy virtue, despite my mummer's status. The loose reputation that actors hold is undeserved. I would ask that you keep that in mind."

She moved to go but he still held her elbow clasped firmly in his hand. She tugged. He refused to let go. "Kindly let go of me, good sir, or you will regret it."

A knowing look came into his eyes. "What would you do, Madeleine?" he asked tauntingly.

Before she could think of something totally outrageous that would embarrass or defy him, a young girl appeared before them.

"Papa?"

The girl was younger than Evan and had dark, wavy hair that fell just below her shoulders and dark, inquisitive eyes. Her complexion was milky white, with rosy blooms on each cheek, her mouth a pink rosebud. She reached out her arms.

Immediately, he released Madeleine and lifted the child up, kissing her soundly upon each cheek. The girl giggled and squirmed and he placed her back upon the ground.

Madeleine was amazed at the change that came over him. She had found him arrogant and caustic. Now he smiled and looked as any proud father might.

"Lyssa, I'd like to present Madeleine to you. She will be singing with the troupe that has come to the faire."

Lyssa locked her arms around her father's leg and buried her face in his knee. Pulling away slightly, she glanced up at Madeleine after a moment's time. Seeing Madeleine looked at her, the girl mashed her face once again into his leg.

He patted her head gently. "Lyssa's quite shy," he said quietly. "She wasn't always." A hard look came across his face, clouding the pleasant expression that had been there momentarily. "At any rate, she doesn't take to strangers well and doesn't often speak around them."

Madeleine nodded. Though she had none of her own, she was good with children. Kneeling beside Lyssa, she asked, "Have you ever been to a faire, Lyssa?"

The child lifted one eye away from her father's leg and peeked at Madeleine. "No," she whispered and planted her face firmly back into his knee.

"Well, it's time you went to one. I know for a fact that your papa had this faire come to Stanbury especially for you."

Once more Lyssa peeped out. "He did?" She continued watching with wide eyes.

"Of course he did. Your papa loves you very much, Lyssa. Why, of all the little girls in England, your papa has the reputation of loving you the very most."

"Really?" The girl's head was now totally

lifted from Garrett's knee.

"Yes, everyone knows that, you silly goose." Madeleine smiled at her.

"I'm not a goose," Lyssa said stubbornly, her bottom lip sticking out.

"You could pretend to be one," Madeleine told her. "All you have to do is think like a goose—and quack!"

She folded her hands under her and bent her arms, making a motion up and down as if she had wings. She hobbled along and began quacking, softly at first, and then louder as Lyssa began playing along.

"Come, now, you can't just quack like one, Lyssa, you've got to act like one, too."

Soon, she and the young girl were moving along the ground, honking and squawking, their arms flapping up and down.

"Papa, Papa, you have to quack, too."

Lord Montayne shook his head. "No, sweet girl, an earl does not go about quacking in public."

Lyssa's bottom lip poked out again. "Then don't be an earl."

He looked around. The closest people were on the far side of the meadow, well out of earshot. Still, he hesitated.

Madeleine looked at him pleadingly. "Please?" she mouthed.

He squatted down. "I'll stop being an earl.

Just for a few minutes," he told his daughter.

The earl made the best bird of all, his squawks and honks loud and very obnoxious.

"You sound very much like the real thing, my lord," Madeleine told him.

"He's not a lord," Lyssa said. "He's a goose."

He groaned and quacked one last time. "This goose must stand, Lyssa," he said and rose to his feet. He then held out his hands to them and they both stood, too.

"I'm afraid I sound so real that someone will want to cook me."

Lyssa smiled at him and took his hand in hers. She placed her free one in Madeleine's. "Can we see the faire now, Papa?"

Lord Montayne looked at Madeleine and she answered for him. "Things are not quite ready yet, Lyssa. It takes a few days to assemble everything." The girl frowned. "We could go and see what's being done. That way you would know what you want to do once things are ready."

Lyssa's answer was to tug on their arms and propel them along with her. They walked slowly, Madeleine pointing out the different wares to be sold.

"Over here will be things every woman needs—spices, salt, honey, soaps. Down this alley you'll find coal, iron, tools, and knives will be sold."

They moved further along and Madeleine stopped them again. "Here are where shoes and various cloths can be purchased. My favorite is the velvet because it's so soft and the colors are rich."

"I have a velvet tunic, Madeleine. I got it for Christmas. Aga made it for me. She says I'm beautiful when I wear it."

"Aga? Who's that?"

Lyssa ducked her head, her shyness returning after such a long outburst of familiarity.

"It's Lyssa's nickname for my mother," he replied. "We're not sure how she stumbled upon it but Mother has remained Aga, nevertheless."

Madeleine led them to a more open space, away from the stalls. Hammering echoed throughout, as many had been pressed into service. "Here will be the horses, Lyssa. Men will come from all around to size up the horseflesh. A lord might buy a mare for breeding new stock, while a reeve might be sent to purchase several horses to help in the farming. You'll want to bring your papa around to see the ponies."

"Ponies!" Lyssa exclaimed, the shyness nowhere to be found once ponies were mentioned. "Can we come see them, Papa, can we, can we, please?"

"I'm sure that's something I can arrange," he assured her. "There'll also be dancing and singing, Lyssa, and the mummers will put on several shows. Madeleine helps out there."

Lyssa's eyes grew round. "What do you do, Madeleine?"

"First, I play a few songs to help quiet the crowd. Some have pretty melodies, while others tell stories."

"You're a troubadour?" Lyssa asked in amazement. "Troubadours have to be men."

"Not this one," Madeleine said. "I also help narrate some of the plays. If we're short-handed, I even play a part now and then, all in costume."

"I want to hear you sing," Lyssa told her. "I like to sing."

"You do?" Madeleine looked at the girl's father. He shrugged. "Can you sing a song for me now?"

Lyssa shook her head and wrapped her arms around Garrett's leg again.

"Not again, little one," he said and pried her away. He lifted her high above his head and then lowered her until she rested atop his shoulders. He began strolling back the way they'd come until they reached the shade of an old oak.

He lifted Lyssa again, placed her on the ground, then wiped his brow and sat with his back against the trunk.

"You've worn me out, child." He motioned for Madeleine to sit.

It took her a moment to kneel and she took special care to arrange her leg.

He then winked at Madeleine. "Oh, I'm so tired. Maybe you could sing us a song, Madeleine?"

As Lyssa watched her eagerly, Madeleine saw him shake his head slightly. "No, my lord, I'm sorry. I cannot sing unless I have my lute with me." She paused, meeting his eyes. "I wish I could sing without it but I can't."

"I can sing without a lute," Lyssa said quietly. "I sing to my dolls every night before I go to sleep."

"Then would you please sing for us, Lyssa?" Madeleine asked.

The child began. She started slowly, a bit hesitant, but she grew in confidence as she continued.

It was obviously a song the girl had made up but she had perfect pitch. They both clapped loudly when she finished.

Her father hugged her. "I did not know I had such a talented daughter. You are very good, Lyssa."

She beamed at his words of praise.

Evan suddenly appeared and jumped into Madeleine's lap. Jealously, Lyssa climbed beside him. Evan pushed her aside but Lyssa was determined. She returned to her spot and held on to Madeleine tightly, despite Evan's nudges.

"Quit shoving," Madeleine ordered Evan. "I'll not share a story otherwise." Both settled down and listened quietly as she told a tale from the Arabian Nights.

When she finished, Evan jumped up, tired of being still for so long. "Can you play with me?" he asked Lyssa.

She turned to her father, who nodded. The children ran off, holding hands.

"It seems Evan's found a playmate," Madeleine said. "I'm glad. He's been lonely with no children his age in the troupe."

"I'm amazed Lyssa went. She's said more in the last hour than she has in the last year, Madeleine. You've woven a magic spell about her."

Madeleine laughed. "No, it's nothing I did, my lord."

"It was," he insisted earnestly. "I had no idea she sang so well. I've never heard her sing before."

"You should encourage her. If she's shy, it's a good way for her to learn to open up."

"Would you give her lessons?"

"Why me?"

"She's relaxed around you. Maybe she could learn something of the lute, too. I'm encouraged by what I've seen today." He took her hand in his and pressed it gently. "She likes you, Madeleine, and she's been through . . . a difficult time."

"But do you trust me, Lord Montayne? I lied about who I was. You believe I stole your cloak.

Don't forget, you also think me a jewel thief." She smirked a bit as she said the last remark.

"I do trust you, Madeleine." There was no hint of sarcasm in his voice. "Will you help Lyssa?" He looked at her eagerly. "I'd pay you, of course."

Madeleine hesitated briefly but the thought of making the enchanting girl—and her father—happy helped her decide. It also wouldn't hurt to have some additional coins for her trip to France.

"Yes, I'd be delighted to work with your daughter, my lord."

Lord Montayne helped her to her feet and they both brushed off the bits of grass that clung to them.

Neither saw Royce as they passed by the group of men working to create the fences that would hold in the horses.

"Married, Madeleine?" he said under his breath. "And yet you dally with his lordship. We shall see about that." He drove the nail through the wood in one angry blow.

CHAPTER TWELVE

ASHBY NOTICED HOW unusually quiet Garrett was throughout dinner. He had grown to be a taciturn man in the time since Lynnette had left but the silence tonight was overbearing. He wondered what Garrett was contemplating, for beneath the silence his friend was pensive.

Garrett's mother caught Ashby's eye. He could see the questions written on Edith's face. He smiled at her reassuringly. He'd fostered with her and her husband, Ryker, from the time he was eight years of age and he loved her very much. Stanbury had become like his own home since he'd lived here for close to a score. He was closer to Garrett than his own brothers and had tried to be a good friend throughout the years, especially during times of trouble. Luke's death. Lynnette's leaving. Each time he'd helped Garrett pick up the pieces.

Now, Edith continued to look puzzled. He smiled again at her and turned to Garrett. He'd do his best to draw his friend from the cocoon that surrounded him.

"Have you seen the faire being created right before our eyes, Garrett?"

Garrett grunted.

"I take that as a yes?" he pressed on.

Garrett's face cleared and he focused on his friend. "Yes, Ash, I walked about some today. Lyssa was with me."

"Papa! You're talking about me."

A blur dashed by the table and vaulted into Garrett's lap. He gripped the table to prevent being thrust backward in his chair.

"Careful, my sweet," he gently chided Lyssa. "We almost went crashing to the floor."

"Sorry, Papa," she said softly then perked up. "Would you like to hear my song again?" She wrapped her arms around his neck and whispered in his ear.

Ashby and Edith exchanged astonished looks. The child seemed like a different person. He'd seen Lyssa range from sullen to sweet over the last two years, from silent to barely speaking—but never jubilant, never as a child her age was meant to act. Something significant happened today. A smile tugged at his mouth. He had an idea who might be involved.

Lyssa climbed down from Garrett's lap. She

seemed unsure what to do now with all attention focused upon her. Her hand went to her hair, where she methodically began twisting a strand around her finger.

Ashby spoke up. "You said you had a song, Lyssa? Could we hear it, please?"

Lyssa nodded but remained silent, her finger still twirling in her hair. She looked from Ashby to Edith and back again. He tried to encourage her once more.

"Come, Lyssa, we are the perfect audience to hear your song for the first time. I know you must sing better than your papa, and surely you'll sound better than I can. The ladies fairly knock themselves down to escape hearing me when I try to serenade them."

Lyssa giggled. "I sing to my dolls every night. And I sang for Madeleine and Papa today."

He shot a look at Garrett, whose eyes remained hooded. His elbows were propped upon the table, hands locked under his chin.

"Who's Madeleine?" asked Edith.

"She's Papa's friend, Aga," said Lyssa impatiently. "Can I sing my song now?"

"Of course," Edith told her but she kept her eyes upon her son for the moment.

Ashby noticed Garrett ignored all glances that came his way, choosing to concentrate on Lyssa instead.

Lyssa sang with joy. The words she'd made

up were simple but the tune was sweet. Her tiny voice soared throughout the great hall. She seemed to grow taller as she sang and never once faltered.

When she finished, thunderous applause echoed in the cavernous room. Everyone present, from her family to the servants, seemed amazed how she'd opened up. She ran to Garrett and hugged him fiercely.

"You did well, Lyssa. It's time to tuck you into bed."

Garrett picked his daughter up and they left the great hall. Edith's gaze followed them.

"He hasn't put her into bed in such a long time, Ashby. What is going on? Who is this Madeleine?"

He sighed. "I wish I could say more, Edith. I'm afraid you'll have to ask your son." He rose and left the room, curiosity urging him on.

He ascended the stairs and went to Lyssa's chamber. Garrett was inside, kneeling next to his daughter at the foot of her bed.

"And God bless Papa and Aga and Ashby and Annie and Cook and my dolls. And God bless Madeleine. Amen."

Garrett helped Lyssa into bed, arranging the bedclothes and settling her dolls around her. He leaned over and kissed her goodnight.

Ashby leaned against the wall outside the door. As Garrett exited, he fell into step with him.

Casually, he asked, "Madeleine is now your friend—and Lyssa's?"

Garrett stopped in his tracks and faced him. "All I know is that she worked a miracle today, Ash. She had Lyssa playing and talking. Madeleine showed her where everything will be set up for the faire. Lyssa climbed into her lap and listened to a story. Lyssa sang for us and, by God's teeth, she's good! Then she went off to play with a boy Madeleine's been caring for. She was . . . happy."

Garrett ran his hand through his hair, shaking his head. "I still don't know who Madeleine is, Ash. But after today, I don't care."

He wanted to point out to Garrett that more than one miracle had been wrought today. Little Lyssa might be talking and smiling but her papa was showing his own spark, as well. Ashby hadn't seen Garrett care about anything for a long time. It was nice to see his friend come so alive. Ashby missed the kinder, gentler Garrett of past days.

"Mayhap the mysterious Madeleine has even more tricks up her sleeve," he said cryptically.

GARRETT RETURNED TO the great hall, a feeling of satisfaction filling him. He longed to be a better father to his daughter. The simple task of tucking her into bed for the night had left him surprisingly content. He vowed to spend more time with Lyssa in the future. Act with more patience toward her. Get to know her better, especially since Madeleine was helping Lyssa to come out of her shell.

His mother caught his eye and waved him over. He stopped to fetch two mugs of ale from a passing servant and offered her one. She took it and he drew up a chair beside her, the warmth of the nearby fire seeping into him.

"Who is Madeleine, my son?" she asked pointedly.

Her question startled him. He took a long draw of the ale, stalling for time because he also sought the answer to that same question.

"Why do you ask, Mother?" he asked glibly.

She looked at him shrewdly. "Do not answer a question with another question, Garrett. I am no fool and would not have you treat me as one."

Though usually placid in nature, he knew the steel that ran through him was all Edith.

"I know better than that, Mother. You are a capable woman who could run Stanbury or any of my businesses without any help from me or others." He paused. "Truly, I don't mean to put you off."

"Then answer my question. I want to know who the woman is who has made such a difference in my granddaughter's life." She smiled wistfully. "To see Lyssa behaving as a child her age should warms these old bones."

"You're not old, Mother."

She sighed. "Sometimes, I feel very old, Garrett. But Lyssa keeps me young. It was nothing short of a miracle to see her sing with such abandon. Freely giving of herself with a joy that seemed immeasurable."

He smiled. "It was delightful to behold. It has been far too long since I have witnessed her acting as a child should."

Edith studied him carefully. "Lyssa said that Madeleine was your friend. What does that mean?"

He shook his head. "I wish I could tell you, Mother. Madeleine is a member of the mummer's troupe. She serves as one of their troubadours."

Her eyes widened. "A woman who is a troubadour? Why, that is unheard of."

"She is the first I have come across to perform in that role. You must come and hear her play and sing. I swear, it is as if the heavens have opened up and the very angels are using her as their vessel."

"Why, Garrett, you are almost waxing poetic. It is very unlike you. Why does Lyssa call this woman your friend? I cannot imagine any man being friends with a woman, much less a stranger. One from a mummers' troupe."

He thought a moment. "I have spent time in Madeleine's company, both with Lyssa and on my own. Madeleine is unlike any woman of my acquaintance. Mother. She can be quite reserved and yet, at times, I have seen her become lively and cheerful. Mostly, I have witnessed this when Lyssa is present. Though Madeleine has no children of her own, she is drawn to them and they to her."

Garrett pushed his hands through his hair, frustration building within him. "She is quite the puzzle to me. She can be abrasive when addressing me yet I am intrigued by her every word. I haven't felt so alive in many years. I have challenged her. Argued with her. Laughed with her." He sighed. "And I have watched her with Lyssa and seen the changes she has made in my daughter's life."

His mother placed a hand on his arm. "I know you have been lonely for years, Garrett. Ever since Lynnette left. I am torn between my concern for your involvement with this woman and yet I want to support any relationship that not only brings happiness to Lyssa—but to you."

"It's not what you think. I have no true relationship with Madeleine," he assured Edith. "We are little more than acquaintances."

"Yet I see in your eyes that you wish it could be much more."

With a few words, his mother had cut to the

heart of the matter. He did want more from Madeleine, more than she could give him. Yet he was willing to take whatever crumbs he could from her, hoping that might be enough to soothe his soul.

"I plan to enjoy the little time I will spend in her company while the mummers remain at Stanbury," he said brusquely. "Madeleine has already woven a spell about Lyssa and is drawing her out. If that's all that occurs before the troupe leaves, I will be more than satisfied."

He rose, wishing to be alone. "I must speak to Ash," he said, using his friend as an excuse to leave the great hall.

As Garrett retreated, he thought of how Madeleine had also bewitched him—and wondered if he would muster the courage to let her go when the time came.

MADELEINE STAYED BUSY the rest of the day. There was much to be done since the faire opened in two days' time. It would be in operation for almost a week and then culminate with the summer solstice. Not much emphasis was placed upon this day in France but in England, particularly for the people she now resided with, this event seemed to have special significance.

"Think, Maddie, 'tis the longest day of the year," Gwenith told her. "Some think it a night of eerie superstitions but Mama always told me 'twas a night for passion to run wild." Gwenith's eyes sparkled for a moment. "Anything can happen during solstice." She sighed and then looked a bit sheepish. "Most anything, I suppose. At least that's when Evan's papa swept me off me feet with but one kiss. Oh, he was a rascal, that man."

Madeleine smiled at her friend. Today, Gwenith had a bit of color in her cheeks and she was sitting up talking animatedly. Evan had been in and out and Gwenith finally felt well enough to pay him some attention. Her cough still sounded ferocious but it appeared less often, though the dark circles still remained under her eyes.

"Where did you meet Evan's father?" Madeleine asked, curious.

Evan burst into the tent. "Are ye going to read to Mama again?"

Color swept up Gwenith's cheeks as Evan leaped into her lap.

Madeleine laughed and met Gwenith's gaze. "You're just in time." Keeping her voice low and soothing, she started the book she'd been entertaining them with the past few nights.

Evan nuzzled his mother's cheek and sat

close to her as Madeleine finished up.

"That 'twas nice, Maddie, dear. Thank ye." Gwenith stroked Evan's hair, a contented look upon her face.

Evan suddenly sat up. "Mama! I made a new friend today."

"Ye did? What's his name?" Gwenith asked eagerly.

"It's not a he, Mama. It's a she. She's five." He held up five fingers on his hand. "She likes to run and she's gonna see me in the show."

"That's nice, my sweet."

"She's friends with Maddie, too. Maddie told us a story about a castle and a fairy princess. And there was a mean witch and a . . ." He paused and frowned. "What's he called again, Maddie?"

"A warlock, Evan. That's a man who's a witch."

"That's right, Mama, a warlock." He shivered. "'Twas a very scary man he was but the hero saved them all."

Evan stood, ready to go again, but not before he imparted one more piece of information. "Maddie has a friend, too. He's Lyssa's papa, and she called him *me lord*. I thought lords were very scary, like warlocks, but Lyssa's papa was nice."

Evan kissed his mother's cheek. "I'm gonna see if Osbert needs me help, Mama. I'll be back."

"Don't be gone too long, Son. 'Tis almost time ye were abed."

Gwenith waited till Evan was out of earshot before turning to Madeleine. "So ye've a friend who's a lord?"

Madeleine blushed, which made Gwenith chuckle. "Tell me all, dearest, and no holding back."

She was reluctant to share the entire story with Gwenith. Early on, she had revealed to Gwenith that she was married but hadn't provided any details as to why she was not keeping company with her husband.

"You remember when you found me on the docks, Gwenith?"

"Aye."

Madeleine filled Gwenith in on her encounters with Garrett, leaving out their kiss, of course. That was something she'd keep to warm herself when the nightmares got bad.

"The earl's daughter is a precious little angel. She and Evan got along so well. It was good to see Evan have a companion near his own age."

"And ye, too, Maddie?"

Madeleine flushed as Gwenith gave her a knowing smile. "Ye keep people at arm's length, Maddie. Oh, not Evan and me, but I've thought ye needed more than us."

She shook her head. "You've become my family, Gwenith. You, Evan, the troupe. You've all taken me in and been so kind. Don't go seeing things where they aren't," she gently scolded.

"It's already there, Maddie," Gwenith softly said. "There's something between ye and this lord. Oh, stop shaking yer head at me, girl. I know ye."

She reached over and took Madeleine's hand. "I knew from the moment I laid eyes on ye that ye're no commoner, Maddie Bouchard, or whatever yer name is. I don't know what ye're running from or why, but I do know I love ye like me own flesh."

Gwenith leaned forward and wrapped her arms around Madeleine's neck. "I want ye to be happy."

She let go and fell back into her pillows. "Don't live life with regrets, Maddie. Don't look back. Look ahead."

But what could she look forward to? She longed to return to France and leave her burdens behind, but if she did, she feared what would happen to Gwenith and Evan if her friend didn't fully recover.

Yet, more than anything, she longed to see Garrett again. To spar with him. To see that gentle smile he withheld from the world. To feel his mouth on hers.

Her head ached. Maybe some air would do her good. She bent and kissed Gwenith's cheek and brushed the hair back from her friend's brow. It frightened her how Gwenith had wasted away in just a few short weeks. Though she still bloomed with optimism, her cheeks were sunken, her eyes dull, and her flesh seemed to hang on her bones. Madeleine blinked back the tears just as Evan came in. He kissed his mother goodnight and allowed Madeleine to tuck him in.

She left the tent. The camp was settling down for the night. A few mummers still gathered around the dying fire, talking and joking, but most people were ready for a good night's sleep. She continued toward the open area, which would soon be covered with wares and crowds of people interested in buying and selling their goods. It was a different kind of life—but one she'd come to appreciate. The people might not have two coins to rub together but they were rich in all that mattered. They had an honesty about them and a love for what they did. Madeleine realized that these past few months had been among the happiest in her life.

Thankfully, those around her had dispelled the horrors of Henri for a time, which had helped her soul begin to heal. She listened to the crickets' soft music, longing for the nights she and her father sat together outside and listened to their chirping. She glanced up to the star-filled night, at peace for the moment.

"Madeleine."

The peace instantly shattered. She turned and saw a frowning Royce approaching her. He did not seem to be in good spirits and she sought to dispel his sour mood with humor.

"Good evening to you, Royce. Aren't you in a black mood? If I didn't know better, I'd think—"

"Enough, Madeleine," he said angrily.

His tone immediately put her on guard. She had heard it too many times from Henri.

"What's wrong, Royce?" she asked carefully.

"I thought you were married." He spit the words out at her. His blue eyes, usually so merry, were now as cold as ice as he looked at her with suspicion.

Her stomach roiled, a queasy feeling settling in it. "I am. I told you so."

"Have you told Lord Montayne?" His eyes narrowed as he studied her.

"Why would I bother to tell our lord host of my marital status?" she tossed back.

"Why, indeed? I would have thought that unnecessary. Until I saw you together this afternoon."

Madeleine quickly thought back and realized Royce must have seen them walking with Lyssa.

"Yes, I was with Lord Montayne earlier to-day. He asked that I show him and his daughter around. I was happy to comply."

"You seemed awfully cozy."

"Royce, please. I was merely doing the earl a favor. I love children so, and his daughter is a very sweet girl. In fact, she and Evan have become fast friends."

"I saw how he looked at you."

She stammered, "Wh-what do you mean?"

He took her by her arm, his fingers like steel pressed against her tender flesh. "I know what a man wants when he looks at a woman like that, Madeleine, and it's not a tour of the faire grounds."

"Royce, let go," she said quietly. "You're hurting me."

He jerked her close to him. She was so near she could see the stubble along his chin and her stomach churned. Usually, she could swallow the nausea until Henri was through beating her. This time, Madeleine didn't know if she could now. She was out of practice—and so very afraid. The thought that she had no control of this situation made her hysteria rise. Her heart pounded violently against her ribs as dread filled her. She couldn't form a coherent thought. All she wanted was to be free of this man. To run and hide. To find sanctuary.

His other hand went around her nape, his fingers tightening. Terror seized her, holding her in place as much as his strong hands. As Royce's eyes bored into her, something snapped within her.

Why was she so afraid?

This man was not her husband. He held no power over her. No man did. Within seconds, her fear morphed into fury. She might have taken the abuse in the past because it was at the hands of her husband. This time, it was different.

She was different.

Madeleine determined she would never allow herself to be bullied by a man ever again. Though she knew that physically she was no match for Royce, she could scream to the bloody heavens if she had to in order to bring help. Causing trouble for Farley and Elspeth was the last thing she wanted to do, however, seeing as how they had been so good to her. She would make an effort to reason with Royce.

If it failed, only then would she act, hoping the consequences of her actions wouldn't reflect poorly on the owners of the troupe.

"Royce, please," she said calmly. "You must release me now. I insist."

"Is this how the mighty lord looked at you, Madeleine? Did he want you as much as I do? Would you do for *him* and deny *me*?" he sneered.

"Take your hands from her," a voice commanded from the dark.

CHAPTER THIRTEEN

"**T**AKE YOUR HANDS from her."

Garrett was surprised at how steady his voice remained despite the anger thundering through his body. The thought of any man touching Madeleine against her will sickened him. He clenched and unclenched his fists, wanting to tear the bastard from Madeleine and slam him to the ground.

The couple turned in his direction. Garrett could see the fear and alarm written across Madeleine's face. He now recognized the man as the one called Royce who'd whisked Madeleine away from him at the other faire. He'd been jealous of the mummer at the time, but he was furious at the man now.

Garrett took another step toward them. Royce still clasped Madeleine's arm in a tight grip, one that would surely leave bruises on the morrow. He sized up his adversary. His chest was broad and thick and his arms were well-muscled. The moonlight caught the ice-blue eyes that stared daggers at him.

"Unhand the lady now," Garrett demanded.

Royce thrust Madeleine from him, releasing his death grip. She immediately began rubbing her arm, tears glinting against the moonlight.

"Are you all right, Madeleine?" Garrett asked softly.

"Yes, my lord"," she replied, no louder than a whisper.

"I refuse to ask your Mr. Farley to vacate the premises because of the actions of one individual," he told Royce. "However, *you* are to leave and never return to Stanbury. I will not tolerate the abuse of women in any manner."

Royce balled his hands into fists, ready to attack. "I have never abused a woman in my life." He made to charge Garrett but Madeleine jumped in front of him.

"Royce, are you mad? Have you forgotten the law? Reason has fled you for I know you'd never assault a nobleman. 'Twould be death to do so!"

Royce froze at her words.

Garrett clenched his hands into fists as Madeleine turned and threw out her hand.

"No, please, my lord. This was simply a misunderstanding, more my fault than Royce's."

What? Her fault? Anger coiled in Garrett's gut. Had Madeleine led this man to think he could have his way with her then changed her mind? He had no patience for cock teasers.

She stood very still but he caught the slight tremble in her voice and body.

"I beg you to reconsider, my lord. Royce is an integral part of several of our plays. It would be impossible for Farley to replace him now and would affect many in our troupe, not to mention the many who've come to Stanbury to sell their wares. Please, my lord. Do not be hasty in your decision."

Garrett raked a hand through his hair. He'd like nothing better than to punish Royce with his fists and banish him from Stanbury. Yet he needed Farley's troupe to stay. He couldn't risk losing Madeleine.

He inclined his head to her. "As you wish, Madeleine." He turned to Royce. "If I hear of or witness another scene like the one I came across this evening, there will be no forgiveness a second time. Leave Madeleine well alone—and stay far from sight—else I'll banish you from Stanbury. Be gone!"

Royce stood eyeing Garrett for a long moment, a surly expression upon his face. Finally, he turned and trudged off in the direction of the tents.

Garrett took a step toward Madeleine. Her

trembling grew more visible now. Tears flowed freely down her cheeks, glistening in the bright moonlight. He held out his arms. He didn't know if she moved to him or he to meet her but, suddenly, she was there, enfolded within his embrace.

He ached for her as silent sobs racked her slender body, her thin shoulders shaking. He held her tenderly, murmuring soothing words to her, stroking her silken hair over and over. Eventually, her sobs ended and the shudders subsided— but she remained in his arms. He made no move to kiss her, choosing to comfort her instead.

He realized it didn't matter. Although he had fantasized about kissing her again, he was content now to simply hold her. After witnessing the scene with Royce as he held her against her will, Garrett did not want to take the chance of scaring her away.

Besides, he liked the feel of her next to him. True, he'd rather be running his fingers through her long hair, stroking her breasts with his hands and tongue but, for now, this proved enough.

"My lord?" Her voice was hesitant. She eased away from him slightly and met his gaze.

"Yes, Madeleine?"

"I . . . I want to thank you. You see . . . well, Royce has never behaved thus. I . . . ." She couldn't go on.

"I understand, Madeleine." He drew her to

him again for a brief moment but he knew he must let her go. Reluctantly, he dropped his arms and took a step back.

"May I accompany you to your tent?"

She nodded. He did not take her arm, much as he desired, but remained by her side. He slowed his gait to compensate for her slight limp but they still reached the tent much too quickly.

"Will you be all right?"

She nodded. Before he could let her go, he took her hand and raised it to his lips to press a gentle kiss to her fingers. An electricity seemed to crackle through the calm, June night.

She stared at him, her mouth half-open as if to speak, but no sound came out.

"I will see you on the morrow," he said.

"*Au revoir*," she answered softly and stepped inside.

MADELEINE DID NOT see Lord Montayne until late the next day, though she did spend time with Lyssa. The girl and Evan had turned out to be inseparable companions, one not daring to make a move or take a step unless the other was nearby.

She spent a hopeless morning trying to help Hannah with some of the costumes. Several of them needed to be mended and all needed to be pressed in time for tomorrow's opening performances.

"Madeleine, you are all thumbs!" Hannah chastised. "Just leave. You are causing me more work than I had before you arrived."

She gave Hannah an apologetic look and took her leave. She passed Farley, who wore his usual fretful look and bellowed loudly at his wife. "What's to be done, Elspeth? You can't replace talent like Benton."

Elspeth snorted. "Benton's talent is only marginal, Farley. 'Tis likely someone else in the company could do what that foolish boy did."

Madeleine interrupted. "What's this about Benton?"

Farley grunted. "The young fool off and ran away with some chit he'd just met. Where does that leave me?"

Benton designed and painted the backdrops the mummers used in their productions. She smiled at the big man. "I used to paint some, Farley. I did mostly portraits but I'm sure I could help out however you need me."

Farley captured her in a bear hug, practically cutting off her air supply. He danced around with her. "Did you hear, Elspeth? Madeleine has saved the day."

"Who'll save yer ample ass if ye don't let go of such a sweet morsel?" his wife demanded.

Farley's eyes widened and he dropped his arms from Madeleine. "Now, my dear, don't go there again." He grinned wolfishly at Madeleine. "She'll be jealous even when I'm fat, old, and gray."

Elspeth snorted. "Ye are fat, old, and gray, ye simpleton." Yet she affectionately patted his rump. "Now, me wee girl, 'tis a good thing ye know a thing or two about paints, because Benton left things half-done. Come, I'll show ye everything to do." She linked arms with Madeleine and led her off, Farley cackling behind them.

Madeleine pressed into service any spare body she could find. The troupe, used to pitching in and lending a hand to whomever needed help, was more than willing to aid her. Before nightfall, every backdrop had been completed and every prop was ready to go.

At twilight, she realized Lyssa was still with her. The girl had been her shadow all afternoon. Madeleine had reassured a nervous Annie that the child would be safe with her. She promised the servant she would return Lyssa to the castle before the evening meal, though she made no promises how clean she'd be.

Despite her young age, Lyssa had proven quite adept with a brush. Madeleine found a few scraps of canvas and urged Lyssa to draw something for her.

"Anything you'd like, Lyssa. You're free to put whatever you want upon the cloth."

The child concentrated so her brow wrinkled. Within a few minutes, she had a good likeness of Evan before her.

"That's excellent, Lyssa. You have quite a talent," Madeleine praised.

"I can sing and I draw, Madeleine."

Suddenly a shadow appeared on the page. Madeleine raised her head to find Garrett there, his head cocked to one side as he studied his daughter's work.

"You did this, Lyssa?"

"Yes, Papa," she said meekly.

He crouched down and studied the sketch. "This is very good, Lyssa. Very good, indeed." He patted her head affectionately. "I think you draw and sing equally well. Why have you not shared this with me before?"

Lyssa frowned. "You're always busy, Papa. You go to London a lot. I don't ever see you."

Garrett ruffled her hair. "Then mayhap I will change that, my girl."

She hugged his neck, a sweet smile on her face. "Madeleine draws, too, Papa. She's even better than me."

Garrett eyed Madeleine. "Madeleine seems to have many talents."

"Oh, I haven't drawn in a long time, my lord," she replied, conscious of her paint-splattered tunic and the strands of hair that had escaped her braid. "I only did so as a girl. My own papa indulged me."

"Show me something."

"Why not?" Madeleine picked up a flat, sand-colored rock. She concentrated for a few minutes and then presented it to Garrett.

He recognized Lyssa at once. In but a few simple lines, Madeleine had captured his daughter's essence, the brightness of her soul. "This is remarkable. I insist you give Lyssa not only singing lessons but drawing lessons, as well."

"Once the faire begins, I would be happy to do so, my lord. We should be here for another two weeks or so, I'd imagine. I think Lyssa and I could meet several times."

"I insist upon being present when you work with her."

"Why, my lord?"

"I have my reasons," he said cryptically.

"She might be stifled by your presence. It may make her uncomfortable."

"No, that won't be a problem." He looked around for Lyssa, who'd quickly tired of the adult conversation and run off with Evan again. "Come, child. Annie grows impatient. She wishes to put you in a bath and fill your belly with meat and bread."

Garrett swept Lyssa upon his shoulders and she squealed her delight. He raised a brow at

Madeleine. "The faire opens tomorrow?"

She nodded. "I hope you will bring Lyssa to see the mummers perform."

Garrett took in the high color on Madeleine's cheeks, the sweet curves hidden beneath her flowing clothing, the intense heat in her gaze as she met his eyes. "We wouldn't miss it."

As he'd promised, Garrett didn't miss one performance that first day. Every time Madeleine took her place, he was there.

He'd sat spellbound, watching her, listening to her. It mattered not if she told of Beowulf and Grendel or sang of unrequited love. Her music made him lightheaded and lighthearted.

During the other acts, he often found his mind wandering, fantasizing about making love to Madeleine. He knew his lust was wrong, knew he was still wed to Lynnette, but the thoughts continued nonetheless. He wanted Madeleine next to him in his bed, night after night. With each kiss and every stroke, he would break down and solve the mysteries surrounding Madeleine, until she was thoroughly his.

"Papa," Lyssa whispered loudly in his ear, bringing him back to the present.

Lyssa sat in his lap, transfixed by the proceedings on stage. The play had all the classic elements an audience required, including this final, crucial sword fight between the hero and villain. Lyssa wrapped her arms around his neck tightly as the swords clanged loudly against each other. The audience gasped with each blow.

Finally, the villain stabbed the hero, who collapsed as the crowd groaned. Yet, while preening, the evildoer accidentally tripped and fell, striking his head. He was out cold, helpless, and the audience cheered the hero on, urging him to rise—despite his fatal wound—and finish off the rogue. Cries of anguish rippled through the crowd when the hero failed to move.

But, no, wait, the doctor appeared, and magically brought the hero back to life. The hero roused the villain for one more round and thrust his sword into him until he landed the fatal blow. The villain died, the hero lived, and the crowd went wild with applause.

Lyssa bounced excitedly up and down. Garrett had no cause to calm her high spirits. She'd been still for too long. She jumped from his lap when Madeleine made her way over to them after all bows had been taken.

"Did you enjoy the performance, Lyssa?" she asked.

"Oh, yes." The little girl's eyes were shining with excitement. "The best part was when Evan brought the sword out to the hero. Don't you think it was the best part, Madeleine?"

She laughed and squeezed Lyssa's shoulder. "Of course, sweetie. Evan did the very best job today."

"You did, too, Madeleine. I want to sing just like you."

"Then we must think on when to have your lessons."

"Now, Papa. I want them now." Lyssa clapped her hands excitedly. "But I want to see the faire. Can we?"

"Let me check quickly on Gwenith," Madeleine said. "She's been doing so much better since we arrived at Stanbury. I'll only be a minute."

As she left, Ashby wandered up. "How did you like the little drama, Lyssa?"

"I want to sing like Madeleine. I want to be a mummer."

Ashby chuckled. "What would your papa say about you leaving him and traipsing about the countryside?"

"Oh, Papa won't mind. He likes Madeleine and she does it."

"He does?" Ashby murmured, raising an eyebrow at Garrett.

Garrett scowled. "Enough, Ash. Go off and find yourself some company. Yours is not required here."

"Seems you're in a great hurry to get rid of me, Garrett."

"No. I only know how impatient you are when you could be looking for a pretty maid."

"Fair enough." He swept into a bow. "Good day, Lyssa." As Madeleine approached them, he bowed again. "And good day to you, Madeleine." He winked at her, a roguish smile on his features.

"Good day to you, Sir Ashby."

"Come, Papa." Lyssa tugged on Garrett's hand. She took Madeleine's in the other. "I'm hungry."

Madeleine thought a moment. "You might want to sample some of the flatbread, Lyssa. 'Tis made with honey poured on top and sprinkled with cinnamon and sugar."

"Oh, yes, Papa, let's go have bread."

Garrett purchased several pieces. As promised, the treat was sweet and filling. They visited several of the booths, taking in all the various trinkets and wares. Madeleine pointed out some of the cheeses that were especially good, and Garrett promised to have his steward come and buy several rounds.

A kitten suddenly crossed their path, stopping at Lyssa's feet and meowing plaintively. Lyssa knelt to pet it, and the tabby scrambled into her lap.

"Sorry, my lord," called a heavy woman, waddling in their direction. "He escaped from the bunch." She bent to take the kitten but Lyssa shook her head and held on to the furry creature tightly. It began purring loudly.

"He likes me, Papa! Listen."

Garrett leaned down and heard the noisy purring. He gingerly stroked the kitten under its neck. Looking at the woman, he asked, "How much?"

The woman named her price and Garrett removed a coin from his purse, tossing it to her.

Staring at the coin and then him, she stammered, "'Tis much too generous, my lord."

Garrett gave her a rare smile. "This kitten has found a good home. Go find a place for the rest of the litter."

The woman thanked him profusely and went on her way.

"Thank you, Papa. I shall love him forever and ever." She nestled the kitten under her neck and he playfully licked her ear, causing her to giggle.

"What shall you name him, Lyssa?" asked Madeleine.

"I shall call him Luke," she informed them.

Garrett sucked in a breath. "Why would you choose a person's name, Lyssa? Why not Patches or Scratch or—"

"Papa," interrupted Lyssa, "his name is Luke, like your brother. Aga told me you loved him very much and I shall love my Luke even more." She kissed the kitten on the top of his head and skipped away.

"Madeleine!" Edgar came hurrying toward them. "There's a bit of a problem that requires your attention."

CHAPTER FOURTEEN

MADELEINE PUSHED THROUGH the small crowd that had gathered near a stall selling fritters and fruit tarts. She saw what had to be Evan sitting on the ground. At least she assumed it was Evan.

"How did he get his head stuck in a bucket?" she asked, trying to bite back a grin.

Edgar shrugged. "I don't rightly know, Madeleine. You know our Evan, though. Where there's Evan, trouble's bound to catch up."

"Mmmppmmpphh!" The muffled sound came from beneath the bucket.

Edgar tapped on the surface. "I brung Madeleine!" he bellowed. "She'll be getting you out in no time."

He turned back to her. "Won't let no one near him. Keeps pulling up on it and falling down. I knew you'd know what to do."

At that moment, Evan fell back upon the ground, feet kicking wildly as he tried to extract his head from the bucket.

"It's Madeleine, Evan," she said in the calmest, most authoritative voice she could muster. "Quit squirming about and sit quietly. I want to see how tightly you're wedged in."

He obeyed her immediately, his small chest heaving as she reached her hand inside. The wooden pail sat firmly wedged around his head, mashing his nose to one side. His hair was warm and damp.

"You're a brave lad, Evan," she said, patting his shoulder. "We'll get you out, but it requires patience on your part. Can you be still?"

The bucket nodded. The group assembled lost their battle to hide their smiles.

Madeleine turned to Edgar. "I need pig's grease—and plenty of it."

The mummer practically flew from his spot to do her bidding, almost bowling Lord Montayne over in the process.

"'Scuse me, my lord." Edgar bobbed his head several times and raced off.

Lyssa ran forward and dropped down beside Evan. She patted his hand as she tried to look under the bucket.

"Can you hear me, Evan?" she hollered.

A muffled "Yes," came from within.

"Feel my kitten, Evan." She took his hand,

guiding it until he touched fur. "This is Luke, my new kitten. He likes being petted."

Evan sat, bucket atop his head, stroking the small furball until Edgar arrived.

"Back with the grease, Madeleine. Don't ask how I got it."

She laughed and took the pail he held. Kneeling, she told Evan, "You'll smell awfully bad in a moment, Evan. Breathe from your mouth when it gets foul."

Taking a handful from the container, she rubbed the grease around Evan's neck and the edges of the bucket that imprisoned him.

"May I help?" the earl asked.

Madeleine shook her head. "Oh, no, my lord. You'll get yourself dirty."

He laughed. "Madeleine, I was once a little boy. I know what it's like to be dirty."

She studied him thoughtfully. She could just imagine him as a young boy, dirt smudged on his cheeks and matted hair. Then she pictured a bucket atop his head now. Her robust laugh filled the air.

"If you wish," she said, a smile lighting up her face. "I could use an extra pair of hands." Madeleine thought it unusual that a nobleman would even care about a peasant child's predicament but Lord Montayne was proving to be different from any man she'd met.

She plunged her hands back into the pail and

he did likewise. As their hands touched in the grease, his eyes met hers. A shiver rushed through her. His hands clasped hers for a brief moment before he released them. He scooped a goodly amount of grease from the pail and she followed his lead.

Together, they lubricated Evan's neck, working the oily filth into his hair and along the sides of the bucket. Each time their fingers met, her belly fluttered as if butterflies had been loosened inside it. She bit her lip, trying to concentrate on the task at hand.

As Lyssa distracted Evan with her chatter and the kitten, Madeleine nodded to Lord Montayne. He grabbed the top while she slipped a hand on each side of Evan's head, gently pushing on the bucket as the nobleman tried to wiggle it off.

"Yow!" Evan hollered as his wooden helmet came free. A rough, red stripe creased his forehead, surrounded by globs of grease coating his thick, unruly hair. Lyssa giggled. The infectious sound spread and the entire group gathered began bubbling with laughter. Evan looked sheepish but even he joined in the fun.

"You're a mess, Evan," Madeleine told him. "We'd better clean you up."

"I'll take care of him, Madeleine," Edgar said, yanking the boy to his feet. "Come with me, young man. We'll have you fit and fine in no time."

After one more stroke for the kitten, Evan trotted off.

Madeleine sighed and turned to Lord Montayne, nervous to meet his eyes.

He gave her a brilliant smile. "We make quite the team, Madeleine."

"Thank you, my lord." She swallowed hard. "I fear you'll need a change of clothes, as well."

He wiped some of the excess fat still on his hands upon the grass. "That's no problem, Madeleine. We'll just plan on starting Lyssa's lessons tomorrow." He grinned at her. "Go freshen yourself up. You can't play your lute with slippery fingers."

She observed the greasy smears covering her tunic and her sticky hands. "Good advice, my lord."

THE NEXT FEW days sped by quickly. Madeleine took part in the dramas several times a day, checking in on Gwenith between performances. During her longer break, when York acted as narrator, she spent time inside the castle with Lyssa. She was amazed at the talent the young girl possessed.

In one short week, Lyssa had caught on quickly to different chords on the lute and could already play a few simple songs. They also practiced painting and, for her young age, Lyssa showed promise.

The earl attended every lesson in the small, sunny room provided for their instruction. He never interfered during the lessons but his dark eyes constantly burned as he watched her working with his daughter. Madeleine wished she could forget his presence and, instead, lose herself in conversation with Lyssa.

This proved to be impossible.

Lord Montayne commanded any room he sat in, whether he spoke or not. She continually found herself out of breath, the rhythm of her heart beating erratically, though she'd done nothing strenuous. She couldn't understand why she had trouble breathing when he was nearby, much less why she became clumsy in his presence.

She concluded their lesson for the day, ready to spend a little time alone before she returned to the faire.

"Here, Lyssa, let me clean those brushes." She took them from the girl's hands before she made a mess. "Why don't you and your papa go find Luke?"

Lyssa giggled. "Cook got mad at Luke again. He licked all the cream off a pie."

Madeleine laughed. "Then you'd better go rescue him before he finds more mischief." She gave Lyssa a push toward the door and began to tidy up. She waited for Lord Montayne to follow his daughter, but he remained seated.

"My lord, mayhap you should think of hiring a tutor for Lyssa. Someone skilled in the fine arts. One day, Lyssa will be designing tapestries for the walls in the great hall and weaving them herself. She may even paint portraits of the family and important visitors."

"And sing for their entertainment in the evenings," he added.

"Yes, she will. I'm sure your guests would enjoy her music."

Garrett scowled. "We rarely have guests at Stanbury."

Madeleine was taken aback. He hadn't been abrupt with her since she'd come to Stanbury. She knew his fierce reputation, though, having overheard talk of the Earl of Montayne's black moods. He was curt and demanding toward servants, drank far too much, was a hard man in business, and rode out after highwaymen spotted in the area. Some had disappeared, while some lived to tell tales of horror before they escaped.

She had not witnessed that side of him since the mummers had arrived at his estate. He had been polite and, in the company of his daughter, even lighthearted.

"I did not realize, my lord," she said.

"My apologies, Madeleine. I shouldn't have

been gruff with you. We . . . have a bit of an odd situation here at Stanbury."

Madeleine knew it had to do with his wife. She remembered Ashby mentioning how the marriage had changed him. She knew not if Lynnette was dead or merely away on a long visit since she'd seen nothing of the countess and no mention was made of her. Not even Lyssa spoke of her mother.

"Odd, my lord?" she asked.

He sighed and Madeleine ached for the hurt that sprang to his eyes. "My wife left me for her lover four years ago. I searched every farm and manor between here and London but I never found a trace of her. She abandoned her husband, her home, and her daughter," he continued, "disappearing completely. Lyssa was barely a year old, just starting to walk."

His eyes glittered with a fierce bitterness like she'd never seen. "Even if Lynnette turned up this day, I could never, ever forgive her for leaving Lyssa."

Shocked by his story, Madeleine suddenly wondered what Henri had told his friends about her disappearance.

Despite Lord Montayne's notorious reputation, she doubted strongly that he had beaten his wife. He simply wasn't that kind of man. No one could look so pained over his wife's departure and be responsible for causing her to flee.

Without thinking, Madeleine touched his cheek gently, her palm resting along his stubbled face. He held his hand over hers for a moment, then slowly entwined his fingers with hers. Her heart skipped a beat and then began dancing wildly.

He drew her hand away from his face and studied it before bringing it, palm up, to his lips. The heat from his lips scorched her flesh. Time stilled. Only they existed in this moment.

He finally eased her hand away from his lips but he didn't release it. He transfixed her with his warm, brown eyes and, for the first time, she noticed the flecks of gold in them.

"Can we go back to the faire, Papa?"

Lyssa's question broke the spell of the moment. As the young girl entered with the kitten in her arms, Madeleine quickly turned, slipping her hand from the earl's grasp. She crossed to Lyssa and stopped to rub Luke's ears, his noisy purring filling the small room.

"I must return, Lyssa, you are right. I'd quite lost track of the time." Madeleine smiled nervously. "Bring me my lute and you may come with me. We'll find Evan, and you might be allowed to help him hand props to the mummers this time."

"Did you hear, Papa? I get to help Evan." She skipped over and retrieved the lute, handing the delicate instrument to Madeleine carefully.

She refused to look his way. Taking Lyssa's hand, she said, "Let's see if Annie wants to go with us." They exited hurriedly from the chamber, but Madeleine still heard the nobleman's low curse.

AFTER THAT CHARGED encounter, Madeleine had avoided being alone with him. Garrett saw she maneuvered situations so that someone was always present. Annie was invited to watch her lessons with Lyssa and Madeleine often brought Evan along for good measure. Madeleine had also been introduced to Edith and Lyssa's grandmother was thrilled when she could sit in and hear her granddaughter sing or watch her paint.

That afternoon, Madeleine cut the lesson short. "There's an added performance tonight, thanks to it being the summer solstice. Farley wouldn't pass up an opportunity to squeeze in an extra show for the longest day of the year."

"Will you be singing in the play, Madeleine?" Edith asked. "I've enjoyed visiting the mummer's stage with Garrett and Lyssa. Your voice is quite charming."

"Yes, my lady, and it's a special show. Both York and I have a role. Afterward, there's to be singing and dancing and a large bonfire will be lit.

Would you like to attend, my lady?"

"No, but I'm sure Lyssa will want to be there."

"I don't know, Mother," Garrett said. "She's awfully young. It will be late before those festivities begin."

"I suppose you're right, Garrett. Mayhap we'll watch it from my tower room. That way, if Lyssa falls asleep, I can easily put her to bed. But you go, Son, and enjoy yourself. Ashby, too. He told me he wasn't leaving for London until after the solstice bonfire."

GARRETT AND ASHBY watched the mummers in their final performance of the day. As soon as the play ended, Ashby was all smiles.

"You're all on your own now, Garrett. I beg my leave of you."

"The ravishing Hannah?" Garrett asked.

"It's a possibility. She's lost none of her sweetness these past few weeks. If only I could look at her and not have to listen." Ashby sighed. "Why the Good Lord decided to give the girl an angel's face with a donkey's bray, I'll never understand."

Garrett laughed. "And we all know it's her face that interests you, Ash."

"Do you mock me, Garrett? Would you be so cruel?"

"That and more."

His friend turned thoughtful. "Have you plans now yourself? Will you be spending time in the company of a certain songstress?"

Garrett smiled enigmatically. "Off with you."

Ashby left and Garrett wandered around the faire for a few minutes. It did look as if romance were in the air. Everywhere he turned, he saw couples strolling arm-in-arm, stealing kisses here and there. Loneliness washed over him, as if he were sitting in the surf on an empty beach. He even spied Royce, arms linked with another woman. The man gave him a wide berth and went in the opposite direction.

He found himself in the tent area where the mummers slept. He had a quick impulse to check on Gwenith.

As he approached the tent, Evan rushed out, running smack into him.

"Oh, sorry, me lord. Are ye looking for Maddie?"

"No, Master Evan. As a matter of fact, I was looking for your mother. Is she here?"

Evan's eyes grew round. "Yes, me lord, come right on in." He held his hand out in a gentleman-ly fashion and Garrett entered the tent.

Gwenith was propped up on a low pallet with several pillows. Obviously, she had heard their exchange for she said, "Do come in, Lord Montayne."

Her pallor was stark white against her vivid red hair. She put a hand to her head and smoothed down the wayward curls. "Gets a bit wild sometimes, me lord. Maddie does her best to tame it."

"It's very pretty hair you have, Gwenith."

She eyed him in an appraising manner. "So what brings ye here? Ye wished to see me?"

Garrett found himself slightly nervous as she sized him up. "Well, yes, Gwenith. Madeleine speaks of you often. And Evan is a sturdy lad. He's been spending time with my Lyssa. I suppose I simply wanted to meet you."

"Yer Lyssa is quite a bundle of joy, she is. Such a little lady already with dainty manners. She's been to see me most every day now, bringing me flowers and little treats from yer cook."

"She has?" His daughter had undergone a metamorphosis under Madeleine's tutelage. Visiting a total stranger, bringing her gifts. It amazed him how much Lyssa had changed in a fortnight.

"Yes, me lord, she's a good girl." She fell silent.

Since he hadn't thought about what he'd say to her, he, too, remained quiet.

Finally, she spoke. Once again, she had that

air about her, as if she were evaluating him. "I trust ye would not hurt Maddie, me lord."

"God's blood! Of course not! Why would you ask such a thing?"

"The dying have some liberties, I think." She paused a moment. "Of course, I did not mean physically strike her, me lord. I meant hurt her heart. Maddie was in a sad state when I met her. Something awful happened to her. Can't say for sure what, and I wouldn't pry, but alls I know is she's vulnerable. Don't give her more cause for pain."

"I see," he said, although he wasn't sure he did. Madeleine struck him as someone with confidence and plenty of common sense, not the wounded bird Gwenith painted. Yes, she had secrets she had yet to reveal, but he saw Madeleine as a very capable, talented woman.

He stared at Gwenith for a minute but could think of nothing else to say, so he rose. "Well, it was a pleasure meeting you, Gwenith."

She studied him a long moment before replying. "'Twas interesting meeting ye, me lord."

Garrett removed himself quickly from the tent. He walked along the lane, buying a few trifles for Lyssa from the sellers. They were hasty in their actions, ready to pack their wares and head toward the bonfire now that dusk approached. Garrett could hear the music and shouts from that direction and proceeded that way.

Many had gathered around the woodpile that would soon be lit. A few impromptu speeches were made, while several toasts were offered up. The crowd, agreeable to the toasts, shouted its approval.

Then he heard more shouts rise from those gathered.

"Play us a tune, Madeleine!"

"Yes, tell us a story, dear!"

"Come on, Madeleine. Won't be solstice without a tale!"

Garrett saw her reluctantly make her way to the center of those gathered. "I don't have my lute, I'm afraid," she apologized.

"Then we'll just look at ye a bit," yelled a happy drunk. The crowd hooted at his comment. Madeleine blushed prettily.

Edgar yelled, "'Tis just a story we need, Madeleine. You need not sing."

"All right," she said, pausing and tapping a finger on her lips. "This is a tale of what England was like long ago." She launched into a story of life before the Romans came and how the Druids had danced at celebrations such as the one tonight, their chants of "Eye-Ay-Oh," buzzing as bees would.

She painted a picture of the Romans as they came, conquering the simple folk and chasing the Druids far away. Garrett found he couldn't take his eyes from her, spellbound as much by her beauty as the tale she wove.

He was startled when he heard her say, "And to this day, the Druids will dance beneath the pale moonlight . . . so beware!"

The crowd, enraptured by her story, erupted into thunderous applause at its conclusion. Someone passed her a mug and she took a hearty swallow from it, wiping the foam from her lips with her sleeve. The people cheered again, and she moved from the center of their attention to the edges.

Garrett slowly made his way through those gathered and followed her on a parallel path. She finally removed herself totally from the group and began crossing the meadow. He knew where she was headed, a boulder at the far end of the pasture that edged the forest and overlooked the entire open meadow. He'd seen her sitting on it once before.

Sure enough, she went straight to the massive rock, climbing awkwardly up to its large, flat surface. He watched her lie down upon it and slip her hands beneath her head. He approached quietly, propping his elbow on the stone ledge.

"Stargazing?" he whispered.

Madeleine sat up hastily, surprise written across her face. "You startled me! I didn't hear you come up."

"Mind if I join you?" he asked, not waiting for

her response, but easily hoisting himself up next to her. She moved away from the center. With a grin, he stretched out his legs as she had, cushioning his head with his hands, making sure to keep some space between them. "It's a beautiful night," he said easily. "The stars are bright tonight."

"Yes, they are," she murmured stiffly, giving him a suspicious look.

"Madeleine?"

"Yes, my lord?"

"You may lie back down again. There's plenty of room here for both of us. I promise I won't push you off," he said playfully. To try to reassure her, he shut his eyes and waited.

Garrett sensed her hesitation. With his eyes closed, he seemed more aware of her than before, her lavender scent invading his senses.

She waited, obviously undecided about what to do. Then he heard the rustling and she eased back down on the rock. Not close to him, but he still felt the heat of her body.

He did his best not to move, though he could feel his heart ready to leap from his chest. He didn't want her to feel threatened but he so wanted to touch her. He longed to know everything about this wondrous woman who'd turned his world upside down.

His mind raced through the many women he'd seen over the years. None of them held a candle to Madeleine. She had an inner spirit that shone through, enhancing the beauty on her surface. How could he find out who she really was—and what secrets she still kept from him?

MADELEINE'S HEART POUNDED fiercely as she stared at the night sky. She felt very awkward and self-conscious being so near him. She realized she held her breath and expelled it quietly. Lord Montayne said nothing. His eyes remained closed. She tried to relax, putting her hands under her head for support.

Why was he here?

And yet she knew. She'd known it was but a matter of time before they found themselves alone. She just hadn't pictured it in this way.

She stole a glance at him, starting from the feet up. His muscular legs vanished under his rich, black tunic. He wore black often but the dark color suited him. His chest was broad, and both it and his arms were muscular. His profile was, for lack of a better word, simply beautiful. She had never thought a man beautiful before she'd met Lord Montayne.

He suddenly rolled over to one side and faced her, one arm propping his head up, the other resting in front of him. He seemed very large and strong compared to her. She was afraid to move. His very nearness made her feel so small.

"Who are you, Madeleine?"

Her mouth went dry. "Madeleine Bouchard, member of Farley's mummers."

"Bouchard?" he echoed. She thought quickly. "Yes, it's a French name, my lord. My relatives came to England during the Norman invasion."

He eyed her speculatively. "Then you've noble blood in you. I thought so."

"Nay, my lord, you are mistaken. One of my ancestors simply served the nobility. Somewhere along the way he was granted a patch of land to farm. My father farms it to this day."

"Why did you leave your home, Madeleine?"

A cuckolded husband would never understand why she'd left her own husband. She knew she could never admit the truth to him. Yet she couldn't bear for him to think ill of her.

"I was to marry a neighbor but he caught the fever and died. I then was promised to his brother, but he, too, became ill and died. The third brother wanted little to do with me but we still became betrothed at the wish of our fathers. He was killed when a mule kicked him in the head."

She sighed. "People began to say I was cursed. Some called me a witch. Some thought evil would befall any man who came around me. My parents, though they loved me dearly, felt it best that I should leave."

"And so you chose to go with Farley's troupe?"

"Yes. They were gathering in London, which is where I was headed when you and I first met. I knew I must reach them before they took off."

"Your parents actually approved of this plan? Sending you alone on the road to London?"

"Of course not! They wanted me to go and work at the neighboring lord's estate." She snorted. "Can you see me milking cows and threshing wheat? I think not. I had my eye set on far better things. I knew I could sing and act as well as those who came through at our local faire each year, so I took off on my own."

"How did you know of Farley's troupe? That he was organizing in London at the time?"

Madeleine didn't miss a beat. "They'd come our way every spring for several years. I'd become friendly with several members, including Gwenith. I knew where they'd be gathering and decided to take my chances with Farley and Elspeth."

Garrett looked her directly in the eyes. "I don't believe a word you've just told me, Madeleine."

She bolted upright. "*You* are no gentleman, sir. How could you doubt a lady?"

"I thought you were a farm girl, Madeleine."

She blushed, the color rising from her neck to

the tip of her head.

"Lie back down," he said, "and tell me some more about yourself. I always did enjoy a good tale."

Madeleine didn't move. She was furious with him for not believing her and angry with herself that she was such a poor liar. Oh, if only they'd met under different circumstances. If only she weren't destined to leave Stanbury and seek sanctuary in a convent.

"Come, Madeleine," he commanded. His voice was soft but she recognized the tone, one she was conditioned to obey immediately.

She eased back onto the rock, her body stiff, her mouth set. Returning her hands behind her head, she acted as if she had not a care in the world. She stared straight ahead, though she did not see the stars above. Her mind was filled with Garrett, while she could feel the heat he radiated. He smelled of leather. He smelled male. It drove her to distraction—and it made her mad. At him. At herself.

He eased closer to her. Her eyes remained fixed on the heavens above. He reached out and tilted her chin so she faced him. Her bottom lip trembled slightly at his touch. After a moment's hesitation, he lowered his head to hers until their lips met. He brushed them softly and slowly against hers. His hand slipped from her chin and he stroked her jaw gently.

Lazily, he ran his tongue over her lower lip.

She found her lips parting without thought and he eased his tongue into her mouth.

He deepened the kiss and she shifted her arms from behind her head and wrapped them around his neck, urging him closer. Madeleine ran her fingers through his hair, wanting him to touch her everywhere as his tongue mated with hers. Sensations unknown to her rippled through her limbs. An ache began between her legs as a fierce longing swept through her. He feasted on her mouth as she sprang to life.

He broke the kiss, his lips trailing along her jaw and to her throat, where he licked and nipped. His hand covered her breast, gently squeezing it.

Suddenly, she shoved him back. "*Married!*" she gasped. "'Tis a sin!"

Garrett smoothed a wayward strand of hair from her face. "I don't feel married anymore. Lynnette has been gone for so long. All I know is that the ache I've known can be filled with you, Madeleine."

He cupped her face within his hands and bent to kiss her again. She whipped her head from side-to-side, struggling from his grip.

"No, I can't!" she wailed. She pushed him away and slid down the rock and took off in a half-run, half-walk since her knee ached fiercely.

"Madeleine, wait!" he called to her.

She stopped and spun around. "Leave me alone!" she cried. "God forgive us."

CHAPTER FIFTEEN

MADELEINE FLED ACROSS the meadow, her skirts held high. Her limp made the going hard and she cursed Henri with every step.

She reached into her pocket and withdrew Henri-the-Pebble. "I hate you, Henri, I truly hate you, and I hope you rot in Hell!" She spat on the small stone and then flung it from her. "Take that, you rotten bastard!"

She continued toward her tent, stealing a few cautious looks over her shoulder. Thankfully, Lord Montayne did not follow.

Reaching the tent, she moved aside the flap. A single candle burned by Gwenith's pallet. She was fast asleep, as was Evan, snuggled next to his mother. Madeleine extinguished the candle, slipped her shoes off, and made her way to her own bed in the corner.

She lay down and pushed her face into the

pillow to choke out the sobs as she had learned to do to avoid even further punishment from Henri. Hot tears soaked the pillowcase. She could not control them. Her insides ached, a deep, throbbing pain that was more than physical. She felt the hurt down into her very soul.

God had given her almost more than she could bear with her mockery of a marriage. She had escaped before she became another added rumor for Henri's fourth wife to muse upon. She was willing to atone for breaking her wedding vows by living out the rest of her life in a convent, devoting herself to a life of prayers, dedicated to Him alone. If Henri chose to divorce her, so be it. She would have rid herself of a monster and have gained sanctuary in the process.

But now God tested her resolve in another way. She desperately wanted the Earl of Montayne. She needed him more than anything on this earth. Yet he was the one thing she could never have. Would a loving God put temptation in her path? Was this a test of her faith?

Thank the Just Almighty that she remembered her own marriage vows before things went beyond a kiss. She reminded herself that even if she were not wed, it *was* a sin for her to be with the nobleman, even if his lawfully wedded wife had abandoned him for parts unknown.

She never wanted him to know she, too, was

married. He was a man. Even if he learned that Henri had beaten her, he would not condone her actions. Most men beat their wives and a man would naturally side with another man. Lord Montayne must never learn the truth.

Avoiding him would be next to impossible. He was the lord of Stanbury and might show up anywhere on that property unannounced. Though it pained her, she must end the lessons with Lyssa. That would keep their contact to a minimum. She would also need people around when she saw him. They could never be alone again as they had been tonight. She feared she would give in to temptation otherwise.

Madeleine sighed, wiping away tears. She had enjoyed working with Lyssa far more than she'd let on. At times, she had secretly thought of Lyssa as her own daughter, reveling in such a fantasy. She felt sorry the girl would be hurt by the situation but Madeleine must avoid Lord Montayne as much as possible.

But couldn't she think about him for just a little while? Surely God wouldn't begrudge her that small pleasure. Those few moments tonight with the earl were the happiest she'd known since she'd left her parents and moved to Chateau Maraine with Henri.

Madeleine pictured Garrett's boots first, then worked her way up his strong, powerful body. She imagined his lips on hers, the feel of his hand along her jaw, the touch of his tongue against hers. Her belly fluttered again and she moaned softly, longing for him and a life out of reach.

A fresh flood of tears sprang from her eyes, tears of desire and loneliness. Madeleine curled into a ball and fell into a restless sleep.

THE LESSONS WITH Lyssa ended without Madeleine having to justify anything to Garrett. Gwenith had taken a turn for the worse during the night. Madeleine remained constantly at her side, only leaving for brief spells to take her turn on stage. Eventually, she took no breaks at all from the sickroom, leaving York to narrate each performance in her place.

"Will Mama die, Maddie?" Evan asked, four days now into their vigil.

Madeleine fought tears as his wide, fearful eyes told her that he knew there was no hope. She leaned over and picked him up and brought him onto her lap. She held him close, stroking his hair.

"It's not for me to say, Evan. Only God knows." She hesitated. She was a person who always faced the truth. She'd never been dishonest with Evan and couldn't begin lying to him now. "But I do fear your mama's days on earth are few," she added softly.

A tear glided down Evan's cheek. "I've always been nice to Mama, haven't I, Maddie? Even when I've been a bit bad?"

Madeleine smiled at him. "Of course you have, Evan."

Gwenith wheezed, causing them to start. "Maddie?" she croaked. "Ale."

Madeleine poured her a cup and held it to Gwenith's cracked lips. She drank but most of it dribbled down her front.

"Evan," she whispered.

"Right here, Mama." He knelt next to her and she took his hand in hers.

"I love ye, sweet boy."

Evan sniffed. "I love ye."

"Listen to Maddie, all right? Be my good boy."

"I always listen to Maddie."

"I know ye do." Gwenith choked and Madeleine held a cloth to her friend's mouth as a wave of blackened blood oozed onto the rag.

"Is there anything I get for you?" she asked.

"No." Gwenith turned to Evan. "Be a good boy and go to Cook and get me some leftover bread." As soon as he exited the tent, Gwenith faced Madeleine. "Much as I'd like, I cannot ask ye to take Evan."

"Oh, Gwenith, I'd do anything for you. You know that."

Gwenith studied her a long moment. "Then take him to Lord Eversleigh, down Sussex way." She named an estate and said it was along the coast. "Evan is his son. He'll do right by the boy." She coughed again and grimaced. "If he'd make him a stable lad or something, that'd please me nicely."

"Will this Lord Eversleigh doubt me?"

Gwenith smiled tiredly. "Nay, Maddie. Evan's the spitting image of his other three sons and they all take after their papa. He'll believe ye. Just tell him Gwenith sent ye. And Maddie?" She smiled through her pain, a sad, sweet one of dreams lost. "Tell him I never stopped loving him. My thoughts were with him to the last."

With that, she was gone.

Madeleine took Gwenith's hand and kissed it tenderly as tears streamed down her cheeks. She held it close until the warmth ebbed and then gently placed it next to Gwenith's heart. Her own heart now shattered into a thousand pieces. A piece of her had died with Gwenith. But she would do as her friend had asked.

"I promise you, Gwenith, I will take Evan to his father. If he'll not have him, then I will care for him always."

Madeleine rose and left the tent. Several had gathered outside in the growing gloom. She turned to Osbert. "Tell Farley that Gwenith has passed. We need to seek permission from Lord

Montayne to find a spot for her burial. And find Father Kelvin, too. Gwenith must have last rites."

Elspeth stepped forward and put an arm around Madeleine. "I'll get Hannah and Ruth. We'll help prepare Gwenith."

Madeleine shook her head. "No, I must."

Elspeth squeezed her arm. "I insist. Ye're worn to the bone. Find Evan and care for him now. Take him to our tent. Ye'll both sleep there tonight."

The next few days passed in a blur. Father Kelvin presided over the funeral mass and Gwenith's internment. The faire continued but Farley excused Madeleine from performing until after the burial. Then Edgar came bearing interesting news.

"Just think, Madeleine. Lord Montayne has asked the mummers to stay on for a week after the faire ends. It's a house party he's having, and he'd like us to entertain his guests. It means extra money in all our pockets!"

Madeleine was still numb from Gwenith's death and hardly took in Edgar's news. Nothing seemed of interest to her anymore.

Then she realized Edgar had said extra money. This would enable her to complete her pledge to Gwenith and see Evan to his father in Sussex. From the channel's coast, she could sail directly to France. It would be time to forget her sorrows and move on.

"What kind of money, Edgar?"

"Well, Farley said it'd all be a bonus we'd be getting, with his lordship paying a goodly amount for us to stay on awhile."

"That's good news, indeed, Edgar," she said.

Farley found her soon afterward. "I hear that Edgar already let you in on our good news." He was beaming. "To be asked to stay for a house party is a great thing, Madeleine. But," he added, "Lord Montayne especially asked for you to narrate our plays. He said York has a pleasant voice and all but he thought his guests would be amused by a woman acting as troubadour. Are you up to it, Madeleine?"

Heart heavy, Madeleine knew she could not let Farley and the rest of the mummers down. She owed them too much. "Of course I will do it, Farley."

Farley's face lit up with a warm smile and he wrapped her in a bear hug. "That's my girl," he cried. "A mummer puts one foot in front of the other, no matter what the circumstances are."

THE NEXT DAY the faire ended. The peddlers moved on with their wares. The crowds dispersed to return to life as they knew it. The troupe's tents remained at the far edge of the meadow, though, since the mummers had been asked to stay on. They rehearsed several new plays for Lord Montayne's guests, who began arriving shortly after the faire's end.

One afternoon, Lyssa came to play with Evan and began talking excitedly about the changes. "Madeleine, you should see all the people. No one ever visits us, except Ashby. Aga says he's not a visitor, he's just a silly man."

Madeleine laughed. "I couldn't agree with you more, Lyssa. Every time I've spoken with Sir Ashby he's been silly, indeed."

"But he likes Luke," Lyssa pointed out, watching her tabby chase the string of yarn Evan trailed behind him.

"Then Sir Ashby must be a nice man, too."

"I miss you coming to the castle, Madeleine," Lyssa pouted. "Papa said you're busy."

Tears brimmed in her eyes. "Yes, Lyssa, I was caring for—" Her voice trailed off and she swallowed hard.

"Evan's mama."

"Yes, Gwenith." Madeleine's heart was heavy as she said the name. "She was my very good friend, and I miss her a great deal."

Lyssa frowned. "Are you Evan's new mama?"

She hesitated. "That's a difficult question, Lyssa. I am caring for Evan now."

"Lyssa! Come play with Luke and me," Evan called.

The girl left Madeleine's side and ran toward the boy and her kitten.

"Who will be responsible for Evan when the troupe disbands for the winter?"

Madeleine turned and saw Lord Montayne standing before her. The sun burnished his dark hair until it gleamed. His eyes glowed at her from his tanned face. Her heart lurched at the sight of him.

Calming her flutters, she quietly answered, "Gwenith asked me to take Evan to his father. I will be doing this after your house party has ended and the troupe moves on."

"So you'll leave the mummers?"

She nodded. "For a time. It's important I get Evan to his father." She watched the two children playing with the kitten, their squeals of delight bringing her momentary happiness. "He's never met him, you see. It's an unusual circumstance."

"Will the father accept him?" Garrett asked. "I assume he's a bastard?"

Madeleine shrugged. "Such an ugly word for so sweet a child." She met Garrett's gaze. "Gwenith seemed sure that his father would do right by him."

"How will the boy feel, being left in the care of strangers?"

"You are interested in the feelings of a mummer's bastard, my lord?"

"I simply wondered how he'd feel being apart

from you, Madeleine. I know how lonely I've been without you." His voice held great tenderness as he took her hand. "You're all he's got now."

Madeleine tugged at her hand, but Garrett refused to let go. "I must honor Gwenith's final wish, my lord. Evan should be with his father." She tugged harder, and he held on even more tightly. "Please give me my hand, my lord. I'm rather attached to it."

"So am I," he replied. He lifted it to his lips and grazed her knuckles before relaxing his hold. She jerked away from him as if he'd scalded her, and he laughed.

"I have missed you, Madeleine."

"And I have missed you not at all, my lord."

"Ever the little liar. And whose wife are you today?"

Madeleine caught her breath in a moment of panic. Then she relaxed, catching the teasing light in his eyes. "I have been many a man's wife since I was yours, my lord. I think today I'll be Edgar's."

"And make poor Edgar's wife in heaven jealous?"

It amazed her how he remembered such small details. "I'm sure if I make Edgar deliriously happy, he'll forget all about his dead wife," she said flippantly.

Garrett grew suddenly serious. "You're coming to the keep tonight, Madeleine?"

"Yes, my lord," she assured him. "We have been hard at work on several new dramas for your guests."

"Good," he said and turned to go. "I will see you tonight."

"Yes, my lord. The entire troupe will be ready to do your bidding. Your guests shall not be disappointed."

⇶⇷

THE CASTLE WAS aflutter with activity after having gone so long with no guests to speak of. Annie, Lyssa's nurse, confided in Madeleine how surprised they had been when Garrett announced the upcoming house party.

"Ye could have knocked me down with a feather, Madeleine. I can't right remember guests for ever so long at Stanbury. Not since the mistress done up and left."

"Are there many who've come?" she asked.

"A good twenty or more. Stanbury's large enough for them, that's for sure, and 'tis right for the master to start entertaining again. Lady Edith has walked around with a smile on her face for a week."

Madeleine thought of the house parties she'd given as the wife of one of the leading champagne merchants in Reims. Of course, they'd all been Henri's friends and business associates. She'd acted merely as hostess at these affairs but had enjoyed them for as long as they lasted. They broke up the dull routine of her sheltered life and she also had the opportunity to play and sing for those gathered.

Henri had showed a mix of pride in her accomplishments and yet had rebuffed her in private for not maintaining the high standards of his home. She knew, too, that once the guests made their way back to their own homes that Henri would find some fault so great with her that he would mete out the appropriate "punishment". It had become standard behavior in their chateau and made her all the more thankful to be away from that prison.

The mummers would perform every night for the next seven nights at Stanbury. The audience was an eclectic group. Some were wealthy landowners who finagled an invitation once they'd heard those were being issued. Others were past friends of the family and the rest business associates of Lord Montayne's from London.

Madeleine overheard Edith lamenting that her dearest childhood friend, Lady Ancil, was too ill to attend, and promised she'd do fifty *Our Fathers* for that bit of good luck. She'd run away from Henri while they were guests of the Ancils and the noblewoman would have recognized her on the spot.

The troupe waited each night until the evening meal had been served before they came out. Madeleine usually sang a few songs before the night's play began. Sometimes she sang a duet with York, which turned out to be quite successful.

Farley mentioned they'd have to try that more often once they left Stanbury.

Madeleine took comfort in that she'd be gone from Stanbury soon. She hated staying in one place so long for fear Henri would discover her whereabouts. She'd even had a few nightmares of Henri finding her. No, her time with the troupe had run its course, and she must meet her obligation to Evan and then return to France.

She'd not informed Farley about her leaving. It hadn't come up again since before Gwenith fell ill. Madeleine would simply tell him that she was taking Evan to his father and would return as soon as she could manage. He didn't need to know about her plans to cross the channel for France. She knew she owed him more but her fear outweighed any loyalty.

Every evening, Madeleine told a story after the play ended. Ashby called for one that first night, and it became a ritual for Garrett's guests. They seemed most enthralled with the tales from the *Arabian Nights*. They also enjoyed the legends surrounding King Arthur. Her mother had told her these stories every night for years. Madeleine had dreamed of someday finding her own Arthur and creating a world of beauty and goodness not unlike Camelot.

It surprised her when several guests gave her gold coins for her efforts.

"Look not so startled, Madeleine," Ashby said as he pressed a coin into her palm. "You are most entertaining and it makes them feel better to reward you in this manner."

"Thank you, my lord," she murmured.

"Ashby, Madeleine. After all, we are old friends." He winked at her and went on.

Madeleine found herself very pleased with the additional funds. They would make her trip go much more easily. She would have more than enough to pay for her passage to France. This way, she could give the jewels she'd saved to the Mother Superior of the convent she joined, thus guaranteeing her keep for the rest of her natural life.

The group had only one more day at Stanbury before they loaded their belongings and headed further west. Madeleine promised, after Lyssa's insistent pleadings, that she and Evan would spend the day with the young girl. Annie saw to the packing of a picnic lunch for them and so they set off to explore, Luke tagging along.

The threesome followed a stream into the

forest that surrounded Stanbury. They stopped at a shady spot for their meal. Cook had provided hunks of bread and cheese, cold chicken, and sweetmeats. They enjoyed their feast then lay on the blanket playing with Luke.

The heavily wooded forest blocked out much of the sunlight. Madeleine did not realize that the sky had become dark or that rain was on its way until a sudden thunderclap startled them.

"Quickly, children, let's pack up and head back to the castle. I fear we're about to get caught in a downpour."

Evan and Lyssa gathered up the leftovers and placed them in the basket.

"Let's put Luke in the basket, too," Madeleine told them. "He'll never be able to keep up with us. Besides, he's acting a bit skittish because of the thunder."

Just as Evan reached for the kitten, a loud thunderbolt rang out. The kitten scrambled up a nearby tree, running out onto a slim branch that hung over the water. He clung to the limb, clearly terrified by his first storm.

Lyssa wailed. "We can't leave without Luke!"

"Shush, love, of course we won't." Madeleine, though tall, could not reach the kitten. "Come, Evan, climb upon my shoulders and mayhap you can reach Luke."

She bent and let Evan scamper up on her shoulders, his legs hanging down, swinging happily. She stood under where Luke was perched but Evan could not grasp him as the kitten moved back and forth with every noise that rang from the sky. Madeleine urged Evan to stand upon her shoulders but the little boy did not have the skill to do so.

Lyssa was crying heartily now. Drops of rain hit Madeleine in the face. She hesitated, knowing she must go up into the tree and reclaim Luke or Lyssa would be heartbroken. But the thought of climbing that high made her heart rebel, pounding so loudly she thought it might pop from her chest.

Madeleine had never understood her fear of heights, which had been with her from her earliest memories. Only her greater fear of Henri suppressed it long enough for her to escape from Frothmore by climbing from the keep's window to flee through the sally port. That had been a much greater height than this tree but she'd still been deathly afraid.

Oh, Mary, Mother of God, be with me now, be with me now. Please, please, be with me now. This prayer echoed over and over in her mind.

Mouth dry, her stomach in knots, she said, "I must go up and get Luke. Stand back."

She lifted her foot and placed it into a knot-hole as she grabbed the lowest branch available. Hoisting herself up, her knee groaned under the strain. Madeleine climbed until she could go out on the limb Luke had chosen to cling to in his fear. She eyed the kitten, his fur now soaked, wondering whose fear was greater. All she wanted was to return to the sweet ground where she belonged. God had not meant for her to be as a bird, flitting in this tree.

"Come on, Luke," she said to him in gentle, coaxing tones. "Come see Madeleine, my good boy."

Lightning crackled, causing Luke to slowly back further onto the branch. A loud boom rang through the forest and the terrified kitten skittered even further away, his fur standing on end.

"No, sweet kitty, come here," Madeleine begged. She scooted out as far as she dared on the slender limb. After stretching, she had the kitten within her grasp.

Madeleine stroked him to calm him. "That's my boy," she purred and clasped him in her hand just as thunder roared again.

The children began clapping, jumping up and down with their joy. Suddenly, Madeleine felt the branch begin to give. Her eyes widened and she tightened her grip on Luke.

"Evan," she said cautiously, not wanting to frighten them, "the branch seems as if it could break at any moment." She paused, licking her lips. "I'm going to lower Luke to you. Please do your best to catch him."

"Yes, Maddie," Evan said, his eyes round. He held his arms up. Madeleine pried Luke from his perch, said a quick prayer, and dropped him.

Evan made a perfect catch. He handed the yowling kitten to Lyssa and stared back up at her.

"Can I help ye, Maddie?"

She heard how frightened he was. "No, just stay there. I'll—"

But she never completed her sentence. The limb, which had been groaning under her added weight, snapped without warning and dumped her into the ice-cold stream, her leg buckling from her weak knee. She landed clumsily on rocks that bit into her flesh as her leg twisted under her.

A scream tore from her throat as blinding pain flashed through the injured leg. Fortunately, the water was not very deep so she remained at an awkward angle, half on her side, half on her back inches from the bank of the stream. At least she wouldn't drown.

Lyssa began crying as Evan jumped in and tried to lift her. Madeleine gasped as the pain returned in waves and she began retching violently.

Finally, she opened her eyes. "You must go for help, Evan. I cannot get out and you're too small to hoist me." She grimaced and bit her lip, trying to control the pain shooting through her back and leg.

"Go, Evan. Take Lyssa with you. Hurry, please."

Evan took Lyssa's hand and they began running. Luke howled pitifully as he was jostled along.

Madeleine waited until they were out of her sight before she cried out. If she leaned back, she could rest her head against the bank. She did so and then surrendered to the pain.

CHAPTER SIXTEEN

GARRETT SMILED TO himself as he gazed up at the darkening skies. His guests had enjoyed a week of perfect weather, which meant he'd been suffering through a week of being the perfect host. He'd tired of his group of visitors almost immediately, but having the special show each evening for Stanbury guests was the only idea he'd had to hold the mummers here after the faire ended.

Now they were scheduled to leave on the morrow, as were his guests. What would he do? Could he go back to life as he'd known it before he'd met Madeleine? He'd not been the same man since that April night when he'd first seen her. Thoughts of her stayed with him from his waking every morning until he collapsed in a heap upon his bed at night. Too often, she invaded his dreams, as well. How could he manage without her?

He'd entertained all manner of wild thoughts, from offering her a position as Lyssa's tutor to holding her in one of the far north tower rooms to serve as his mistress.

Garrett knew she'd turn down both offers.

He turned to the group assembled. "I'm afraid we'll have to adjourn inside for our pleasures, my friends. Looks like a storm is brewing. Mayhap we can continue our bowling later."

"Could the mummers perform early?" asked Lady Sanvale hopefully. "Or that wonderful girl, Madeleine, could tell us more of Beowulf or the Norman invasion." The noblewoman shivered. "I swear you'd think she'd been there herself, she describes things in such great detail."

Several chuckled at her remarks. Garrett added, "I know Farley promised some special entertainment tonight for us, with it being their last time to perform. Why don't you rest a bit, Lady Sanvale? I'll see what can be arranged."

There were murmurs of assent as the group began heading back to the castle. The first raindrops hit at that moment and Edith led the way, the ladies squealing like young children.

Garrett hung back, happy to be in his own company for once. He walked slowly home, savoring the quiet surrounding him, even if he had to become soaked to enjoy it.

He'd just entered the outer bailey, thankful that none of his company was in sight, when Annie dashed up to him, an anxious look on her worn face.

"Oh, my lord, I wasn't expecting this storm." She wrung her hands nervously.

"Speak up, Annie, what's on your mind?"

"I let Lyssa go on a picnic with Madeleine and little Evan. Now there's this downpour and look at those dark clouds that way. The little mites'll be soaked to the skin. I don't want them to catch their death of cold."

"Don't worry, Annie. I'll saddle Ebony and bring them back. Where did they go?"

"Lyssa wanted to picnic by that stream, just beyond the edge of the forest."

"Then think how dry they'll be," he reassured her. "Those trees are a thick covering. I'll wager they feel but a few drops."

Garrett strode off toward the stables had Ebony saddled. He mounted the frisky horse and turned him out the gates and across the meadow, heading toward the woods.

The sky had darkened considerably. A streak of lightning tore across the heavens, followed by a noisy thunderclap and he heard Lyssa's cry from a distance. He spurred Ebony on.

Halfway across the meadow, he spotted the two children scrambling toward him as the rain arrived full scale and a steady downpour began.

Garrett dismounted, alarmed that he hadn't spotted Madeleine with them. She would never leave the children on their own.

The pair was wet to the bone, shivering with the cold. Lyssa had lost one of her slippers. Both children were in tears. Garrett felt a chill rush through him.

"Me lord!" gasped Evan. "Ye must help." He bent down and put his hands to his knees, leaning over as he tried to catch his breath.

"What's wrong?" Garrett demanded. His harsh tone caused Lyssa to burst into fresh tears.

"She's hurt, Papa."

Madeleine.

"Maddie fell trying to save Luke, me lord," Evan added. "He'd climbed in a tree when the storm began and was afraid to come down. Maddie went after him, and the branch broke."

Lyssa wailed even louder. "Luke was very bad, Papa," she said. "Now Madeleine's hurt." She squeezed the kitten and he hissed, swiping a paw at her. A thin line of blood appeared on the back of her hand. Lyssa burst into new tears and tossed the kitten upon the ground.

Garrett thought quickly. He didn't wish to leave the children here but he wanted to reach Madeleine as quickly as possible. He knew they were too small to ride Ebony alone. The horse was a handful for even the best of riders.

"Let's get you home quickly," he told them.

"Come, and we'll ride Ebony together."

"No. Maddie's hurt. She fell in the water. Get her out, me lord. I can walk with Lyssa back to the castle."

Garrett saw the little boy straighten to his full height. He knew instinctively that the boy would get his daughter back to the keep safely.

"Stanbury is in sight, Evan. Can you see it?"

He nodded. "We'll go straight there, me lord."

Garrett knelt and lay his hand on Evan's shoulder. "You're a brave lad, Evan. Do me proud and take Lyssa home. Find Sir Ashby and tell him what's happened. He'll know what to do." He squeezed the boy's shoulder. Scooping up Luke, he handed the feisty kitten back to Lyssa. "Take Luke and go with Evan. Don't give me a surly face. Luke's but a kitten and he's very frightened now. You'll have to be a brave girl and take him home. Go now."

They began rushing, hand-in-hand, in the direction of Stanbury. Garrett remounted Ebony and galloped the remaining way across the meadow. He tied the horse to a tree and entered the forest. From Annie's description, he had a good idea where to look. He'd spent many hours in these woods over the years and he knew them better than anyone at Stanbury.

He found Madeleine immediately but nothing prepared him for what he saw. She'd managed to pull herself partially onto the bank but half of her body remained in the stream. Though late June, he knew the water had to be freezing. There was no telling how long she'd been immersed in it.

He ran to her and saw she was unconscious. He lifted her from the water, her skirts heavy and clinging to her. Her chilled body was deathly pale and still.

For a moment, he thought her dead—but then she gasped. Her eyes flew open and he saw the pain and fear held in them.

"'Tis all right, Madeleine, I'm here." He brushed the wet hair from her brow. Her skin felt like ice. He must warm her. He couldn't lose her as he'd lost his brother.

She began weeping and moaning softly. "Oh, God, it hurts. Not again. Please, not again."

He lifted her shoulders and placed her head upon his lap. "What ails you, Madeleine? What's hurt?" he asked gently, as he stroked her clammy cheek.

"'Tis broken," she said bitterly.

"What?"

"My leg." She began laughing hysterically. He tried to calm her but didn't succeed. Finally, her laughter subsided into weeping.

"You'll be all right, Madeleine," he assured her. "We'll get you back to Stanbury. You'll heal."

She stared into his eyes, her own a stormy color. "Heal? I'll never be whole again."

ASHBY ARRIVED AT the edge of the stream soon after with Lord Marbury's physician. "Thank God old Marbury never ventures three steps without his doctor in tow."

Hating to leave her, Garrett stepped out of the way so the doctor could examine Madeleine, pushing and probing. Garrett leaned around and was horrified when he saw the awkward angle of Madeleine's leg. It sickened him just to look upon it. No wonder she'd been in such pain. Thankfully, she'd passed out again.

"We brought a cart," Ashby said. "I wasn't sure how severely she was hurt. The children were very upset. We can lay her across it."

"Thanks, Ash." Garrett gave him a weak smile.

Ashby placed a hand upon his shoulder and gave it a slight squeeze.

"My lord?" The physician rose. "I cannot do a complete examination here but this woman is seriously hurt. The leg is definitely broken. Beyond that, I cannot venture to say. She may have internal injuries."

"Then let's bring her back to Stanbury. Do

whatever it takes, man, just help her."

The doctor rigged a temporary splint from two branches of a nearby tree. Once it was in place, the three men were able to lift Madeleine and carry her the short distance to the cart. She swam in and out of consciousness on the short trip to Stanbury. Garrett was aware of every jostle the cart made. He cradled her head in his lap, hoping to ease the jarring as Ashby held her leg in place.

Garrett supervised Madeleine being taken to a small upper chamber, where the doctor examined her carefully. After some minutes, he asked Garrett to step in. The physician wore a grave expression on his face.

"I was correct, my lord. The lower leg was damaged, broken in two places." He shook his head. "There's more that troubles me, though."

A fresh wave of fear swept over Garrett. Injuries of any kind could prove fatal. "What mean you?"

"This woman has been sadly mistreated. Her knee is misshapen, as if it had been broken before and not mended properly. Does she walk with a limp?"

"Yes," Garrett said slowly, anger building within him.

"Well, it may take her a very long time before walks again," the doctor said bluntly. "The knee joint was weak before. It's impossible to tell at this time if it is strong enough to hold her weight as the bones in her leg try to mend. She has a long recovery ahead of her." The doctor frowned. "There's more, my lord."

Fear raised the hair along his arms while anger knotted low in his gut. Garrett nodded for him to continue.

"She's been badly abused. Her legs are scarred rather severely, her back almost as much. Scars like these would not come from an accident. She has been beaten severely, numerous times."

Speechless at both the accusatory tone as well as the unthinkable revelation, Garrett sucked in his breath. "I'll have you know, I caused no harm to this woman."

The physician nodded. "As I suspected. Most of the injuries are not recent, save for her unfortunate fall from the tree." He paused, glancing back at his patient.

"I gave her something to sleep, to help the pain, but only time will tell." The physician eyed him with interest. "I recognized her as one of the mummers."

"Yes." Garrett's voice was barely above a whisper. "She is also tutor to my daughter," he added.

"I see," said the man, a glimmer in his eyes. "Well, as I said, I've given her something for the pain. She'll sleep deeply for many hours, mayhap even through the night. 'Twould be good if someone could stay with her."

"I'll arrange it. Thank you."

The physician hesitated a moment. "I will check her on the morrow, but I leave midmorning with Lord Marbury."

Garrett watched the doctor leave and then turned to stare at Madeleine's still form.

Marbury's physician had no reason to lie to him yet Garrett found it hard to understand what he'd heard about Madeleine. Doubts lingered. Surely the man exaggerated.

Knowing he shouldn't pry, he couldn't resist. He had to know if the physician had spoken the truth. He cared too deeply for this woman. He had to see for himself.

He moved closer to the bed and eased back the sheet. As if in a dream, he gently rolled Madeleine to her side and lifted her tunics, inching them up slowly. With every move of the cloth, he saw the scars on her milky white flesh. Some were deeply embedded. Others appeared pink, much more recent. Some seemed as if they had been burned into her flesh, others cut into it. Garrett had seen many types of wounds on the battlefield but the purposeful torture of an innocent woman sickened him.

He continued to raise her skirts. Her back and buttocks were also marred. His pulse pounded in outrage at the thought of Madeleine's tormenter. Garrett put her clothing back into place, smoothing the fabric as best he could.

He returned Madeleine to her back and she made a few small whimpers in her sleep as he recovered her.

In utter shock, Garrett knelt on the floor next to her. What kind of animal could do this to another human being? Savagely beating or burning her until she was so disfigured?

He swallowed the bile that rose in his throat. What kind of suffering had Madeleine endured? For how many years? What fiend had attacked her over and over? His gut said she'd been on the run when he'd met her, trying to protect herself from her abuser. Had it been fate that she'd chosen Garrett's name?

A white-hot anger blanketed him. If her abuser had appeared before him at that moment, he would have killed the man with a single blow. He tried to calm the fury that seared through every pore of his body, causing him to tremble violently. Anger wouldn't help Madeleine now.

When he was a child, Ryker used to beat his mother often. He still remembered his feelings of helplessness when Edith came to the table the next day, her face a mass of bruises, her body moving stiffly. He'd hated Ryker for many things, but especially for this.

Garrett leaned over and pressed a tender kiss upon Madeleine's brow. He took her hand and held it to his cheek, oblivious to the tears that fell down his face.

He whispered, "I swear, Madeleine, that I will protect you from whomever did this. You will be safe with me."

He then bowed his head and wept.

CHAPTER SEVENTEEN

S*HE KNEW SHE'D angered him. The signs were many. The cold, calculating stare. The set of his mouth. Even his stance. She knew what was coming.*

She ran, lurching first down the tower steps, then out of the chateau. If she could reach the vineyards, she'd be safe. Crossing the inner bailey she passed curious glances, but she had no time to stop. From the outer bailey, she found the gate already raised. She called for the bridge to be lowered. It fell and she hobbled across.

The vineyard lay beyond, its lush, green vines calling to her. She could hide there. Hide from the anger, hide from the shame, but most importantly, hide from the punishment that awaited her if she were caught.

She rounded the corner and froze.

Henri stood between her and freedom, his arrogant smirk chilling her to the bone.

"Did you think you could escape punishment, Madeleine?" He reached for her and she screamed.

"MADELEINE? WHAT IS it—the pain?"

Her eyes flew open at the man's soft words. Her vision was slightly blurred and she blinked several times trying to bring things into focus. She did not recognize her surroundings. She did, though, recognize the familiar agony.

Suddenly, she felt pressure on her shoulders and tried to throw off the hands holding her down.

"Madeleine!"

The voice was commanding, causing her to cease her struggles. Gently, she was pushed back into soft pillows.

Then she saw Garrett hovering over her, concern written across his tired features.

"Shall I call the physician again? Do you need something for your pain?"

What was going on? Henri had punished her, she was sure of it, her throbbing aches told her as much. So how had Garrett come to be at Chateau Maraine?

Then the events of earlier that day came rushing back to her. The sudden storm. Luke in the tree. The limb crashing down. The icy water.

She breathed a small sigh of relief, knowing she was at Stanbury. Henri was only a ghost of a memory. For once, he was not the cause of her misery. The pain was of her own making.

"Madeleine? Shall I call for the doctor?"

She looked up again at Garrett's troubled face and was surprised at his distress.

"No, my lord, do not send for a doctor. Save your money and mine. I have managed pain before. It's an old friend." She made an effort to smile. "Are the children all right? Did Luke manage to survive his first thunderstorm?"

Garrett expelled a long breath. "Both Lyssa and Evan, as well as that mangy beast, are perfectly fine. You," he continued softly, "are not, I'm afraid."

He slipped his hand around her limp wrist, his thumb massaging it lightly. The sweet gesture brought her comfort despite her misery. "Your leg is broken, Madeleine," he told her.

"I know."

He looked at her quizzically. "The doctor said it's not the first time something has happened to that leg."

Madeleine knew he wanted her to fill in the blanks of her story but she remained silent.

After a moment, he shrugged and continued. "You will require much rest before you are up and about. My mother and Annie have promised to take good care of you. Mother even brought one of her chemises for you to wear." He smiled at her. "The lilac sets off your eyes nicely."

Panic suddenly coursed through Madeleine. Her jewels were sewn into her clothing. "My clothes!" she cried. "Where are my tunics?"

He leaned down and picked up her wet tunics and dropped them back onto the floor. "I'll have them washed for you."

"No!" she cried vehemently. "I must do that myself." She leaned across him and tried to reach for the tunics but the pain flared. With a soft cry, she fell back onto the pillows.

"Do not concern yourself with the task, Madeleine. It will be done for you."

She gritted her teeth. "Would you please hand them to me, my lord?"

He frowned but did as she requested. She held the tunics close, afraid to let them out of her sight. "I will take care of it myself."

Garrett sighed. "Whatever you say."

She sat brooding for a moment and then abruptly said, "I must return to the mummers, my lord."

"Why?" he exploded. "You can't even walk now, Madeleine. You may not walk for months. I can't let you."

"What did you say?" Icy fear filled her.

"You must stay at Stanbury, Madeleine. Farley's mummers will go to their next stop, but you need time to heal."

"Will it truly take that long to recover?"

Garrett gave her hand a quick squeeze. "The physician only said it will take time, that's all. You may stay here as long as you like. If you're worried about your keep, you may give Lyssa more lessons while you recover."

"I would enjoy spending more time with Lyssa. But what of Evan, my lord? Gwenith gave him to my care. I had planned on taking him to his father, Lord Eversleigh in Sussex, when the mummers left Stanbury on the morrow."

She clasped his hand tightly. "Is there any way Evan can remain here until I can honor Gwenith's last wish? He could help in the stables or the kitchen, mayhap?"

Garrett placed his free hand atop hers, patting gently. "Master Evan is as welcome as you, Madeleine. I'm sure I can find something for him to do to keep him from mischief."

"Then you would be the first, my lord."

She gave him a smile but found her eyes drifting shut as relief washed over her. Her last conscious thought was she and Evan were safe.

Thanks to Lord Montayne.

GARRETT REACHED TO pick the wet clothes off the bed now that Madeleine had fallen asleep. He started to lay them across the chair to dry.

"That's odd," he said to himself. Although they were still damp, the garments were unusually heavy. He slipped his hand around them until he reached the hem of her skirts. Hard lumps lay within the layers.

He ripped open the hem and several pieces of jewelry fell to the floor. A sapphire bracelet caught his eye. He could not be mistaken. The piece matched the ring Madeleine had sold for Gwenith's care, the one he'd bought from the old jeweler.

He tore at all the hems until the tunics were empty, then bent and examined the precious gems sparkling on the floor. Diamonds. Rubies. Emeralds. More sapphires. He spied three rings, two more bracelets, and a necklace, all of excellent quality.

They had to be worth a small fortune. No wonder she'd been so concerned about her tunics. Where had Madeleine gotten such priceless pieces? He refused to believe she was a thief. She seemed too good, too kind.

A thought struck him. Did they belong to the man who'd hurt her? Had she taken them as revenge? In order to escape? Or was she the noblewoman she'd so vehemently denied?

Garrett placed the clothes over the chair but kept the jewels for safekeeping. He sent Annie in to sit with Madeleine before heading to his own chamber, all the while wondering about the mystery that was Madeleine Bouchard.

FARLEY'S BOOMING VOICE awakened Madeleine the next morning. She groaned. Every bone she possessed felt stiff. Her leg throbbed painfully, feeling as if liquid fire had been poured upon it. She thanked God with a quick prayer that a true physician had helped her this time. She had a much better chance of healing properly.

Farley burst into the room seconds later, Elspeth trailing behind him. She took one look at Madeleine and burst into a brogue so thick, no one for three hundred miles could have understood her. She flew to Madeleine's side and kissed her hands, her cheek, her brow, and the hands again, tears flowing freely from her.

"So you did this over a wee kitten?" Farley growled.

"It would seem so," Madeleine replied meekly. "Though who knew the branch would break, taking me with it." She was still groggy, but she found it easier to get her words out this morning than last night.

"Well, we'll miss you, girl. When you can travel, know you'll always have a place with us."

Madeleine was moved by his words. "I thank

you, Farley. If it's meant to be, I'll return to you." She was saddened by the look on his face. "You do have York."

"York?" Farley snorted. "He's a handsome lad with an aversion to work. I guess I'll make do with him for now." He frowned down at her. "Are you in much pain, Madeleine?"

She didn't want to worry him. "There's some, but not more than I would expect."

Elspeth straightened, her tears beginning to subside. "Lord Montayne says ye're to remain here until ye're well. Evan, too." She stroked Madeleine's arm. "You'll be missed, Madeleine. Ye, Evan, and that precious Gwenith."

Elspeth stood, wiping the remaining tears on her sleeve. "Must be on the way now. Had to come and say our goodbyes."

Madeleine bit her lower lip, losing her battle with tears. "You took me in. You did so much for me. I'll miss you both."

"We'll miss you, too." Farley sniffed loudly. "Must be on our way, though."

He and Elspeth took their leave, passing the richly dressed physician as he entered the chamber. His face was lined with deep furrows, as if he frowned from sunrise to sunset.

"Good morn," he said brusquely. "I've come to see you before I leave with Lord Marbury. We travel back to London, you know. My lord is quite close to our king."

Madeleine assumed by his air that he looked down upon attending a lowly mummer but he had done a competent job. He examined her briefly, seeming to be satisfied with what he found. "I've left some herbs for you. A creature named Annie has them. She's gone to fetch you something to break your fast. Be sure to stay off the leg as much as possible."

"Sir?"

Madeleine knew she must confirm what Garrett had mentioned. "Will it be months before I walk again?"

He shook his head slowly. "That, I cannot say. Only time and prayer will give you that which you seek. I bid you good day." He quickly exited the room.

Annie returned soon afterward, helping Madeleine to relieve herself and then trying to feed her.

"Annie, I'm not totally helpless. Please, let me feed myself. I'm not a babe in this bed, but a grown woman."

"I would think ye a child after going up the tree after a mongrel."

Madeleine sighed. "It was important to Lyssa. You cannot tell me that you yourself wouldn't be a fool over that sweet child."

Annie softened. "Aye, I do see yer point," she amended. "I'm sorry ye're hurt so badly."

"Maddie!"

Evan rushed into the room, flinging himself onto the bed, rattling dishes and tipping over Madeleine's broth. She knew not which hurt worse, the blinding pain in her leg or the spilled broth that burned her side.

"Child! Get up at once!" Annie chided.

Evan stubbornly shook his head, refusing to listen. "Me Maddie needs me, Annie. I cannot leave her now."

His face was so earnest even Annie could not stay mad at him for long.

Madeleine grimaced and shifted slightly. She hadn't the heart to reprimand him. She could see the worry and fear in his eyes. He'd just lost his mother. She knew he was scared of losing her, too.

Annie clucked her tongue. "Very well, little boy. Ye can stay a few minutes, then it's nothing but quiet that'll come from this chamber."

The servant replaced the wet coverlet with a dry one and took the dishes out, giving them a bit of privacy.

Evan waited until Annie left. "Oh, ye look bad, Maddie. There's a big bruise here and a little one there," he added, touching her brow and cheek. "What are we to do now?"

"Lord Montayne has said we may stay here for the present. When I am well, you and I are to journey to your father's house."

Evan's eyes grew wide at the thought. "I

have a father?" His excitement quickly changed to doubt. "Mama never said that."

Madeleine laughed. "We all have fathers, Evan. Yours just happens to live in Sussex. His name is Lord Eversleigh."

Evan pondered this information. "So my papa's a lord?"

"Yes," Madeleine said. "But he's a wife and three other sons, Evan. Your mama was not his married wife but she loved him very much, nonetheless."

Madeleine placed her arm around Evan. He curled up next to her. "Your mama hoped Lord Eversleigh would make you a stable boy at his home. Would you like that, Evan?"

The boy's eyes lit up. "Oh, yes, Maddie, I do love the horses. I think they like me a little bit, too."

"Then we'll see if Lord Montayne will let you practice being a stable boy here. We'll be here for a while, Evan. As soon as I'm able, I'll write to your papa and let him know we're coming."

From the doorway, she heard Garrett say, "That's not necessary, Madeleine. I wrote to Eversleigh this morning about the boy. But where did *you* learn how to write?"

CHAPTER EIGHTEEN

MADELEINE GLARED AT Garrett as he stood in the doorway. *The man eavesdropped with more ease than Evan,* she thought, steeling herself for the coming conversation.

Evan scampered over to him and hugged his leg.

"You wrote my papa, me lord?" The boy smiled and squeezed Garrett's leg again.

"Yes, Evan, and I'm sure we'll hear from him soon. Now, I do believe Lyssa was looking for you."

"I'm going to tell her about me papa." Evan puffed up with pride. "He's a real lord."

"Go look for her then. I'll tend to Madeleine." Garrett glanced at her, a gleam in his eyes.

She lay helplessly in the bed, trapped for another inquisition.

Evan ran over to her, planting a sloppy kiss

on her cheek. "Got to go, Maddie," he said and ran from the room.

As Garrett strode confidently toward the bed, she forced herself not to squirm as he said, "Now that prying ears are gone, I'll ask again. How did you learn to write?"

"How do you know I can write, my lord? I might have been telling little Evan that for comfort and then asked you to pen the letter for me later. Did you think of that?"

Garrett shook his head. "You have a ready answer for everything, don't you?"

"In this case, I do. I can write, you know. My papa was not a serf. I explained it all to you before."

Garrett groaned. "Yes, I remember now. Norman invasion, aided his lord, rewarded with land, first betrothed died, second betrothed died, third betrothed kicked in the head by a mule and died, ran away, joined the mummers, wound up here. Is that the right order for the lies?"

Madeleine wanted to slap him. How dare he make fun of her! "You seem to have everything memorized. Mayhap you'd make a good troubadour. They must commit to heart hundreds of stories to be any good at all." She sighed. "The better ones know thousands."

He raised his eyebrows expectantly, a smile tugging at his mouth.

"Oh, of course, I can read and write," she told

him, her exasperation growing. "My papa taught my brother and I listened carefully. I actually caught on faster than Peter, which made him want to bash my nose a few times."

"And did he?"

"Bash my nose?" She chuckled. "Of course he did. Always when no one was looking. He'd claim I tripped and landed face down, hence my bloody nose. He was always causing me grief."

"Was?"

She nodded. "Yes. He's dead now. Eventually, I was the one left to help Papa with the accounts. I have quite a head for figures."

"How did Peter die?"

She cleared her throat. "On the way to town. He was alone and accosted by highwaymen." A single tear slid down her cheek. "My parents never got over his death. Peter was always the favorite one."

He burst out laughing. "You are incredible, Madeleine. Racked by pain, alone in the world, responsible for a little boy, at the mercy of a wicked nobleman, and you still spin your tales. No wonder my guests praised you so highly." He turned to go. "I'll be back, mayhap in a few days, or when you're ready to tell me the truth."

Madeleine reached for the cup on the table next to her and hurled it toward his head. He ducked and, still laughing, left the chamber, closing the door behind him.

"You bloody bastard!" she called after him. "Goodness." She suddenly laughed at herself. "I've been in England so long I'm now cursing in the language. I wonder if I should say my rosary in English," she mused.

Finally finding herself alone now, her first thought was to check her tunics, which lay across the back of the chair next to the bed. She tossed back the bedclothes and struggled from the bed to the chair, groaning as the pain flared. Heaving herself into it, she fingered the hems of her tunics. Panic seared through her.

The jewels were gone.

"No," she whispered. "That cannot be."

Her fingers searched without success. Someone had discovered her hidden treasures and taken them. The tunics were clean, so she knew they had been taken to be washed while she slept.

Which of Garrett's servants had discovered her secret stash? The hems appeared intact so whoever had found the gems had not only claimed the jewels but repaired the stitches, as well. Tears welled in her eyes as an ache filled her, a hurt so deep it was as if someone had run a sword through her.

She was in no position to seek out the person who had stolen her jewels. She had barely made it from the bed to this chair and dreaded having to return to the bed again. Madeleine forced herself to do so, however. As she lay there, she realized no one would have the audacity to steal under Garrett's roof.

Fear encircled her heart as she realized it could only be the Earl of Montayne who had discovered her cache. She was already at his mercy, being unable to leave with the mummers because of her injuries. Now would not be the time to confront him in her weakened state. Once she healed, though, she would have to brave facing him and demand that he return the gems to her. They were her property and would allow her to journey with Evan to Lord Eversleigh, as well as give her the means to continue to survive in England.

For now, Madeleine decided she would play ignorant and bide her time.

LORD MONTAYNE WAS as good as his word. Madeleine didn't see him again for a fortnight, though half his castle's population had visited her in the first few days she was in bed, including several of the guests leaving to return to their own homes. One in particular, Lady Sanvale, was especially kind. Madeleine noticed the sparkle in the silver-haired woman's eyes every night she had entertained with her stories and songs. She felt especially honored when the dowager countess came to see her.

"You are remarkable, my dear," Lady Sanvale said, patting her hand. "And so very brave! I don't know of many men who'd rescue a kitten the way you did, risking your life for a child's happiness." She removed something from her surcoat and took Madeleine's hand, patting her again as she placed something heavy and cool in her palm.

Madeleine opened her hand to find a beautiful brooch. "Oh, dear, my lady, I cannot accept such a valuable gift."

Lady Sanvale silenced her. "My child, I'm an old woman. Not many live to be my age and I've decided to make my own laws as I go along. You have brought me happiness and I would return some to you. Now take this. You may have need of it someday."

Madeleine's eyes glimmered with tears. She leaned forward and kissed the other woman's withered cheek. "I thank you for your generosity, my lady."

Others also visited, including many of the servants who'd come to see her perform during the faire. Lyssa came daily and even Lady Edith honored her with a visit.

But Garrett did not come.

He stayed away for two full weeks and Madeleine began to feel as if she might lose her mind after the first few days of bed rest. She didn't know if it was from boredom or lack of his company. She had come to enjoy their verbal sparring and she missed him terribly.

Madeleine began Lyssa's lessons again. Evan sat in on them, too, practicing both music and drawing when he could be excused from his work in the stables. The earl, true to his word, made sure his men kept the boy busy there. For his part, Evan seemed to adore being around the horses. He did come and sleep with her every night, though.

"I'm used to sleeping near ye, Maddie," he told her when he planted himself on the floor at the foot of her bed after that first night. "Ye might need me. I'll be here to help protect ye."

"Then come lie next to me, Evan. The floor's too hard."

Of course, Lyssa became jealous and also wanted to sleep with her. They'd had quite a time convincing the girl she belonged in her own chamber. It was moments like that in which Madeleine was relieved that Annie was the girl's nurse and not she.

Madeleine awakened early, as was her custom, and rose immediately. She practiced getting around several times a day, wanting to strengthen her leg and her own stamina as much as possible. She'd learned in the past not to let injuries slow her down or Henri would make it worse for her. Her husband despised any display of weakness and took cruel advantage of anyone in that state. Madeleine had learned to fight the pain at first and then worked with it. After three years with Henri, she knew just how far she could push her body and what its limitations were.

The leg, still in its unwieldy splint, was heavy, but she managed it well. She hobbled around the room several times, exhausted but pleased with her progress. She whispered a fervent prayer to the Holy Mother, hoping the splint was helping her bones to mend properly. She smiled to herself, picturing the arrogant physician. She wished he could see what she'd already accomplished in so short a time.

A light rap sounded on the door and it opened quietly. Her heart skipped a beat at the sight of the Earl of Montayne bearing a tray. On it sat bread and ale, with a large wedge of cheese. Her stomach rumbled at the sight of it and she felt her face flush.

He entered the room and closed the door. Concern for her was written on his features.

"Should you be trying to walk, Madeleine? It's a bit early, don't you think?"

She shook her head fiercely. "Nay, I must!" she insisted. "It's important that I move about. It helps to heal more quickly."

Concentrating on each step as she moved slowly and deliberately toward the bed, she swung the damaged leg stiffly along. She glanced up and saw him watching her, a pained expression on his face. He looked as if he were ready to sweep her up and carry her to her destination. It was the last thing she wanted from him. She gave him credit, though, for he stood still and waited until she finally reached him.

He helped her onto the bed, lifting her against the pillows and smoothing the covers over her. The very nearness of him brought her absurd pleasure.

He placed the tray on the bed and she reached for the ale, suddenly very thirsty. Her hands trembled as she took the cup and brought it to her lips, realizing her efforts had depleted most of her strength. He raised his hand to hers and steadied it so she could drink more easily.

Madeleine drank deeply. These turns around the room always left her drained. She wished her host would leave for she had no wits about her now. Still, he'd stayed away for a long time and she thought to question him why.

"My lord?" she asked. "Is there something special about today?"

"I wish you would call me Garrett. You are a guest in my home. All my friends call me Garrett."

A giggle escaped from her, knowing how Henri had referred to the English earl. "I've heard said your enemies call you the Devil Himself."

He grinned. "Better you call me Devil than

nothing at all." His expression grew serious. "I do wish to speak with you about an important matter. Last night, Lord Eversleigh arrived at Stanbury."

She gasped. "So soon?" An ache like the one she'd felt upon Gwenith's death filled her suddenly.

He nodded. "He'd like to leave today with Evan. He's meeting the boy for the first time now."

Her lips began to tremble and she bit the lower one, trying to still it. "May I see Evan before he goes?" she asked quietly.

"Of course. You know he'd insist upon it."

"Yes," she said softly.

"Lord Eversleigh would like to see you in about an hour. I'll have Annie or someone come help you dress."

Madeleine nodded and turned her face away as he left the room. Sorrow began to weigh upon her soul. Her appetite had diminished and she pushed the tray away as hot tears fell. She dried her cheeks, though, and was ready when the nobleman came to see her. He was very tall, with dark hair and dark eyes that sparkled with the same mischief she saw every day in Evan's eyes. She was struck by the uncanny resemblance Evan bore to this stranger. It would be obvious to anyone that they were father and son.

Eversleigh strode across the room and bowed

to her. He dragged a chair next to her bed. Surprisingly, he took her hand in his.

"Tell me about my dearest Gwenith." There was no mistaking his wistful tone, nor the tenderness in his eyes as he spoke his former lover's name.

Madeleine found her own eyes welling with fresh tears. "She was the best friend I ever had. Gwenith rescued me at the lowest point in my life and brought me around to the happiest times I've known."

Eversleigh smiled. "That's my girl." He sighed. "She was the most alive, most vibrant person I've ever known."

"And very beautiful," Madeleine added.

"Yes." Eversleigh beamed. "With that impossibly red hair and wide smile. She quite stole my heart." He shook his head in amazement. "She stole my wife's, too. Even after Lady Eversleigh found out about Gwenith being with child—my child—my wife hadn't the heart to throw her out. Most wives would storm and rage. Mine made booties for the coming babe."

"Gwenith did have a way about her," she agreed with a smile. She felt the mirth fade from her lips and squeezed his hand. "You were very much in Gwenith's thoughts at the end, my lord. She told me she'd never stopped loving you." Madeleine's eyes misted over. "Those were her last words."

Eversleigh stood abruptly and cleared his throat. "Why did she leave?" he thundered. "I could have cared for her. She'd never have gotten sick, never left Evan motherless, never . . ." His voice broke and he sat in the chair again, his head in his hands.

Madeleine wished she had the answers the nobleman so desperately wanted.

Eversleigh remained that way for several minutes before raising his head. "Thank you for being her friend. For caring for my son. He's very fond of you. In fact, if you'd like, you may journey to Sussex when you are well and care of him there. Would you consider it?"

Madeleine longed to do that very thing. She'd become so attached to the little tyke in such a short time, she had no idea how she'd manage without seeing him on a daily basis. Yet Evan had his own life now with his father. She, on the other hand, had to return to France and embark on her new life there.

"I will keep that in mind, my lord," she told him. But she could see he knew she would never interfere.

Loud steps came from the corridor and Evan and Lyssa pushed her door wide, bounding in as only the young can.

"Maddie, did ye meet my papa? Isn't he wonderful?" Evan ran to one side of her bed and Lyssa joined him on the other.

"Yes, Evan, Lord Eversleigh is very nice. I think you'll have a wonderful time living in Sussex."

Evan glanced quickly at his father and then said, "Papa said ye could come with us. Will ye, Maddie?" He gazed at her lovingly, making her heart ache all the more.

Her voice was thick as she replied, "I'll consider it, Evan. But for now, I must remain behind and get well. You do understand that, don't you?"

Evan threw himself into her arms, wrapping his own around her neck. "I'll miss ye so, Maddie, just like I miss Mama." He squirmed away and studied her face a long time.

"What are you doing, Evan?" she finally asked.

"I'm remembering what ye look like, Maddie. I'm forgetting what Mama looked like already. I don't want to forget ye, too."

Madeleine's face puckered and she reached for him, holding him fast. "I do love you, Evan. I will always, always love you. You'll remember that, won't you?"

"Of course." He scrambled toward the door, followed by Lyssa, his ever-present shadow. "I've got to tell me horses goodbye now, Maddie." He frowned. "But I won't miss that Barth at all, with his creepy one eye. He's a mean one."

Madeleine smiled wistfully at the retreating figure, knowing she'd never see him again.

GARRETT STEPPED INTO the doorway. Madeleine's face was buried in her hands. He watched her shoulders jerk with spasms as if she were sobbing but the absence of noise was eerie. The room remained absolutely silent.

As he headed toward the bed, he heard her murmur, "You're my own little love, Evan, the only child I'll ever have. I will love you always."

"What do you mean by that?" he demanded.

She lifted a reddened, tearstained face to him. "What?" she asked, obviously startled to see him.

"You are a young woman, Madeleine, not more than three and twenty. Surely you'll have many children."

She shook her head vehemently. "No, no, I haven't been good enough to deserve children."

Puzzled by her strange comment, Garrett eased down on the bed next to her and took her hands in his. "You are one of the kindest souls I know, Madeleine."

She squared her shoulders. "No, my lord, you don't really know me at all. I've done things I could tell no one about, especially you. But God knows—and I will make it up to Him." She slipped her hands from his and brushed the tears from her cheeks.

He shrugged. "All you need to do is confess,

Madeleine, and then get on with your life." He thought of the scars she bore, sure that she'd been the one sinned against.

"No, my lord. I have thought of a way that will please God and solve all my problems."

He waited patiently for her to elaborate.

"I intend to enter a convent."

Garrett grabbed her by the shoulders and shook her, as if to knock some sense into her. "What? You can't. I won't let you."

"Don't you see you are one of the reasons I must do this?" she asked him, the pain evident in her voice.

"I won't let you go, Madeleine." He took a deep breath. "I love you."

CHAPTER NINETEEN

MADELEINE FROZE AT his words. No man had ever told her this. She was stunned at the depth of emotion that raced through her trembling body.

Garrett released his grip on her shoulders and loomed over her, inches away, his eyes intense, willing her to keep looking at him, only at him, and nothing else.

"I love you," he repeated softly, his large palms cradling her face as he brought his mouth down on hers.

She had thought their kiss atop the rock in the meadow was earth-shattering but it paled in comparison to this one. The first had started gently and built, while this one began possessively and became more so. She could feel the passion pouring from Garrett into her—and she responded to his call. His assault on her mouth was rough and tender at the same time, savage yet sweet. Emotions unfamiliar to her came in wave after wave, as an invading army would, never letting up. She couldn't think, couldn't breathe, couldn't imagine being anywhere, except in his arms.

How could something so wrong feel so right? Why had she been denied these feelings her entire life? Why had God so cruelly coupled her with an old man full of spite and hate when there were good men like Garrett to be found?

He finally released her and she instinctively moved back toward him. He chuckled, a low, soft laugh, one that held satisfaction even as his eyes glowed with triumph.

"You will not enter a convent, Madeleine." He cupped her face again in his strong hands, as if the need to touch her superseded all others. "Where do you think I've been these last two weeks?" he asked softly. "I went to see the bishop. He knows Lynnette deserted me years ago. I have petitioned for a divorce on grounds of abandonment."

His words shattered Madeleine to her core. *Divorce?* The notion was almost unheard of, and only then used by men who locked barren wives away in a convent and sought freedom from their vows in order to marry a fertile woman. Then understanding struck her with great force.

He did this for her. For them. Garrett wanted a

life with her. With her!

He rubbed his callused thumb across her smooth cheek. "It will take much time and more than a healthy donation to the bishop's coffers but then we'll marry, sweetheart. No convent for you. You were made to be loved . . . by me alone."

Garrett kissed her again, this time a sweet, tender kiss, sealing his pledge to her. "I've never truly loved another, Madeleine," he said, his voice raw with emotion. "Never."

Her tears fell at his words and before she could stop herself she replied, "I love you, Garrett, with all my heart."

"And never another man?" he asked, his tone serious.

She shook her head. "Nay, I've loved no other." She wiped at her tears. "But we cannot do this, Garrett, 'tis wrong of us. God would—"

"God wants His children to love one another and be happy, Madeleine. You are happy with me?" he asked, hesitation in his voice. "I have a reputation for coldness, though I've found that in your company I'm all heat and fire." His eyes blazed with desire for her.

Madeleine thrilled at his words and couldn't help but tease him a bit. "You are never cold with me, my lord." She cocked her head to one side. "Arrogant. Argumentative. Hardheaded perhaps, but never cold."

He laughed at her words. "You bring out the best in me." He studied her a moment. "I know you are devoted to God and that it makes you uncomfortable kissing a married man. I promise I won't kiss you again until I am freed by the Church."

Madeleine saw the determination in his eyes. He'd seemed so sad and yet so angry when she'd first met him. She realized how unhappy and lonely he'd been and felt grateful that she'd brought a little bit of sunshine into his life. As long as he promised not to touch her, what harm was there in giving him something to live for, something that renewed his energy and his outlook on life?

Besides, she truly loved this man, loved for the first time ever. The depth of her emotions surprised her. Love for Garrett swept in and filled her heart before she'd known what was happening. She couldn't imagine being parted from him and wished she could commit to him in body and soul for the rest of their lives.

Yet Henri lurked in the shadows. Where only minutes ago she'd struggled to move about this room, now her struggle must be to stop this. Now. Before it was too late.

Though this was the only happiness either of them had known in years, she must make Garrett see how impossible a love between them was. She could not let her selfish heart rule her head and give him hope for their love. Would she not do the same thing Lynnette had done by leaving him in the end? It was a cruel ploy.

She must beg God to give her the strength to withstand this temptation. Her love for Garrett was too strong. She must put a chance at momentary happiness with him aside, for what if she gave him hope of a future together and then disappeared? She could imagine only too well how he would withdraw from life. If she vanished after pretending they would have a life together, her rejection might break him for good.

She found voice for her brave words, though they rang hollow in her ears. "I am damaged goods, Garrett, a poor troubadour with a limp. I have a regretful past and no future, nothing to offer you. I cannot accept your love."

The heat in his eyes frightened her. Madeleine saw her words only challenged him. Garrett would be resolute in his quest for her. She prayed for strength and hoped God wouldn't let her down.

He moved toward her but she placed her hand upon his chest.

"You said no more kisses," she reminded him.

"No more—after this one," he said and lowered his head to hers one more time.

FOR THE NEXT two months while her leg slowly healed, Garrett held to his promise. He did not kiss Madeleine. He longed to every waking moment and dreamed of her at night, but he refused to break his pledge. Though she did accuse him on more than one occasion of looking at her like a hungry wolf before devouring a sheep.

"I said nothing about looks, Madeleine. I may gaze upon you any way I like. And you may look at me with a certain fondness tomorrow, for I have a surprise to share with you.

"I find I don't care much for surprises, my lord."

He smiled at her. "Oh, I think you'll be happy with this one."

The next morning, he entered her chamber, careful to mask any emotion, his cloak gathered about him.

She cocked her head to the side and pursed her lips. "I suppose you've come bearing some gift to take my mind from my worries, my lord. Mayhap you have a sweetmeat or one of Cook's tarts hidden within the folds of your garment? Go ahead, hand it over and be done with it."

He moved more closely to where she lay in her bed, propped up with pillows, and opened his cloak.

She drew a sharp breath in, her eyes widening in shock. "My lute!" she cried.

He handed her the instrument and watched the joy spread across her face. She clutched it closely to her breast, her whole body trembling as her eyes glistened with tears.

"What think you of surprises now?"

She took his hand and kissed it fervently. The heat from her lips scorched his skin. "Oh, my lord, my lord. You don't know how happy this has made me. This, my most treasured possession, restored to me at last!"

Then the smile died on her lips. He saw anger spark in her eyes as she pushed his hand aside. "You've had my lute all this time! Why did you not return it to me? I gave back your cloak, the very one you wear now. What wickedness possessed you to keep my lute from me? Oh, you are as black-hearted as Satan Himself!"

"If you'll remember, Madeleine, I stumbled upon you at a faire far from Stanbury, never expecting to lay eyes upon you again. Yes, you graciously returned my cloak to me that day but your beloved instrument was in my solar at Stanbury. I'd actually put it away for safekeeping, fearing Lyssa might discover it and cause some harm."

He sat beside her and took back her hand, entwining his fingers with hers. She tugged but he refused to give it up.

"I'm afraid to say I didn't give your lute a second thought, especially since you played one at each performance of the mummers. It was only when I stumbled across it that I knew I must return it to you."

He squeezed her hand. "Tell me you're pleased at having it once again."

She stroked the lute's smooth wood with her free hand. "Yes," she said, her voice barely a whisper. "I will forgive you." She hugged the instrument. "I shall never let it from my sight again."

He excused himself, overcome by witnessing her strong emotions. He felt a tightening in his chest, ready to burst as he exited the room.

Knowing that time spent in Madeleine's company would never be enough, Garrett decided he must press the bishop harder for his petition to be granted. For what increased in his heart every day he spent in Madeleine's company would not cease until he could freely hold the key to her heart without guilt.

EVERY DAY, MADELEINE worked with Lyssa on her art and music and had begun teaching her letters, as well. The child caught on quickly and the hours flew by.

They were working so intently that neither of them heard Annie until she appeared before them. "Time for a bath and a bite to eat."

Lyssa frowned but knew better than to protest. She followed Annie through the door, calling back to Madeleine, "I'll see you on the morrow."

Madeleine awaited the tray that was brought to her room every night. She often ate alone, savoring the quiet time, sometimes composing new songs in her head. She usually entertained in the great hall after the evening meal, so she enjoyed this time spent in solitude.

After finishing a light meal of cold chicken and bread, she heard a rap on the door.

"Come in," she called, knowing it was Coster. Each night he carried her down the steep stairs, which were much too difficult for her to navigate alone.

The big serf entered the room wearing his usual sheepish grin. "How are you tonight, Madeleine?"

Madeleine welcomed him. "I'm doing well, Coster. How is your daughter feeling?"

Coster gently scooped her up. "'Tis almost time, me wife says. Agnes can't catch her breath and waddles about like a duck. That's a sign, that it is, Madeleine. The babe'll be here before we know it."

He walked carefully along the shadowy

hallway, his touch as gentle as his ways. Cook teased her unmercifully, saying how Coster was smitten with her and Madeleine noticed he did blush when she looked him directly in the eyes.

The fragrant smell of warm bread mingled with the sweat of the men who'd worked a long day greeted them as they proceeded down the staircase to the great hall. Coster brought her across the room to the cushioned stool she sat upon every night as she worked her magic on the crowd.

Madeleine caught Garrett's eyes upon her, reading the jealousy in them as she rode in the huge arms of his servant. He had offered to bring her down himself each night but she had told him no, thinking it unseemly for the lord of the manor to wait on her in front of his people. She reminded him how, despite his simple ways, Coster had served the earl's family faithfully going on two score now.

While she'd tried her best to put distance between her and Garrett, it gave her a small thrill to see the longing in his eyes as Coster placed her on her feet and then helped seat her.

"I'm off to check on news of the babe," Coster whispered to Madeleine.

"God be with Agnes," she replied.

October had just arrived and Madeleine was grateful she was near the roaring fire. Her fingers were cold and she warmed them before reaching for her lute. She sang a few songs first, all written since her accident, and they were warmly received, the loud applause causing her cheeks to flame. She hoped those gathered would think it was her nearness to the fire that caused the rosy glow.

"I'd like to tell you tonight of the mighty Roland," she said as she lay her lute aside.

"'Tis another song, Madeleine?" called out Cook.

"No, though I do know a few songs about him. I'd rather tell you this story instead."

Those in the great hall gathered closer, anticipation on their faces.

"Once there was a famous king named Charlemagne, King of the Franks. He was a wise and just ruler who loved his people very much. That is why, while he was fighting the Saracens in Spain, he decided to leave, because he received word of some trouble at home.

"He asked his nephew, Roland, along with a small band of knights, to guard the rear of his army while he returned home. They were charged to hold the pass at Roncesvalle. In spite of his reputation for bravery, Roland and his men were quickly attacked by the Saracens. It was a mighty force, four hundred thousand strong."

Gasps echoed throughout the hall. "Four hundred thousand?" asked Cook.

Madeleine nodded and continued. "Roland

fought bravely at the front of his small group, swinging a sword named Durendal. The battle was long and hard but, in the end, the numbers against the Franks were too great."

"Poor lads," someone whispered.

Many nodded their heads in agreement.

"Roland was urged by his friend, Oliver, to sound the oliphant, a powerful horn Charlemagne had given his nephew. Only Roland could do so. It was said that the uproar would be so great that the ground would shake and chimneys would fall at its noise. Men would cry out, plunging fingers in their ears to keep the sound away. Yet Roland refused, saying that it should only be used in the most deadly of peril."

"What did he think four hundred thousand men were?" came a question from the rear.

"Let her finish," Cook begged and gestured at Madeleine to continue. "And then?"

"The fighting continued and Roland's group of knights fell, one by one, until he was the only remaining soul. He blew the oliphant, which Charlemagne heard. But by the time the king arrived, Roland lay at death's doorstep. Charlemagne held his nephew in his arms as he breathed his last breath."

The crowd remained spellbound for a moment but Madeleine did not continue. Finally, someone called out, "Did Charlemagne kill the Saracens and avenge Roland's death?"

Everyone leaned forward expectantly, waiting for her answer. Madeleine smiled mysteriously and said, "That is a different tale for another time."

There were good-natured grumblings and, slowly, people drew themselves to their feet, ready for bed after the night's entertainment. Madeleine watched them leave, remembering how Yves had often said, "You must always make them want more, *ma cheri*. Always give, but not too much, and they'll want to hear you again and again. *C'est bon, non?*"

Suddenly, Garrett appeared before her. "May I help you to your chamber?"

Coster had not yet returned from checking on his daughter. She hesitated. Walking was becoming easier for her. She practiced each day for longer periods in her room but stairs were still beyond her.

Garrett held a hand out to her. She took it tentatively. She liked the idea of being in his arms more than she should.

"Perhaps you can assist me as I try the stairs," she suggested. Her next words tumbled out in a nervous rush. "I removed the wrap from my leg yesterday. I probably need to stop babying it."

Garrett swept her up in his arms. "Quit your babbling, Madeleine. You can try the stairs on your own another time. This time"—he grinned crookedly at her—"I am here, and I wouldn't pass on this opportunity for the world."

He mounted the stairs easily, his masculine scent and very nearness overwhelming her senses.

"Truly, Garrett, I can walk," she croaked. "I must." Her voice cracked.

He frowned at her. "What's wrong?"

"Nothing. I simply forgot to drink during my tale. I'm parched. I'm fine."

He proceeded down the hall, passing her chamber. "You missed the door," she told him, her voice deep and raspy.

"You need wine. I have some in the solar. I'll give you a cup and then take you to bed."

MADELEINE EYED HIM speculatively, her brows arching. "Your solar?"

Garrett smiled enigmatically at her and then squeezed her playfully, a squeak spurting from her lips. As he walked down the stone corridor, he wanted to jest with her some more but found his own mouth now dry. The thought of bedding her caused him to stir. He was so aware of her nearness, each breath she took, each blink of her eyelids.

Now he finally had her in his arms after weeks without a single touch and he wanted nothing more than to make love to her.

He regretted his rash promise of two months before. He had been full of hope that the bishop would send his petition immediately to Rome but that had not been the case. Despite Garrett's insistence and liberal contributions, the cagey holy man had not acted swiftly, putting him off with one excuse after another. Garrett despaired of his suit reaching the Pope before the spring.

He wondered how much more he could take, seeing Madeleine every day, longing to touch her. Now she was gathered in his arms, here in his chamber, something he'd only dreamed of each night. He took a deep breath and eased her onto the bed. Wanting to hide his arousal, he quickly moved to the other side of the room and busied himself with pouring two cups of wine.

But then he lost all the willpower he'd gathered the minute he turned and saw her sitting straight and still on the bed. It reminded him how stiff she'd been against him that night they'd ridden Ebony together, the night they'd first met. She hadn't truly relaxed until she'd fallen asleep in his arms. The memory of her body pressed to his was enough to shatter any control he had left.

He slowly moved toward her, extending one of the cups. She drank a few sips nervously, her eyes never leaving his.

He drained the contents and set the cup onto a table. "Drink up, Madeleine," he urged.

She did as he requested, her amethyst eyes wide as they peeked over the rim. Finishing, she handed him the cup, which he put next to his.

"Thank you for the wine, my lord," she said haltingly. "That was very thoughtful of you."

He sat next to her on the bed. "Do you not know that my every thought is of you?" He lifted her braid and brought it to his lips.

She shivered. "My lord?"

He stroked her hair along his jaw and across his cheek, savoring its silky texture. He traced the braid across her lips, then rubbed it lightly across her face. As he did, his knuckles grazed her cheek and she sucked in a sharp breath. Her eyes met his as he began winding the braid around his hand, drawing her nearer to him.

She tentatively caressed his cheek and he groaned. He placed his free hand behind her neck and brought her lips to his.

The moment they touched, shock waves ripped through him and he moaned. She pushed her palms against his chest but he did not budge.

"Garrett, we—"

"No," he shushed her, kissing her again. "We can't go on as we have any longer. I must have you, Madeleine."

"It's wrong," she murmured into his mouth.

He edged away from her for a moment and gazed into her eyes. "Then morality be damned." Instead, he shifted her into his lap and continued the kiss, deepening it.

MADELEINE'S STOMACH FLIPPED as if she'd turned somersaults. Dizziness made her head spin as if she'd drunk too much champagne. As he kissed her, his hand left her neck and moved to her breast, slowly kneading it.

She gasped.

Garrett continued caressing her as his lips trailed along her jaw to her neck. He rained a shower of kisses there, causing her to tremble. He lifted her from his lap to place her across the bed. Even as he settled her, his mouth was on hers again, urgent in its demands. He stretched out next to her, throwing a leg over hers, trapping her.

He reached for the hem of her tunics and lifted them slightly, touching her calf, stroking her skin up and down, massaging the flesh. He moved to the back of her knee, touching it lightly. Her breathing now came in uneven spurts. Still kissing her, his fingers moved higher, grazing her thigh as he moved to hover over her.

He deepened the kiss, his tongue stroking hers, sucking on it gently, nipping it playfully. She reveled in sensations never experienced before. He continued brushing her thigh, then moved even higher, cupping her womanly parts, rubbing against the seam of her sex gently. Slowly, he pushed a finger inside her.

Madeleine tensed, not understanding what he was doing, even as she began to quiver with need. He slid his finger out gradually and then pushed it back in quickly. She gasped, gripping his shoulders tightly. He continued the movement and she rose to meet his hand each time, whimpering quietly. He stroked her more deeply and more quickly until she cried out, her body shuddering violently as waves of pleasure exploded through her, leaving her limp and spent, wondering what had just occurred.

Garrett eased off her and she watched him quickly doff his clothes. As the candlelight flickered and shadows danced across his muscular frame, she sucked in her breath and gripped the bedcovers. He was perfect in every way—and gazing at her with passion and love as he returned to the bed and wrapped her in his arms. His kiss was gentle now, slow and sensual, and as his tongue mated with hers, he entered her. He began an easy rhythm which she responded to readily. No thought was required. She simply moved until they were one.

Then she shattered again, her cry of joy muffled as his mouth hungrily claimed hers again and again. She felt the tremors running through them both.

Madeleine finally knew love. And knew it well.

He rolled over, bringing her with him and cradled her next to him. He kissed her brow, her eyelids, her cheeks, and her mouth, over and over. She never wanted this moment to end.

"I love you, sweetheart," he told her again and again, nuzzling her neck, caressing her gently. She sighed her pleasure softly in his ear.

Finally played out, he gathered her in his arms. She rested her head on his shoulder. After a while his ragged breathing evened out and Madeleine realized he'd fallen asleep. *How could he*, she wondered, *after such a glorious experience?* Was this what happened between a man and a woman when they loved each other? It was the most marvelous, most divine thing she'd ever known. Their lovemaking bore no resemblance to what Henri did to her. That had been vile and degrading. She thought she'd never want physical love from a man again.

How wrong Garrett had proven her.

Madeleine nestled closer to him, secure in his strong arms. She had no guilt, no shame in what had happened between them. She could die happily now having experienced all his love.

Within a few days, though, she would be up to full strength and must make her way to France. She took heart, recognizing that even once she was far from him, this one night with

Garrett would sustain her for the rest of her life. Knowing complete happiness for the first time ever, Madeleine fell into a deep sleep, no dreams of Henri troubling her.

CHAPTER TWENTY

MADELEINE AWAKENED TO nibbles on her earlobe. She opened her eyes slowly to soft candlelight.

Garrett leaned over her, a trace of a smile on his face. "It's very late," he whispered as he bent to kiss her. "Mmmm, you taste good."

Her heart quickened as he touched her breast, his palm running lazy circles around her nipple. He made love to her once again, more gently than before, yet still filled with passion and longing.

As they lay entwined in each other's arms, Madeleine savored the intimacy created between them this night.

"We won't be able to walk through the great hall," he told her. "One look at the two of us and all will know what has passed between us."

Madeleine snuggled closer to him. "I don't

look any different, my lord."

"No, sweetheart," he said, "you are wrong. Even without the candlelight, I know there is a glow about you that wasn't present before." His fingers idly stroked her arm. "I'm sorry I broke my promise to you."

"Sshh," she quieted him, placing her fingers to his lips. "I could have stopped you."

He combed his fingers through her hair. "No, I fear nothing could have stopped me tonight. One look at you and all was lost. Damnation!" His tone was fierce. "I *will* force the bishop to make good on my petition. I must. I cannot imagine spending a lifetime in limbo without you, my love."

She bit her lip, holding back her tears, and once more swallowed her guilt. She, too, wondered how she could spend the rest of her days on this earth without Garrett's touch. She felt certain she'd burn throughout eternity for her actions this night but the transgression had been worthwhile. Nothing would ever compare to these hours she'd spent in his arms.

"So, my lord," she asked with a trembling voice, "since we have become intimate, mayhap I should know more about you."

"What do you wish to know, my sweet?"

She lay a hand on his chest. "Everything."

He sighed. "I was raised here at Stanbury by Edith and Ryker, a man so wicked he should have sired devils with tails and horns."

She gasped. "You shouldn't speak of your father so, Garrett."

"Why not? He never loved me or my mother." He grew quiet for a moment. "He did love my brother, Luke, but he died before reaching manhood."

She squeezed his hand, wanted to comfort him for the sorrow she heard in his voice.

"Luke died of the fever. I prayed for God to take me instead, but He had other ideas." He paused. "Luke was good at everything. He could fell a deer better and faster than anyone at Stanbury. He would have been a terrific soldier had he lived to maturity, so natural was he at swordplay and in the saddle. I worshipped him, followed him around like a pup, drove him nearly insane."

Garrett seemed miles away so Madeleine left him to his memories. Finally, he spoke again. "Ryker was eventually poisoned by one of his women. He always had several mistresses. Never tried to hide anything from my mother. Marva was afraid Ryker was ready to replace her and so the bitch poisoned him. Told him in front of all present in the great hall just after he'd taken a few bites. He lived long enough to run his sword through her before he collapsed and died. All as my mother and I watched."

Madeleine shivered.

"Sorry, my love. I should speak of more pleasant things."

They lay in the dark as he told her of his estate, his house in London, and of the horses he bred that many nobles bought from him. Then he began to speak of wine. "My family owns estates in Bordeaux, which is in the south of France. The weather is pleasant and we grow grapes that produce Merlots and Sauvignons. I'd never taken much interest in them before, although Ryker made sure I learned about wine and spoke rudimentary French."

A sudden chill froze Madeleine's heart. Somehow, she knew what he was going to say. Her father had only rarely mentioned the absentee English landowner of the vineyards their family tended and always referred to it as Stanbridge land. Madeleine guessed that Garrett's family surname was Stanbridge—and that he was her father's employer.

"I traveled to Chateau Branais, near the Garonne River, only last year for the first time. I spent time there with the man and his son who manage the estate for me. They've done so for years and they do an excellent job. Why," and she could hear amazement in his voice as he put it together, "their name was Bouchard, just as yours is."

"Papa told me that it's a common name in France," she replied quickly. "Much as Baker is in

England."

He seemed excited. She could feel it in the sleek muscles that rested next to her. "But the wife, I can't remember her name, she bore a resemblance to you," he exclaimed. "Madeleine, I might have stumbled across some of your distant relatives!"

She was thankful that it was the dead of night and the light of the candle had long flickered out. If he could have seen her face, he would see her unraveling as he spoke.

Madeleine tried to keep her voice calm. "That could certainly be a possibility." Thoughts of home coupled with her nagging fear of Henri discovering her here at Stanbury brought a deep uneasiness to the pit of her stomach.

"We will visit these Bouchards when we marry, sweetheart. I would love to show you France. It's a beautiful place."

But not as beautiful as England, her heart cried out. "Mayhap," she said, pretending to stifle a yawn.

"Oh, my love, I've droned on and bored you."

"No, I'm not bored, just a bit tired."

He kissed her brow. "I must take you to your own bed. Here, let me help you dress."

Garrett replaced her tunics, chatting lightly as he did, and then dressing himself. "I'm to have a visitor from France at the end of this week, coincidentally."

The overwhelming sense of dread crashed full force upon her. Tamping down her alarm, she inquired, "Someone comes to conduct business with you?"

"Yes. An odd, rather cranky fellow named Henri de Picassaret. He wants to negotiate a land deal. De Picassaret would award me a portion of his champagne vineyards in northern France, close to Reims."

A low roar sounded in her ears and the pit of her stomach turned to ice. Her hands began shaking so she started fussing with the folds of her tunic to hide her distress.

"What does this Frenchman want in return?" she forced out, relieved that she sounded so natural.

"That my ships would carry his own wines to certain ports I frequent, in particular the Hanseatic ports and the Low Countries." Garrett snorted. "We had quite a falling out in London, April last. To be honest, I thought the old man had gone half-mad. But Ash saw him at Lord Ancil's this week and brought a letter to me from de Picassaret. The writing was fluid and intelligent and the arrangement he proposes is far sweeter than what he offered before." Garrett shrugged. "I suppose whatever troubled him then has now been resolved. I am at least willing to meet with him again and see if this is a business venture that I wish to pursue."

Garrett continued speaking but Madeleine heard no more. Panic welled inside her like a pot boiling over. Henri, here, this very week.

If he found her here, he'd kill her. He'd kill Garrett—and anyone who'd had knowledge of her.

She must escape.

Madeleine composed herself. She could give nothing away. She must protect Garrett at all costs. Involuntarily, she shivered.

"Are you chilled, love?" He wrapped his arms around her, rubbing her back. "Let us get you to your bed."

He lifted her into his arms and carried her down the hall to her chamber, placing her in the bed and pulling the bedclothes over her.

"Sleep well, my love," he said, his voice a soft caress before he padded quietly out the door.

But Madeleine knew sleep would elude her the rest of this night.

WHAT HAD GARRETT done with her jewels?

He was the last one with her clothes and she was positive he'd found the precious stones and hidden them away. The day after her fall, she'd spotted her freshly washed tunics neatly placed across a chair—no jewels concealed in them any longer. Instinct told her that Garrett must be behind them vanishing without a trace but he'd made no mention of them. Since she had been in no physical position at that time to bargain or demand anything, her decision to remain quiet about the gems' disappearance had seemed wise. Now, so much time had gone by she didn't know how to approach him, especially with all the tenderness he'd shown her. She also didn't want him forewarned in any way of her planned attempt to flee Stanbury.

Thank the Sweet Lord that Elspeth left Madeleine's bundle of things when the troupe had moved on weeks ago. Annie had brought it to her and Madeleine checked it immediately when she was alone. Several valuable pieces were still in those garments. With those—and the brooch Lady Sanvale had gifted her with—she could get to a port and sail for France and Chateau Branais.

Madeleine pondered where to travel. She was afraid to go the way of Sussex, in part because she might feel the need to stop and see Evan. Garrett would think of that and follow her, preventing her from leaving England by that route.

She'd go to London. The stories trickling out from there spoke of a raging typhus that consumed the city. Garrett's reeve, Stephen, who went to London on business for him sometimes, had returned the last time with horrible tales.

He'd regaled the great hall one night with talk of the many bodies he'd seen stacked in the streets awaiting burial. The reeve's lurid descriptions sickened Madeleine. She'd asked Coster to take her to her room instead of listening to all the gruesome details.

What better place for her to run? Garrett would never think she'd be foolish enough to go to a city facing such an outbreak. Hopefully, she'd be able to get a ship bound for France as quickly as possible now that she was more familiar with the waterfront area and there was no Bertrand to prevent her from doing so.

If she succumbed to this disease, so much the better. Death seemed a welcomed blessing compared to Henri finding her. That would be a living hell on earth, one she didn't think she could survive again, not since she'd known Garrett's love and compassion.

Madeleine busied herself the next few days with the necessary preparations to make her way from Stanbury to London. It was hard to keep a serene appearance but she'd become skilled in her playacting and could hide her true mood. She thanked the Virgin daily for the business that kept Garrett away from Stanbury for several days, unsure she could have hidden her anxiety from him.

While keeping up her lessons with Lyssa and spending time with Edith, Madeleine found a purse in which to place the coins she'd collected from the guests who'd rewarded her for her storytelling. The one thing she regretted was that she'd need to take one of Garrett's horses. Walking to London was well beyond her endurance. Her injuries had healed remarkably, though, thanks to the immediate attention they'd received but it would be impossible to make it the many miles to London by foot. She decided to leave one of her pieces of jewelry in exchange for the horse she must take. Perhaps the brooch from Lady Sanvale would do. Garrett had told her he was fond of the dowager countess.

Her biggest problem was how to get the animal outside the walls without drawing attention. To that end, she went exploring and after a diligent hunt, located Stanbury's sally port. As before, the door was practically hidden by vegetation. She would use the sally port for her escape.

Madeleine decided to engage Coster's help with this part of her plan. Though married and true to his wife, the man was batty over her and a bit simple. Though she'd never traded on her looks, this time, an exception must be made.

Later that day, she waylaid Coster in the outer bailey. "How are you today, my fine gallant?"

He broke out in a huge grin at her friendly greeting. "I'm having a fine day, Madeleine."

She cast her eyes down and shuffled glumly. "I wish I could say the same."

"Something's wrong, Madeleine?"

She raised her head, her eyes filled with tears. "Oh, Coster, I'm so upset. It's my mother. Oh, but you wouldn't understand." She turned to walk away, knowing he'd scurry after her, which he did.

"What's wrong with your mum?"

"I'm very worried about her. She's all alone, down Sussex way. She must be terribly anxious that I haven't returned home by now." Madeleine paused, trying to gauge his reaction. He did appear concerned, so she continued. "I would be home already if I'd stayed with Farley's troupe since they always disband for the winter. She must be frantic, what with her only child missing."

Coster scratched his head. "How can I help you? Say the word and I'll make it happen, Madeleine." The servant stretched to his full height, his chest ready to burst with pride in coming to her aid.

"I would like to borrow one of Lord Montayne's mounts and ride to see her." She batted her lashes for good measure and placed a hand on his arm. "Do you think you could help me?"

Worry filled his eyes. "Have you asked the earl's permission?"

"No," she said quietly.

Coster shook his head. "It's not a good idea. There's danger on the road—robbers and thieves and mongrels—just waiting to eat up a pretty morsel like you."

"Oh, Coster," she cried, "I must go! I love my mother more than anyone in this world. I need to see her." Madeleine let her tears flow freely.

He patted her on the back. "There, now, Coster will help you. Tell me what needs to be done and 'twill get done."

Madeleine had learned that Henri would arrive midmorning the next day, shortly after Garrett himself would return. If she could leave after the castle bedded down tonight, more than likely she would not be missed until she was asked to entertain tomorrow night. That would be more than enough of a head start.

She told him where to tie the horse and placed in his palm the brooch that Lady Sanvale had given to her. "I am trusting you to hold this for me, Coster, for safekeeping. Only if it becomes absolutely necessary are you to tell Lord Montayne I borrowed his horse and you're not to tell him where I've gone, for I don't wish to worry him."

Patting his arm, she said, "Of course, I plan to return to Stanbury and bring his horse back safely, but in the event something should go wrong, you may give him the brooch as payment."

Madeleine could tell even the unworldly Coster was none too sure of this plan but she believed he would carry it through for her.

"Be thinking of what tale you'd like to hear when I return. I will tell it especially in your honor."

He seemed to like this idea a good deal. "Do you suppose it could be a song instead?"

Madeleine laughed. "Whatever you ask for, Coster. If it's a song you want, I'll be thinking it up on the road between here and Sussex."

Coster smiled broadly. "Make it a song then, Madeleine. A very good one."

HENRI DE PICASSARET arrived shortly before the midday meal. Garrett had arrived from the south only minutes before. He'd wanted to see Madeleine briefly but de Picassaret was not a man to be kept waiting. He hurried outside to greet the French nobleman and did his best to hide his shock as de Picassaret dismounted. The comte faced him and Garrett took in how the man had declined since their last meeting. The Frenchman had lost a good bit a weight. His eyes sank so far into his skull that he looked like a walking corpse.

Knowing his duty as a host, however, Garrett greeted him warmly. "Comte de Picassaret, I welcome you to Stanbury."

Henri nodded his head curtly in return. "We have much to discuss, Lord Montayne."

Garrett agreed. "First, though, let us dine. We'll have the entire afternoon in which to conduct our business. Cook has planned an elegant meal for tonight in your honor and I'll provide special entertainment for you afterward."

"I appreciate your efforts on my behalf, my lord," Henri said as he followed Garrett into the keep.

The two men were closeted the rest of the day discussing wines. Henri's manner was almost fawning as he tried to convince Garrett to return with him when he left for France.

"It's in your best interest, Lord Montayne, to travel with me and inspect the vineyards that will soon be in your possession. It is a beautiful time of year in my country," he explained. "Of course, when is France not beautiful?"

"I must agree with you," Garrett said. "I visited there only last year for the first time. Our family vineyards are in Bordeaux. Although I have traded in wines for many years, I had never seen the properties we owned in the south."

"How unusual. Exactly where are the Montayne vineyards? I have visited the region on occasion."

"They are located close to the Garonne, surrounding a property called Chateau Branais."

Henri blanched considerably. "What did you say?"

"The vineyard is at a place called Chateau Branais. Why, are you familiar with it? A family named Bouchard manages the estates. The son, Pierre, is most knowledgeable about the grape."

Henri took a sip of the wine before him. He recovered some of his color. "Yes, I have been in the area before. I may have called upon these Bouchards."

Garrett smiled. "They are lovely people. The father and son worked well together and the wife was quite charming. I'm fortunate to have such good hands supervising my lands."

"I seem to recall they had a daughter when I visited them some years ago."

Garrett looked at him blankly. "A daughter? Odd. They never made mention of her. Possibly she died? That might explain why nothing was said. If she'd married, surely her name would have come up in conversation for I was with them some weeks."

Henri nodded slowly. "Perhaps I was mistaken. I'm sure you are right, my lord."

Garrett stood. "My legs are tired from all this sitting. Would you like to see a bit of my property, Comte? Then we can adjourn to dine in the great hall. You'll not be disappointed with Cook's choices."

Henri gave him a thin smile. "That would be

most delightful, my lord."

It took them close to an hour to conclude their brief tour. Garrett took pride in the farmland surrounding Stanbury and his stock of horses. De Picassaret was complimentary throughout their time together.

Eventually, they made their way to the evening meal. A jester capered as they ate, the bells from his cap tinkling merrily as he wove his way through the crowd. He was followed by a juggler and a man with a pet monkey.

Garrett was pleased with his guest's response to the planned amusements. He looked about for Madeleine, sure she would have made an appearance by now. She had told him before he left that she would prepare a special song for his guest. She must've simply lost track of the time.

He motioned Coster over. "Please fetch Madeleine, Coster. I would like our guest to hear her sing and play," he said quietly.

Coster nodded and shuffled off, an odd expression upon his face. Garrett had no time to think on this, though, returning his attention to de Picassaret.

Almost a quarter-hour passed before Coster returned. Madeleine was not with him. Garrett frowned as the giant-sized serf ambled over to his table.

"Coster, why have you not brought Madeleine back with you?" he demanded.

"Madeleine?" Henri interrupted. "What did you say?"

Garrett turned to address Henri. "It's my troubadour, Comte. A woman, actually. I discovered her with a group of mummers and persuaded her to stay on for a while. She has tutored my daughter in art and music and performs for us here at Stanbury most every night." He smiled. "She's quite talented. A beautiful voice and lovely to look at. She also knows thousands of stories. I'm sure you'll enjoy hearing her play. We just seem to have a bit of a problem locating her."

He turned back to Coster, who was fidgeting from one foot to the other. Before Garrett could say a word, Coster removed something shiny from his pocket and handed it to Garrett.

"I'm sorry, me lord. It's all me fault."

Garrett recognized the brooch in his palm as one that Lady Sanvale wore frequently. He looked at Coster in confusion. "Come again, Coster. You're not making yourself clear. Why would you give me Lady Sanvale's brooch?"

"You're to keep it for now. Madeleine said so."

"Why would Madeleine give me a brooch? Where the devil did this come from?" Garrett frowned at his servant. "Coster, you have much to explain. Start at the beginning."

"I know I did wrong." Coster sighed. "Punish

me, me lord, for I deserve it. I never should have helped her."

His words had an immediate impact upon Garrett. The hall grew quiet as everyone gathered there waiting for Madeleine watched intently.

Garrett's tone was even and controlled. "What did you help Madeleine do, Coster?"

Coster fumbled for the words before they rushed out in a torrent. He explained how Madeleine was worried about her mum and how he'd helped her borrow a horse to reach home for a short visit.

"She promised to return the horse, me lord. The brooch was only if something unforeseen happened to her. You were to have it."

"Where did she go, Coster?"

"Why, down Sussex way, me lord. That's where her mum is."

A cacophony of whispers filled the room. "She's got a mother, he said?"

"I bet her mum is as pretty as she is."

"Why'd she go now, ye think?"

Garrett felt as if he'd been torn in two. As soon as he had declared his love for her, Madeleine had disappeared without a word to him.

Just as Lynnette had.

Why would she do such a thing?

She'd admitted doing things she would reveal

to no man. Was she a thief, as he'd once suspected? He squeezed the brooch in his fist, knowing it belonged to Lady Sanvale. Had Madeleine helped herself to such a pretty piece?

That could not be the case. The dowager countess had a kind heart and had greatly admired Madeleine. It would not surprise him if the old woman had gifted Madeleine with the brooch.

Then why had Madeleine gone? He swallowed hard, thinking of her scarred legs and back. Did her sudden disappearance have something to do with those old injuries?

His love for Madeleine was strong enough to outweigh anything he'd learned about her. To learn the truth about her was taking a chance. But as he lived and breathed, Garrett knew it was a chance he must take.

He forced as pleasant as an expression as he could muster onto his face as he turned to de Picassaret. "I'm afraid I have some unexpected business to attend to. I trust my servants to meet your needs for the short time that I must be gone."

De Picassaret's face turned a deep red. "Lord Montayne, we have business to conduct."

Garrett waved a hand. "I'm aware of that." He paused, aware of the countless eyes upon him. "Have your man draw up the necessary papers. I'll sign them immediately upon my return, then send them posthaste to your estate. We'll be in business together by the next harvest."

When de Picassaret didn't say anything, he added, "Does that suit you, sir?

"Of course." He hesitated. "This woman, Madeleine, must be important for someone like you to drop everything in such a manner."

"No one you need concern yourself about." He turned to Coster. "I will deal with you upon my return," he told the gentle giant. "For now, saddle my horse. I ride to London."

CHAPTER TWENTY-ONE

GARRETT CURSED, LOUD and long, the entire ride to London, disregarding those he passed. He knew they thought him mad but he didn't care. Madeleine had driven him to the point of insanity.

Why had she left?

Had her guilt over the consummation of their love driven her from his arms and into God's? She had told him she planned to enter a convent. Was there one within the walls of London in which she could hide from him? And what of her family? Did Peter and her parents really exist or were they more of her fanciful tales? How could he have fallen in love with someone who lied as easily as birds flew or ducks swam? Why could he not let her go and simply get on with his life?

Because he had no life before they'd met. A

pleasant existence had been destroyed by his runaway wife. That part of his life was still unresolved. Now he chased after yet another woman who had deserted him.

As surely as the sun would rise, Madeleine was his ray of hope. Garrett ached inside with the knowledge that he had no future if she did not share it with him. He needed Madeleine as much as he needed the air he breathed. He craved her, all of her—her humor and intelligence, her warmth and kindness, her willowy body and its hidden curves of pleasure. He would seek her out to the ends of the earth, kiss her into submission, and then drag her home to Stanbury.

He pictured the scars on her legs and back and wondered if her flight had some connection with the abuse she had suffered. He'd not said a word to her about them after they'd made love. He doubted she had any idea he knew just how terribly she'd been scarred. No, when he found her he'd smother her with love before he demanded answers. The truth, this time.

London's massive gates were sealed when he reached them. He rode up, a solitary figure in the still morn. He cursed his luck, knowing he would be denied entrance until sunrise. He dismounted Ebony and paced back and forth, his breath visible in the damp night air.

He'd taken a huge risk by coming to London but his gut told him Madeleine mislead Coster as to her final destination, knowing the serf would eventually pass along the information to Garrett. It was a flimsy excuse. He doubted Madeleine even had a mother, much less one as close as Sussex.

He looked to the great city rising before him and his heart told him the woman he loved was somewhere within those walls. He would find her, his French beauty. As he'd ridden, it became clear to him. Her gestures were typical of the French. Even her very name was French. She could even be related to the same Bouchards at Chateau Branais. He would begin at the waterfront and see which ships were headed to France.

As he waited, he continued to pace, searching his memory for any clues within his grasp. All had seemed well until the arrival of Henri de Picassaret.

Garrett halted in his tracks. *Was that the connection?* De Picassaret was French. Did the nobleman know Madeleine? Or her abuser? Garrett tried to recall if Madeleine had reacted oddly in any way once he'd told her de Picassaret was to visit Stanbury. He had been so enamored with her and the time they'd spent in his bed that he remembered little else.

She had fled when the Frenchman arrived, making Garrett believe there was some connection. If only he'd thought to quiz de Picassaret more thoroughly before he stormed away from Stanbury. The vineyard owner must think him mad.

He remembered the nobleman had indicated he would make his way to London upon leaving Stanbury, as he was ready to return to his home. It could be worth his while to locate the comte. The Frenchman might shed some light on the mystery called Madeleine Bouchard.

The sun broke across the horizon, slowly casting its rays against the gates. A nightingale called for its mate, the sound mocking him. The tired watchman peered down upon him.

"Must warn you, my lord, about the typhus. It raged out of control for a while, though it's been much better these last few weeks. I'm supposed to let all travelers know this before they enter."

The thought of falling to typhus gave Garret a chill but his choice was made. "Hell and be damned, man! Open up!"

The clang of the gate behind him sent a shiver up his spine but it also renewed his commitment. The city was quiet in the bleak dawn with little activity. As Garrett headed for the waterfront, he spotted a few bodies wrapped in sheets, left outside for the early morning death wagon. The greenish stains on the linen reminded him of his vigil at Luke's bedside as he lay dying of the dreaded disease. Besides the fever and vomiting, Luke had been racked with abdominal pains and reddish spots that appeared all over his torso. He had been confused, too, which hurt Garrett most of all, watching his beloved brother slip away, not knowing anyone around him.

Many vessels of all shapes and sizes filled the harbor. Trade was at a standstill. It looked as if few ships, if any, had been let out during the epidemic. If that were the case, it might be easier to find Madeleine than he originally thought.

He first sought out the harbormaster, eventually finding him asleep in a nearby tavern. The place was littered with drunken sailors, sleeping off their night of carousing. He shook the man awake and pulled him out into the empty streets, as much for a private word as to escape the stench of stale, unwashed bodies.

The man recognized him through bloodshot eyes. "Why, Lord Montayne," he slurred. "What brings you to London? 'Tis not our usual time to do business."

"I know, Raleigh, but I have need of information." Garrett produced a gold coin, which Raleigh quickly pocketed. The man wiped his chin on a sleeve.

"How bad is this typhus?"

Raleigh rubbed the sleep from his eyes and pushed back the strands of hair falling in his eyes. "Just about run its course, my lord. The death count has fallen off considerably with the cooler weather. I've been told we'll open up for trade in a week's time. His majesty's counselor was certain of it."

His speech was interrupted by a loud grumbling. Raleigh looked sheepishly at Garrett. "Sorry. My belly rules me, I fear."

"I require your help, Raleigh."

The harbormaster squinted. "What do you need, my lord?"

Garrett quickly explained. "More than likely she'll wish to sail for France. Can you find her?"

Raleigh nodded wearily. "All of the manifests will come my way."

"Not good enough, Raleigh. She would think to travel under a different name."

"If you're willing to spend the gold, I can arrange for the port to be watched carefully. Give me the name and a description of this woman, and I assure you she will be found."

Garrett paused before he spoke as his loss of Madeleine washed over him anew. "She's very tall. Thin as a reed. Her hair is the color of wheat in the summer that's ready to be threshed. Her eyes are a deep amethyst and she has a small scar running across—"

"I know her. It's the same woman as before."

Garrett's insides raced. "What do mean you?"

"Back in the spring, a Frenchman came to me. He described the exact woman you now do.

He was also very anxious to find her."

"Who was this man?" Garrett demanded, ready to slam this man's face into the nearest post. "I'll have his name."

Raleigh shook his head. "Don't recall it. He was a servant but he had plenty of coin to spread around. She had booked passage on a cargo ship bound for Calais but she never showed up to sail."

So he was right. Madeleine was French. He was certain she'd been running from her abuser the night they'd met.

"Was her name Madeleine Bouchard?"

Raleigh grinned, his yellowed teeth prominently displayed. "That was it, my lord."

Garrett completed his arrangements with Raleigh and left for his London home. It would be dark since his servants weren't expecting him but he was weary from his long ride. With no ships sailing for at least a week, he knew Madeleine was stuck in London. Garrett wanted nothing more than his bed for now. The sleep would rejuvenate him as he matched wits with his beloved Madeleine. When rested, he would begin his search for her in earnest.

Although Garrett thought he'd confiscated all of Madeleine's jewels when he removed them from her tunics, she must have had more hidden, counting on selling them to aid her escape. He'd visit as many jewelers as he could. Surely, she would turn up that way.

IT TOOK TWO days before Garrett found a man who remembered her. He was a wizened bag of bones but his eyes sparkled as he spoke of her.

"Oh, yes, my lord, she was a vision of loveliness. I really didn't want what she was trying to pawn, but the poor woman seemed desperate for money. I gave her the best price I could." He sighed. "Would you like to see the piece?"

Garrett had no desire to but his need of further information from the shriveled little man drove him to respond. "Yes. Show it to me."

The jeweler reached under his counter and lifted a necklace, placing it on black velvet for better display.

Garrett glanced at it perfunctorily and then whipped his eyes back, startled that the necklace was indeed very familiar to him.

It had belonged to Lynnette.

How had it come into Madeleine's possession?

He felt a queasiness in his stomach as a moment of doubt flooded him. Did Madeleine know what happened to Lynnette? Was this the unspeakable act she referred to? Was the woman who filled his every waking moment in league with someone who knew where Lynnette was?

He turned to the shriveled jeweler. "You said the woman I described sold this to you?"

"Oh, yes, my lord. 'Tis a nice piece, don't you think?"

"Yes," Garrett agreed. "Very nice. How much?"

IT WAS EARLY afternoon when Garrett climbed the stairs of the dark, dank building. A child wailed loudly in the distance. The smell of urine and stale vomit overwhelmed him. A tattered woman and her young son passed him on the stairs, their eyes downcast, their faces covered with filth. Garrett shuddered at the place Madeleine had chosen to hide, guessing her funds must have dwindled considerably if this was the best she could afford.

It had been easy to find her. She'd given the jeweler a good idea where she could be found in case he had further interest in her stones.

Garrett heard her voice as he neared the top of the rickety stairs.

"*Zut, zut!* When will this end?"

Yes, that was his darling, cursing in French. Quietly, Garrett opened the door.

The alcove was small, with barely enough room for a narrow bed and chair. Stale air hung like a curtain, blanketing the entire space. A fat rat scurried by his foot, as if glad to make its escape from the enclosed place. The only window was cracked down the middle and he felt the sharp wind pouring into the nook, chilling him.

Madeleine was on her knees next to the lumpy bed, her fingers laced together, her head bowed. She was giving God a dressing down, with a few apologies thrown in for good measure. A single shaft of sunlight fell upon her, radiating a halo around her head. His desperate, runaway angel.

"Oh, Sweet Christ, I cannot say any more *Hail Mary's*! I'm so tired and lonely and frustrated. I want only to serve You—but I cannot stop thinking of Garrett."

She sighed, biting her lower lip. "I know I must never see him again, my Dear Lord, for I know marriage vows are sacred. I am so very sorry, indeed. I just want to go home now and see *ma mere et mon pere*. I miss them so much. I promise to go to the convent if You'll only grant me a few days of peace with them."

She crossed herself once and then again. "In Your Name, oh Holy Christ, I offer these prayers. Amen."

Without opening her eyes, she flung herself against the tattered quilt. Once again, her sobs were silent. Somehow, Garrett felt these noiseless tears were a key connected to her past.

He stepped inside and closed the door quietly behind him.

She banged her fists against the bed several times and then croaked out, "Oh, Garrett, I miss you so."

"Then why did you run away?" he asked softly.

Her head snapped up, her face tearstained, her eyes swollen from crying. She began to violently tremble. "No," she whispered, shaking her head back and forth. "It can't be." She rose unsteadily to her feet. "I . . . I don't want to see you," she said stubbornly, her chin rising a notch.

Her words crushed him but he stood straight as a Montayne would. For a long moment, he gazed at her steadily without speaking.

She ran her tongue over her bottom lip nervously. "You must leave, Garrett," she demanded.

He could see her pulse fluttering wildly against her slender, white throat. He took a step toward her and she shrank back. "You take my declaration of love for you and throw it back in my face? Without a word, you forsake both me and Lyssa. Did you think she and I would simply pick up our lives where we left off?"

Tears welled in her eyes. She blinked, spilling them down her cheeks.

"I thought my heart could not be broken twice in this lifetime but you proved me wrong. You broke it again, Madeleine. I cannot imagine what your thoughtlessness will do to my child." He ran his fingers through his hair, his frustration with her growing. In agony, he told her, "You abandoned us. *Just like Lynnette.*"

HIS WORDS WERE stronger than any blow Henri had ever dealt her, for Henri had only hurt her physically. Garrett's words pierced her soul.

She felt the waves of anger that emanated from him. His words were meant to hurt her— and they had. He compared her actions to Lynnette's. She couldn't let him think he was unloved. What Lynnette had done had almost destroyed his soul. In the end, Madeleine would still have to leave him, but she must let him know she loved him and trusted in him.

She prayed God would give her the strength and courage to do what she must do.

She stared at him, his eyes blazing, his mouth set so firmly, and her face crumpled. Oh, God, she loved him so much.

She ran to him and threw her arms around his neck, burying her face in his massive chest. Madeleine clutched him desperately. Finally, he placed his arms around her and held her to him. Tremors rippled through her body as she clung to him. He bent and placed a soft kiss on the top of her head.

"Oh, Madeleine." Garrett sighed and drew her even closer. He brushed his lips against her hair over and over. She closed her eyes and wished they could remain this way forever.

He lifted her chin with a finger and met her gaze. "We must talk."

She nodded and swallowed hard. He led her to the single bed and sat, pulling her down next to him.

He took her hand in his. "Where did you find the necklace you pawned?"

Shocked at the question she'd least expected, she asked, "Necklace?"

He reached into his purse and dangled it before her.

"So that's how you found me," she muttered. Her eyes opened wide as she realized the meaning of his words. "You still believe me a thief!"

She jerked her hand from his, her pride wounded by his words. "That's what you mean by my 'finding' it. You mean where did I *steal* it, my lord? Well, I didn't!" Her chin went up and she glared at him.

"I'm not saying you stole it."

"It was a gift to me," she answered reluctantly, knowing God had finally given her the way to tell her sordid tale.

"From whom?" His eyes darkened.

She could see doubt mingled with love in his eyes. Did he think she was some merchant's bought woman? A married man's mistress?

Madeleine shook her head adamantly. Mayhap it wasn't wise to tell Garrett about Henri in his present mood, not without knowing where his thoughts were headed.

"That I will not say. But have no doubts, the necklace was mine to sell. Why all these questions?"

"Because I had this necklace made especially for my wife. Lynnette wore it always. I'm sure she had it on when she left Stanbury."

"No," Madeleine gasped. "It couldn't be."

"I'm afraid so." He lifted the clasp. "This alone would be enough to convince me. See, the lion engraved here with a sword in his paw. My banner is exactly the same. The stones, too, are identical to the color I had made up. There's no doubt this is my wife's necklace."

Madeleine stood. She had to face the inevitable. He would learn of Henri now. In her heart she knew that her love for Garrett demanded she tell the truth.

"I know where the piece was purchased for me. That may be the first clue in Lynnette's disappearance." She stood quickly, determined to put an end to her charade. "Come, Garrett. I know Ebony must be nearby. We go to The Open Locket. I don't know exactly where the shop is located, though I do remember a heart-shaped locket graces the doorway. This should be enough for us to find it."

GARRETT TOOK MADELEINE'S hand and threaded his way through the crowd, moving down the street to where Ebony awaited. The weak sunshine threatened to break through the cloud cover at any moment. He tossed a coin to the lad that had kept watch of his horse and then placed Madeleine in the saddle. She stroked Ebony's mane fondly. Garrett climbed behind her and she tensed as he put his arm about her waist.

"No, sweetheart," he whispered in her ear. "Please. Do not reject me."

She turned and met his eyes. "Oh, Garrett. How can you forgive me? There's still so much you don't know."

He brushed his lips gently across her mouth, blocking out the world for a short moment.

As they made their way across London, he asked, "How's your mother doing?"

She flushed a deep pink. "So Coster told, did he? I didn't think he'd stay quiet forever but I gave him more credit than I should have. He broke much too fast."

She looked up at him with sudden concern.

"You weren't too hard on him, I hope. He really is a decent sort."

"I will deal with Coster when we return to Stanbury. By the way, where's my horse?"

She gave him a sheepish glance. "Sold," she squeaked out. "I asked for a poor nag, Garrett. Not one up to your usual standards. The brooch I left was worth far more than the horse."

"Where does your jewelry come from, Madeleine? I thought I'd confiscated it all."

"Oh, really?" she replied frostily, but she refused to answer him when he pressed her.

They rode Ebony in silence after that, stopping thrice to ask directions. Eventually, they located the shop. The balding jeweler there was delighted to see customers.

"No one's buying or selling these days with the typhus around," he confided to them. "I'm glad to have your company. Come, tell me what I may show you. Perhaps a ring for the lovely maid?"

Garrett said, "We'd like to inquire about a necklace purchased here some time ago."

"About two and a half years," Madeleine added.

The shopkeeper frowned. "That's a long time to remember a certain piece."

"Here," Garrett said, placing the necklace on the counter.

The man smiled immediately, his yellowed

teeth glowing as much as his eyes. "Of course. The lion clasp. I remember how unusual I thought it was at the time." He picked up the necklace and studied it carefully. "Yes," he confirmed, "I know this piece."

"Do you have any knowledge of who might have come in to sell it? A man? A woman?" Garrett glanced at Madeleine as he asked, "Or do you remember who bought it?"

She flinched at his words. "I don't remember who purchased it my lord but I do recall the seller." The jeweler fingered the clasp as he spoke. "I thought it strange that one such as he would have access to a piece so fine and unusual but he said he was selling it for his mistress who was in great need."

"Can you describe him?" Garrett pressed.

"Oh, easily, my lord. The man had only one eye. Wore a patch over the other. He had sandy red hair and a reddish beard. I remember him quite well."

Garrett grew pale at the description. He gripped the counter for support.

"Garrett?" Madeleine took hold of his forearm. "Are you all right?"

"Yes," he said through gritted teeth. "Thank you." He placed a coin on the tabletop for the jeweler then turned and led them outside.

The afternoon sun had dipped below the surrounding buildings, leaving them in the cool shadows of the October day.

"I know this man," he told Madeleine. "He used to be my head stableman. A lazy, shiftless drunk. Because his wife was quite ill and they had several children, I reluctantly kept him on but I demoted him." He snarled. "I cannot wait to get my hands upon him."

They had only taken a few steps when a man stepped from a narrow alley. "Gimme yer jewels!" he barked.

Madeleine stammered, "But I have none."

"Nay," the thief said. "I just seen ye leave Thomas' place. Ye're bound to have some bauble."

The thief pulled a knife from nowhere. With a quick motion, he sliced Garrett's upper thigh. A bright, crimson line appeared and Garrett gasped in pain and outrage.

"You have chosen the wrong man to tangle with, my friend."

CHAPTER TWENTY-TWO

GARRETT SLAMMED HIS fist into the nose of their attacker, making the thief's head snap back. Crimson blood spurted from the man's nose, giving Garrett a small sense of satisfaction.

The bandit's eyes narrowed. His grip tightened on the knife as he lunged.

Garrett feinted to his left, then delivered a series of powerful blows to the robber's midsection. He crumpled, collapsing into a heap at their feet.

Garrett calmly turned to Madeleine, whose face was white with fear. He pulled her to him. "Are you all right?"

She stammered, "Y-yes. But we must see to you."

Following the direction of her gaze, he stared at the blood flowing down his leg. The pain hit him, sharp and throbbing.

She reached for the hem of her tunic and tore a wide strip from the bottom, tying it tightly around his leg.

"Let us hurry, my lord. We must see to your wound at once."

He sighed. "I do wish you'd quit *my lording* me, Madeleine. Garrett—or my love—would do wonders for my health."

She rolled her eyes. "Get up on Ebony, my dearest Garrett, before I inflict more damage to you myself." She smiled at him sweetly.

"Now that's much better," he said a bit woozily as he gave her a lazy smile.

With her help, he was able to mount Ebony, then he reached and lifted her in front of him.

The light had faded fast and the streets emptied quickly as they made their way to his London residence. He refused to take her back to the room she had been letting.

"We'll send for your things tomorrow, love. But for now, you'll return with me. I wouldn't want to chance your safety."

THREE-QUARTERS OF AN hour later, they reached their destination. Garrett's home was small by Stanbury standards but Madeleine was impressed with it all the same.

She slid off Ebony as a lanky groom appeared. "Had a mishap, my lord?"

"Just a little fracas, John." Garrett eased off the horse with a grimace and handed the reins to his servant. Madeleine quickly took his arm and helped him to the house.

A tiny housekeeper, who barely came to Madeleine's chest, greeted them.

"Hello, Maude," Garrett called out weakly. "This is Madeleine. She's even feistier than you."

Calmly, as though Garrett came in bloody on a daily basis, the servant said, "We'll need to dress your wound, my lord, and then get you something to eat."

Madeleine watched Maude take charge of Garrett, fussing over him as she led him upstairs to his bed, making sure his gashed leg was propped up with pillows.

"Madeleine can attend my injury, Maude. Just bring me a tender chicken with your famous sauce and I'll be fine in no time."

"Chickens are the very thing I need," Madeleine proclaimed.

She and Maude went off in search of chickens and Madeleine asked the servant for wine, as well.

Soon, she returned to Garrett with a tray. He grinned lazily at her.

"I need to undress you, my lord," she told him. "I must see to your wound."

He grinned at her. "Will you see to others things, too?"

Exasperated, she pushed him back onto the pillows and unwound the strip of cloth from his leg. Both his pants and hose were soaked with blood, which had begun to clot. She removed his boots, followed by his clothing.

She cleaned the deep slice first with water then warned him, "This will sting," before pouring wine over the gash. He sucked in air loudly through clenched teeth as the wine touched his skin.

"What are you doing?" he demanded.

"Taking care of you the best I know how," she replied tartly. "I'll either save you or kill you in the process. We'll just have to await the outcome."

"You're worse than facing a herd of bloody Scots," he muttered. "It's not even a scratch."

She ignored him as he rambled on, rubbing the whites of eggs across the wound to provide a soothing balm. As she brought the skin close together, she chanted, "In the name of the Father, Son, and Holy Mary. The wound was red, the cut deep, the flesh be sore, but there will be no more blood or pain until the Blessed Virgin bears a child again."

Binding it with a clean cloth, she leaned back and surveyed her work.

He smiled. "Never have I had such a lovely

nurse." He took her hand and brought it to his lips, pressing a fervent kiss upon her knuckles.

She looked him in eyes. "Oh, no, my lord, you aren't to move a muscle." She removed her hand from his and folded them both primly in her lap.

"Mayhap you are right," he said.

"Of course, I'm right," she retorted. "You must get some rest now."

"Will you stay with me? Please."

She gave in, allowing him to bring her down next to him. He placed an arm about her and drew her close until her head lay on his chest. "Now I am at peace," he told her. He kissed the top of her head.

They stayed that way for some minutes, then Garrett whispered, "I want you."

Immediately, she felt the familiar stirring inside her. She wanted his touch and yet couldn't give in to the temptation. It would only make it harder to leave him. But her heart argued with her mind to seize the moment. There would be no others. Soon Garrett and England would be far behind, and she would only have these memories to sustain her for the rest of her life.

She glanced up at him, and his lips moved to hers. She responded to his kiss, cradling his face in her hands. He needed no further encouragement.

"No regrets," she whispered into his mouth.

"What?"

"Nothing," she said, holding him close to her.

Some time later, when they were spent, he fell asleep.

Madeleine slipped quietly from the bed and dressed. She found Maude humming in the kitchen, the chicken plucked, boiled, and ready to be consumed.

"Oh, my lady, how is the master? Well rested now, is he?"

"He's asleep, Maude. He'll need broth from the chicken, too. We don't want him to get a fever." She hesitated a moment. "And, please, call me Madeleine. I am no lady."

Maude sized her up shrewdly. "You're every inch a lady, my dear. Can't hide that. Can't hide how taken the master is with you, either."

Her cheeks heated with the servant's words and she shook her head.

"Don't be silly, my lady. My master has been most unhappy nearly all his life. Don't think I'll judge you simply because you've brought a little sunshine into his life." She eyed Madeleine speculatively. "Does he know you're a lady?"

Madeleine laughed, taken aback at her astuteness. "No, Maude. He thinks me a thief."

"And he still loves you, nonetheless? I'd reckon the only thing you've stolen is his heart." Maude patted Madeleine's shoulder. "Come, dear. Let's get the master a meal in his belly and then he can have all the sleep he wants."

GARRETT AWOKE THE next morning with a parched throat and a dull ache in his leg. His head was clear, though, with none of the throbbing pain to which he had become accustomed. It was too bad, in a way, for then he could have asked Madeleine to sing to him. Her voice had a way of soothing the pains in his head. He would have enjoyed being her audience of one.

He spotted her dozing in a chair next to his bed. She'd probably been there all night. He reached over and gently took her hand, feeling its warmth. She stirred slightly but did not awaken.

He gazed at her lovingly, wanting to know every inch of her. All his anger from the previous day was spent. He still wondered how she'd come into possession of Lynnette's necklace but she would tell him in her own time. For now, he needed to return to Stanbury as soon as possible and confront Barth. Only when he learned the truth about Lynnette could he start a new life with Madeleine.

He studied her face, glad for once she was silent. Not that he didn't enjoy their verbal sparring. She had a quick tongue and keen mind and Garrett enjoyed their conversations immensely. Still, it seemed a luxury to look upon her beauty in the quiet morning. He looked forward to doing so every morning for the rest of their lives.

He focused on the faint scar that marred her perfect skin. The slightly jagged ridge ran along her cheekbone and he determined it must have come from a ring. Someone had backhanded her with a powerful blow to cause such a blemish to be embedded so deeply. He would kill the man that had mistreated her and not rest until he'd done so.

He gave her hand a quick squeeze and her eyelids fluttered. Despite his sore leg, he leaned up and softly kissed her sweet lips.

"Good morning, my nurse. It's time you woke and tended your patient."

She stretched lazily. "This good nurse needs to be up and about, my lord. Sleeping in a chair is not my idea of a comfortable night."

"You'd rather sleep on that flea-bitten quilt in your rented hovel?"

"Mayhap," she said teasingly.

He started to rise.

"Oh, no. You are to remain abed the whole day. Maude and I have decided that already. You need rest aplenty."

"No, my dear, we leave for Stanbury today. I must—"

Madeleine pushed him back against his pillows, her hands firm on his shoulders. "I know you are anxious to learn the truth about

Lynnette. I'm only asking for this one day for you to heal before you ride to Stanbury. You'll need your strength before you set out on such a long ride."

"You treat me as a babe," he grumbled.

"Just for today, Garrett. I'll heat some broth for you to break your fast."

She returned in a little while with a steaming bowl of the broth she'd promised him, along with ale and bread. As he ate, she redressed his wound.

"The cut already looks to be healing nicely."

"All thanks to your care." His eyes caressed her.

She swallowed hard. "Garrett, there's something we must talk about. Things you ought to know." She twisted her hands together, her brow furrowed as she concentrated on the right words to say.

"It's about—"

"There you are, Madeleine. Might've known where you'd be."

Maude bustled into the room, drawing the curtains as she hummed a bit off-key. "You look much better today, Lord Montayne."

Sunshine streamed into the room and Madeleine began pacing nervously. He wished Maude hadn't interrupted their conversation since he knew Madeleine was about to share something of her past with him.

"You seem to be restless, Madeleine," said

Maude. "Mayhap you could accompany me to market? I've a mind to prepare eels, seeing as to how Lord Montayne is partial to them."

The servant turned to Garrett. "You'd like some eels now, in a bit of saffron sauce? Or would you prefer fried minnows?"

"They both sound delicious, Maude. You make the choice."

She clucked her tongue. "Well, I won't decide just yet. We'll wait until we see what Old James has." She nodded at Madeleine. "I'll get us some baskets, dearie."

As soon as Maude left the room, Madeleine went to him and placed her palm against his cheek. "I will help Maude now." She hesitated a moment. "When we return, I must speak to you."

HENRI DE PICASSARET left the church immediately after mass. He still felt a bit unsure about being in London after hearing the warning from the gatekeeper concerning the waning epidemic of typhus. Yet no fear of illness could have kept him from following the Earl of Montayne as he chased after Madeleine.

The wanton bitch.

Henri felt the bile rise in his throat at the

thought of his wife giving herself to a lover. He had no doubt based on Garrett's reaction to her disappearance that they were lovers. How dare she forsake her loving husband and their vows? Who did the chit think she was to leave him, Henri de Picassaret, man of wealth—and God's chosen one?

He must find her and take her back to France. He'd spent this very morning in constant prayer to the Almighty Father, seeking His advice on how to punish his wife's ungodly behavior. Death seemed too pleasant for one who had sinned as heavily as Madeleine. But, in the end, he supposed God would wish it so. After all, he must find a new wife who could give him children if he were to build a dynasty to revere God's greatness. It was his duty to produce heirs.

It seemed a pity, though, that God had felt the need to test him so. Three barren wives and now the last one who also proved to be an adulteress. It was almost more than a good Christian man such as him could bear.

As a man of God, though, he must accept his fate and walk the path God provided for him, no matter how painful that path became. Still, to be publicly humiliated by Garrett Stanbridge, the Earl of Montayne, was almost more than he could bear. Madeleine's paramour had flaunted their immorality in his face. A man did not get much lower than Lord Montayne. To think that he had almost traded his precious French land to that English swine.

Henri had been searching for his sinful wife in the disease-ridden city and had actually found her at some rundown rooms. But before he could fetch Bertrand to help him spirit her away, Montayne had showed up and snatched her from his grasp. Infuriated, he'd followed them at a distance until they'd entered The Open Locket. Though his curiosity was aroused, it had not stopped him from approaching a burly ruffian on the street. He'd paid the man good coin to take Montayne down and retrieve Madeleine for him.

Of course, now he was being tested even further by God. The man had barely threatened the couple with his knife when he was struck down, compliments of the Earl of Montayne. Instead of taking the earl by surprise and fleeing with Madeleine in tow, the idiot had tried to rob them first. What a waste of his money and time.

If things were to be done right, then Henri must take it upon himself. He'd seen Montayne slashed in the brief fight. He had no qualms about using that injury, or whatever trick was necessary, to kill his wife's lover and reclaim her. Madeleine would have to be severely punished before he let her escape into Death's welcoming arms.

He made his way to Montayne's London home. He stood on the corner across from it, watching, wondering if the unrighteous couple lay fornicating within.

Suddenly, the door opened. Henri stepped back, pressing himself tightly against the building behind him.

An old crone, the height of a child, came out the door. Madeleine followed her, a market basket tucked into the crook of her arm. She turned back when her name was called.

Montayne appeared in the doorway and she returned the few steps to him. He leaned down and kissed her briefly, stroking her cheek with his thumb.

Henri nearly exploded on the spot, seeing the Englishman touch his wife in such an intimate way and watching Madeleine's face fill with pleasure. It was only God's spirit working in him that kept him from screaming to the heavens. Instead, he carefully moved from where he stood and began following his unfaithful wife on the other side of the narrow street. He stayed well behind her, out of her line of vision, while he hatched his plan.

He alone wielded the sword of justice. It was about time Madeleine learned this.

Soon they arrived at the market, an explosion of smells and sounds. The odors of fish and warm bread invaded his senses, as did the sweat of the tightly packed bodies all vying for business. He hated being this close to so many people, worrying what diseases they might harbor. He kept his arms tightly by his sides, not wanting to touch any one of them.

Henri wished suddenly that Bertrand were with him. The servant might be stupid but he was strong and had, on several occasions, helped Henri discipline Madeleine. Hopefully, though, Henri would take her so unawares that she would not have time to react. He must depend on God to give him the strength he needed when the time came.

The women moved from stall to stall, studying the goods to be had. The tiny servant finally stopped at a booth where different fish were sold. She began arguing animatedly with its proprietor.

Henri watched Madeleine move away from her companion and pick up some trinket. She had a dreamy expression on her face which Henri would slap off her the minute they were alone.

It was that look that moved him to action.

MADELEINE INSTANTLY RECOGNIZED the vise-grip that seized her arm. The bony hand belied the power in those fingers. Paralyzed by fear, the cry she longed to voice would not come. Her freedom snatched away in one brief moment, she focused on the familiar black onyx signet ring her husband never took from his hand. It was the sight of this ring that caused her to resist.

She desperately dug in her heels and pulled in the opposite direction, trying to stop Henri's forward motion.

He turned. The look on his face brought terror to her soul. The face of a madman. A scream formed but never came for Henri slapped her so hard that her teeth rattled.

The sunny day went almost black, while stars exploded in a palette of color. Without warning, a second blow followed, and she slumped to the ground in a heap.

MADELEINE AWOKE TO the splash of freezing water hitting her in the face.

Henri stood over her, his mouth twitching rapidly, a sure sign that he was out of control. She might have teased Garrett about being the Devil Himself but she knew that a true demon from Hell now stood above her. There would be no escape this time, no hope to sustain her. She'd lost the love of her life. She hadn't the will, much less the strength, to go on. Unless Garrett was by her side, she had no wish to live anymore.

If she were lucky, she could prod Henri to kill her quickly.

"Do you seek revenge, Henri?" she taunted. "Were you embarrassed in front of your friends for having a wife run off? Did you—"

The kick was swift and vicious, striking her in her ribcage, knocking the breath from her. Pain burst throughout her body but she kept her mouth closed. She would not give him the pleasure of hearing her cries.

Henri twisted his mouth in a semblance of a smile. "Your lover cannot help you now," he said menacingly. "Only I can, Madeleine. Confess your sins to me and I will try to make things right for you with God."

She tried to quell the mounting hysteria in order to answer him calmly. "The only sin found in this room is with you, Henri. You've shown me no love, nor mercy, and you have beaten me in anger. That is your sin, not mine."

The evil smile still played upon his thin, cruel lips. "I know what you do, Madeleine, and you will not tempt me. We shall do this slowly, methodically, so it will be carried out correctly. In fact, we must exact punishment repeatedly for God to be satisfied."

MADELEINE GROANED IN pain. Henri had left her trussed on the cold stone floor. She was unable to move. He'd promised there would be more. If there was one thing Henri did, it was keep his promises.

If this was God's judgment upon her for breaking her vows, so be it. Henri had said that he was taking her home to France. She would simply kill herself at sea, fling herself into the murky waters and find death. She knew by taking her own life she would be damned forever but it seemed a small price to pay to escape Henri de Picassaret.

CHAPTER TWENTY-THREE

GARRETT LEANED BACK in his chair, arms behind his head, and stretched lazily, counting the moments until Madeleine returned from the market. His thigh was stiff but he'd incurred far worse injuries in battle. There'd been several nasty wounds over the years, the most severe given to him by a wayward Scot. A slice to the thigh rated as low as a slight bump on the head but he'd let Madeleine fuss over him because he enjoyed her ministrations.

He could not wait until she was back in his bed.

He'd never been so taken with a woman before. But then, Madeleine wasn't just any woman. He knew that unraveling her layers would take most of this lifetime and on into the next. He looked forward to every minute of it.

Together, they would deal with their problems. He was sure she had been ready to confide in him before Maude interrupted them. Soon, he would learn where she came from and the name of the man that had so cruelly mistreated her. As for Lynnette, that mystery would also be solved. He only had to return to Stanbury and confront Barth. Then he could begin to piece together the puzzle of his wife's disappearance.

Had she truly left him for a lover—or would Barth reveal a different story? Was there a possibility that Lynnette could be dead?

It was hard for him to remember now just what they'd shared together. He'd always been satisfied with Lynnette as his wife. She'd been a bit meek in their lovemaking but he'd assumed that's how it was with all ladies of good breeding. She'd brought him considerable wealth and most importantly, Lyssa—a treasure more precious than gold or land.

Madeleine had changed everything, though. The happiness he thought he'd found in his marriage was a pale shadow against the passion he had for this songstress. Madeleine possessed a fire that lit his soul and Garrett knew this as true love. It went beyond even the physical love they'd made, which was full of heat in and of itself. No, he desired her in every way imaginable. He could not—*would not*—live without her.

But where was she? He was hungry for her, as well as his noon meal. She'd been gone far too long in his opinion. He stood from his comfortable position in the velvet chair, pushing the footstool aside.

He might have known with Maude involved in the marketing it would take longer than usual. The woman drove a harder bargain than his steward ever dreamed of pursuing. If he were smart, Garrett would put Maude in charge of the selling of his wines. He was certain the Hanseatic ports had never seen the likes of a Maude in all their tradings.

He stretched his stiff muscles, glad to move about now that he was up. A brief smile crossed his lips. He would fetch Ebony and head to the market. He was sure to meet up with them. Maude could return here for it would take time to prepare their meal. He could wander about London a bit with Madeleine nestled in his arms.

He grinned again. The thought of her pressed against him as Ebony slowly moved through the streets warmed his blood. Garrett was grateful now that she had sold the horse she'd taken when she'd reached London. It would allow her to ride with him on the return trip to Stanbury. He could almost feel her soft curves, smell her sweet scent.

He donned his cloak and hurried outside, barely favoring his leg now as he called for John to saddle Ebony.

As Garrett started toward town, he decided that he would kiss Madeleine soundly the moment he found her because he would ache until he did so. He wanted her now more than he ever had. He didn't think he could ever get enough of her.

The streets near midday teemed with people. He glanced back and forth as he approached the market, disappointed not to spot Madeleine on her return trip.

Suddenly, he heard Maude's cry. Panic rose in him instantly when he spied his servant rushing toward him, Madeleine nowhere in sight. He leaped off Ebony as she approached.

Hair askew, Maude's alarm was written across her face. "Oh, my lord, my lord. You must do something." She clutched Garrett's arm. "She's gone!"

His heart sank. She'd left him again. This time, it was for good. He would never know happiness. Never be whole.

Then Maude burst into tears. "I didn't see it. I couldn't stop it! Oh, my lord, forgive me. She's all sweetness and sunshine and I know how she loves you so. You must get her back. You must!"

"What do you mean?"

His servant angrily wiped her tears away. "The man, my lord. The man who took her. You must find her. He will kill her."

Fear rippled through him. "Who? What happened?"

Maude shook her head. "Come with me,

Lord Montayne. They can tell you better than I. Old James saw some of it."

She turned and ran through the crowd, tiny as a child, darting in and out. Garrett followed quickly, urging Ebony along, his eyes on Maude the entire way.

The strong stench of fish permeated the air as Maude stopped in front of a stall and motioned him over.

"This is Old James, my lord. He saw it."

Garrett faced a man with a ruddy complexion. "What did you see? Where is Madeleine?"

"Everyone's talking about him!" James exclaimed. "The way he grabbed her. 'Twas the most excitement I've seen in a good number of years." He paused, a crowd gathering around his stall. "I was doing my business with Maude here. From the corners of my eyes, I saw that man. Dressed as a gentleman, he was." James frowned. "Something not quite right about him, though."

A woman with straggly, mud-colored hair pushed her way to the front. "I saw, too, my lord. I saw it all." Her eyes gleamed expectantly. "For a coin or two, I could tell you more." She held out her hand to Garrett, confident he would pay.

He reached into his purse with an unsteady hand. He should never have let Madeleine out of his sight. Handing over the coin, he prodded the stranger. "Go on."

She shrank back a moment as she caught the

look he gave her. She swallowed once before she began. "He was tall, my lord, and as skinny around as my finger here." She stuck it up to show Garrett for good measure. "He had a bulging stomach, though, like he was carrying a babe. Gray hair, too, and a terrible, evil grin."

A raw chill ran through him. A perfect description of Henri de Picassaret.

The woman warmed to her story now. The crowd pressed closer. "Fair rattled her teeth, he did. Slapped her so hard I thought her head would snap off."

"And hit her again!" cried another voice. "She went down fast after that."

Garrett fumed. "None of you came to her aid?"

The group froze at his tone. The woman who'd stepped forward said, "He was gentry. The likes of us know better than to interfere."

His gaze swept over the shabbily dressed crowd and they quickly melted away.

Only Maude and James remained, and James spoke softly. "It happened so fast, my lord. One minute they're here and the next the old devil'd dragged her off. It was none of our business." The fish seller crossed himself for good measure.

Garrett mounted Ebony. He had no time to waste. Without a backward glance, he made for Lord Fenton's. When he'd last met with de Picassaret in London, it had been there. He only prayed Fenton had again played host to the Frenchman.

He rode like a madman through the narrow streets, shouting warnings to those who crossed his path. Madeleine's abuser had found her. It was de Picassaret all along. Now the truth stood before him. Henri's own wife had run from him—and that wife had been Madeleine.

She had tried to put him off when she spoke of the sanctity of marriage vows. She'd been speaking of her own vows with Henri. Garrett's love for her—both physically and emotionally— must have torn her apart.

Yet she loved him. He was certain of it. They had a spiritual connection that ran greater than the physical. He had promised himself he would find the man who'd tortured this woman, who'd marred not only her body but her soul. He would kill the French bastard before he let de Picassaret touch Madeleine again.

But would he be too late?

He reached Fenton's in a quarter of an hour. No groom was in sight to take his winded horse. He looped Ebony's reins to a post and dashed to the door. He rapped the knocker in a steady stream. When no one answered, he beat on the door with his fists.

"Open up!"

He'd about given up hope when the door opened a slit. A young boy of eight or nine poked his head out.

"No one's here, my lord. Lord and Lady Fenton are gone to the country. Can't help you."

He started to close the door but Garrett forced his boot in. "I'm here to see Monsieur de Picassaret. My name is Montayne."

The boy looked at him now in recognition and smiled. "You're the owner of the dark beauty."

Garrett had seen the admiring glances the lad had given his horse the last time he was here. "Yes, my horse is named Ebony."

The child relaxed a bit and opened the door to him, motioning him to come in. "The Frenchman is gone, my lord. I heard him tell Mum that they was going home to France."

"Where is your mother?"

"She went to Bessie's to help her have a babe. She helps with birthings all the time," he said with pride.

Garrett knew it would be hard to track the woman down. He must get what he could from the boy. "Was the comte leaving for France today?"

The boy screwed his eyes closed for a minute. "I dunno. Maybe. I think his servant said something about Tuesday."

"Tomorrow," Garrett said aloud. He tossed the lad a coin and started down the steps. If Henri had already left Fenton's, he'd most likely be down on the waterfront, especially if his ship left on the morning tide. Garrett prayed he would find them there.

He mounted Ebony. The youngster called out to him. "Tell his wife I hope she gets all better."

He whirled. "What did you say?" he demanded, reining in so suddenly that Ebony reared under him. "Speak, boy!"

The child took a step back, his eyes round. "She's in a bad way. She fell down the stairs. She couldn't even walk. The comte's servant had to carry her."

Wheeling his horse in a tight circle, Garrett spurred him through the gate. Between Fenton's and the waterfront he saw nothing but a blur of colors, felt nothing but the pounding pulse of his anger.

He would kill de Picassaret.

At the office of the harbormaster, Raleigh greeted him. "Already back, my lord? I've not seen the lady in question."

Garrett shook his head as he caught his breath. "Which ship leaves for France tomorrow?"

"*The Avril*. It sails at sunrise."

"Check the manifest for Henri de Picassaret."

Raleigh burst out laughing. "No need to do that. Seems the man bought half of England while he was here. Wouldn't surprise me if'n the ship sank under the weight he carries back."

"Do you know where he stays?"

Raleigh cocked his head to one side as he thought. "I'd venture The Wild Duck."

"Tend my horse."

Garrett hurried through the seedy side streets near the port. He reached the inn quickly and inquired which rooms belonged to Henri de Picassaret.

"Not here. Went out with his servant."

Garrett slapped a gold coin on the table. "Which rooms?"

The innkeeper appraised him for a moment, scratching his scraggly beard. "I could let you wait in his rooms." He quickly pocketed the money, flashing a gap-toothed smile. Handing Garrett a key, he pointed toward a rickety staircase. "Up those. Last room on the left."

With trepidation, he mounted the creaking stairs and continued to the far end of the unlit corridor. He slipped the key into the lock and slowly pushed open the door.

The light from a dirty window revealed a lumpy bed and a stack of trunks. There was no sign of Madeleine. He couldn't imagine Henri staying in such a place for very long.

Garrett moved toward the trunks stacked in disarray near the corner. Behind them, under a dirty blanket on the floor, he spied movement. Reaching over the trunks, he gently lifted the blanket.

He stared at the pile of rags for a moment before recognizing an arm, then a tumble of hair. His stomach lurched. He quickly hauled away the trunks around her and knelt.

Madeleine lay on the floor, a small pool of sticky blood under her cheek. How he recognized her, he wasn't sure. Filth matted her long, golden hair. A mass of bruises covered her face. Blood trickled from her nose. One eye had completely swollen shut. Around her throat deep purple contusions were evenly spaced, as if someone had tried to choke the very life from her.

He removed the strips of cloth that bound her wrists to her ankles and lifted her onto his lap, rocking her, stroking her hair, whispering comforting nonsense.

He fought the rage that pulsed with every beat of his heart. Hot tears fell from his eyes as fast as a brook ran.

He shuddered at how savagely she'd been beaten. He would kill the demon known as Henri de Picassaret on first sight. For now, though, he must find help for his beloved. He refused to let her die.

She struggled to open an eye. "You must leave," she said haltingly. Her voice was raspy, much deeper than normal. "He will kill you if he finds you here."

"Who, Madeleine?" He had to hear it from

her.

"Henri. De Picassaret." She hiccupped. "My . . . husband."

What it must have cost her to tell him that.

Madeleine had fled from the fiend she'd married. She bore the scars and the limp from their time together. She'd faced horrors no one should undergo. She'd hid her identity from everyone, even from the man who loved her.

But then they'd found each other. How it must have eaten at her soul when he'd raged on about Lynnette abandoning her marriage when she'd done the same thing, albeit for far different reasons. She must have been terrified he'd learn of this and turn on her.

Garrett cradled her to him. Oh, God in Heaven, he loved this woman.

She tried to speak again. "Please," she begged in a whisper. "Leave. He mustn't find you here." Her eyes were dull, lifeless, and he saw she had resigned herself to whatever fate de Picassaret had chosen.

He shook his head. "I will not leave you, Madeleine. Ever."

He managed to lift her and carried her to the bed. He hated to place her on the rotting mattress but thought it better than the floor. He gently moved his hands over her, searching for broken bones or other injuries. She grimaced as he grazed her ribs.

She began babbling. "He wouldn't let me curl into a ball. I always know to do that. I know to protect myself. What to do. I . . ."

Her voice faded out and she mumbled words in rapid French that he couldn't understand. Garrett wondered just what she had suffered at her husband's hands. He removed his cloak and draped it over her. He wished to kiss her but her lip was split and bruised. He was almost afraid to touch her anywhere.

"I will send for a physician, my love." He brushed the hair from her face, wincing at the new crop of bruises that had been hidden.

"No!" she cried, weak as a kitten's mewl. "I'd rather die than live without you." Hot tears streamed from her swollen eyes. "You foolish man! Why can't you understand? I am married until death parts me from this devil. God has already let Henri punish me for going to your bed."

"You think God *wanted* Henri to do this to you?" Garrett balled his hands into fists. "You are sadly mistaken, Madeleine. I don't know what nonsense he's tried to fill your head with but—"

"Just go," she said quietly. "I don't want you here." She turned her face away, the tears sliding onto the stained pillow.

He strode to the window and leaned out. He searched for a moment and then yelled, "Boy! Boy!"

A youth of about ten ran to the base of the building and looked up. "Yes, my lord?"

Garrett tossed him a coin. "Fetch a doctor here at once. There'll be another piece for you when you return."

The boy took off running.

Garrett came and sat on the bed next to Madeleine. "I'll take you far from Henri de Picassaret. I give you my promise. You need never see him again."

"MY LORD! COME to the window." The boy had returned, hollering for Garrett.

He went to the window and saw the boy was alone.

"No one would come, my lord. They're scared or they didn't believe me that a real lord had need of them. The waterfront is a bad place." He tipped his hat to Garrett. "But I thank you for the coin all the same."

Garrett cursed softly to himself. He went back to Madeleine and took her hand. "Sweetheart, we must leave now. I'll do my best not to jar you."

He wrapped the cloak around her, the same cloak that had warmed her what seemed like a lifetime ago. He slipped his arms underneath her and eased her from the bed. He had some idea of how she suffered. Ryker had beaten him many times before Garrett had finally stood up to him. He still remembered the deep aches, not only in his body, but in his bruised spirit. He would commit himself to nursing Madeleine back to good health, both in body and soul.

He picked his way carefully through the unpaved street, headed toward the waterfront. Madeleine had passed out in his arms. Garrett spied Raleigh and moved in his direction.

The harbormaster hurried to him. "What's this?" He gaped at Madeleine.

"I need a cart. Fast. I must get her from this place. See to it."

The man ran off on bowed legs. Within five minutes, he'd returned, leading Ebony. His horse had been hitched to a small cart. Garrett climbed awkwardly with Madeleine in his arms into the cart's bed. He'd thought to place her down but the cart had no blanket. Not even a bed of straw. Instead, he kept her in his arms.

"Drive me, Raleigh. I can't leave her."

Raleigh gazed at Madeleine with sympathy. "Where to, Lord Montayne?"

Garrett quickly instructed him as Raleigh climbed up into the driver's seat and flicked Ebony's reins lightly.

He closed his eyes. *Just let her live, God. Let her live.* The prayer became a chant in his mind, its rhythm soothing him.

"*Fornicator!*" A devil-like shriek pierced the air.

Garrett's eyes flew open as the cart came to a jarring halt. Henri de Picassaret stood blocking Ebony's path, his eyes wild.

"You snake! You debaucher of God's laws!" He pointed at Madeleine. "She—*my wife*—will pay every day of her life for falling to temptation. You English swine, with your courtly manner and seducing smiles. To think I almost gave you my land."

Madeleine stirred and moaned softly.

Garrett rotated her face away from Henri, who frothed at the mouth as if he were rabid. He restrained himself from jumping out of the cart. His first duty was to protect Madeleine. He would deal with her husband in time.

"Drive through him if you have to, Raleigh, but get us from this place," Garrett ordered.

Raleigh tried to turn Ebony but de Picassaret grabbed at the reins. The horse snorted and whipped his head about but the Frenchman held him firmly. He shook his finger at Garrett.

"You filthy English lecher. I will punish you in God's name as I have punished her."

He could stand it no longer. The thought of this madman's repeated beatings of Madeleine raged through his head. He would tear the man's limbs from his body.

As gently as he could, he placed Madeleine down.

She clutched his arm. "No," she whispered.

"Yes," he returned firmly.

He leaped from the cart, his body shaking with pent-up fury. "You're nothing but a spineless bastard, de Picassaret. You beat those too helpless to defend themselves, you worthless scum."

In a blurred motion, he rushed toward the comte, his fist smashing directly into the Frenchman's nose. The crack could be heard over the shouts of the crowd that quickly gathered around them, cheering on the bloodshed.

His enemy slumped for a moment and then let out a ferocious cry, slamming his fists into Garrett's ears. Garrett reeled from the strength of the fierce blow. The Frenchman cackled with glee over the pain he'd inflicted, his eyes lighting up with sick pleasure. His hands clamped around Garrett's throat, choking him. The strong pressure amazed Garrett. It was the strength of a man gone mad. He wondered how Madeleine had survived as long as she had.

He clawed at Henri's hands and forced them from his throat. Then he gripped the front of de Picassaret's rich, black tunic, now wet with blood. He slammed him against a nearby barrel and pounded him in a blind frenzy, delivering blow after blow to his body.

"This is for Madeleine!"

As Garrett heard a rib crack, the comte emitted a high, girlish scream and collapsed. The crowd roared its approval.

He dropped to one knee and mopped the sweat from his brow as he tried to gain control of his anger. He wanted nothing more than to kill Henri de Picassaret. But could he do so without losing Madeleine's love and trust? Once free, would she want to be with her husband's murderer?

He gazed at her, undecided. Their lives, their love, lay in the balance with his next action.

She cried out, "Garrett! His dirk. It's poisoned!"

Garrett reacted instantly. Moving in one swift motion, he rushed toward his attacker. The comte clutched a blade. Garrett latched on to the bastard's wrist and squeezed with all his might but the madman refused to drop his jeweled dagger. With superhuman strength, he brought it up under Garrett's chin.

He knew with sudden clarity that they were locked in a death struggle. Only one of them would survive this battle.

And the winner would decide Madeleine's fate.

Not a sound came from those gathered around the pair as each fought for control of the deadly blade.

"Whoremonger!" de Picassaret cried and spat

in Garrett's face.

Garrett wrenched the man's wrist and slowly forced the dagger away from him and toward the comte. He pushed the tip of it against the Frenchman's throat, cutting the tender flesh. Blood creased and trickled down onto his cloak.

The comte's eyes grew large in his pasty face. A faint sound came from his narrow lips as he went rigid. A spasm crossed his face then froze in a ghastly mask of death.

Garrett eased his hold and Henri de Picassaret fell lifeless to the ground.

The mass that had assembled shrugged and went on their way, their afternoon's free entertainment coming to an end.

He returned to the cart and climbed into the back of it. At his order, Raleigh flicked the reins and started away from the ugly scene. Garrett eased Madeleine into his arms again, stroking her cheek tenderly as he cradled her.

"He's dead?" she asked, lips quivering.

"Yes." Garrett touched his mouth gently to her forehead. "Henri is dead. And you must fight to live, Madeleine. Don't give up, dearest. I need you too much. I'll always need you, my love."

Madeleine smiled weakly. Her nightmare had ended.

CHAPTER TWENTY-FOUR

MADELEINE AWOKE TO the scraping sounds of a fire being laid in the hearth. A damp chill hung in the early morning air in the master's chamber.

She eased up from the mass of blankets and recognized the tiny servant struggling with the task. "No, Maude, please don't bother. You know we return to Stanbury today. There's no sense in lighting a fire."

Maude faced her, hands on her hips. "The master wants you to have a fire, dearie, and a fire is what you'll get. Now stay in that warm bed and drink the soup I brought you." She motioned to the table next to Madeleine.

Sure enough, a wooden bowl of broth stood awaiting her, steam rising in swirls.

"Maude, you spoil me."

The servant winked at her and turned back to

her job at hand. "No, I believe it's the master who spoils you. I just do his bidding." Maude deepened her voice in a gruff imitation of Garrett. "Maude, make up the master chamber. Maude, warm bricks for the bed. Maude, send for the doctor again. Maude, tend to—"

Madeleine interrupted her, laughing shallowly so as not to torture her ribs unnecessarily. "You've done it all, Maude. I cannot thank you enough for your kindness to me."

The fire now lit, Maude came to her. "I thank you for the change in Lord Montayne. There was always a good man buried in that hard shell until you came around." She beamed at Madeleine. "Now that he has spoiled you, in truth, you'll be rotten to the core now, I fear." She patted Madeleine's hand and smiled fondly at her. "I'll be back in a few minutes. Let the fire do its task, then we'll see about getting you ready for your journey."

She finished the broth and placed the bowl on the bedside table. She sank back into the pillows, her eyes closed, feeling utterly content.

Garrett had pampered her these last three weeks as she healed in his home, indulging her in ways she'd never dreamed. She remembered very little of those first few days. Images and sounds came and went in a blur—yet he was always there. He'd rubbed lotion into her bruises every day. Washed her hair and worked for hours combing out the many tangles. He'd sat and read to her and talked to her, rarely leaving her side. The few times he did, he always called Maude to stay with her. He even slept in the chair next to her each night, though she'd begged him to rest in a bed. He'd refused, a gleam in his eyes.

"Every time you're out of my sight, you get into trouble," he'd said. "If I have my way, you'll spend the next threescore years with me by your side."

She smiled at the sweet memory. She wanted to remember everything about him—every look he gave her, every word he spoke. Garrett had gone into battle for her, slaying the dragon that menaced her, almost losing his life in the process. Thanks to him, she could now wash clean her past. She reveled in her freedom—and welcomed their future. Because they would live it together, as one, their love ever strong forevermore.

The door creaked and she opened her eyes. Garrett came in and quickly closed it behind him. He came to the bed and sat, brushing a stray lock of hair from her cheek.

"Ebony is ready."

Madeleine knew how he longed to leave for Stanbury. Whatever had happened to Lynnette could only be answered there. Still, he'd nursed her until she was whole before trying to unravel the mystery of Lynnette's disappearance. They could build no life together until they learned the truth.

"Are you sure you are strong enough for the journey?"

She saw his concern. She had a few qualms but knew he would refuse to leave her behind. She couldn't deny him this.

"Yes, my lord, as soon as I dress, I will be ready to ride."

"Yes, *my lord?*" His eyes sparkled at the address. He leaned over her, his hands cupping her face as he bent to kiss her.

Her pulse raced in anticipation.

He gently touched his lips to hers, slowly teasing back and forth. She reached up and caressed his cheek. He turned his head and pressed a fiery kiss to her open palm. She moaned softly.

His hands slipped from her face to her neck and his lips met hers again, kissing her with urgency and desire. His tongue slipped into her mouth, demanding and insistent. She responded to him, her arms going around his neck as her own tongue answered his call. Garrett deepened the kiss as her fingers entwined in his hair, urging him closer still. He trailed a line of kisses along her jaw and down her neck. The heat he gave off was immense.

His mouth reached her breast and he slowly dragged his tongue across it. She gasped in pleasure, her fingers pressing him closer. He lazily encircled her nipple and she couldn't breathe. He slowly began sucking and waves of pleasure rippled through her. She arched her back and then cried out in pain.

He stopped immediately. "Madeleine?" he asked hoarsely.

She bit her lip to still its trembling. "My ribs. I stretched them a bit, that's all."

He nodded and rested his hand against them, his thumb stroking her gently. "I'm sorry, my love. I hadn't meant . . ." His voice faltered with emotion.

"Garrett? You've been the perfect gentlemen for weeks, allowing my body time to heal."

"God's teeth, I've tried my best, Madeleine."

She smiled. "Maude tells me my bruises have faded into shades of yellow and pale green."

"They have. Even with them, you are the most beautiful woman I have ever seen."

"I'm sure I look frightful and you are simply being kind." She took his hand in hers. "Despite what I may look like, you haven't kissed me— really kissed me—in a long while. I missed your kiss, my lord. Very much."

She saw passion swirl in his eyes as he gave her a wolfish grin. "If I promise to be gentle, mayhap we can do a bit more? Then we can be on our way."

GARRETT COULD SEE Stanbury in the distance. His belly tightened at the thought of what lay ahead. He'd spent many hours at Madeleine's bedside as she slept, wondering what he would find out when he returned. Had Lynnette truly fled with a lover or had something else sent her away? What role did Barth play in this mystery?

He would soon know.

Garrett sighed aloud, more weary than he'd imagined. The trip took three times the usual length due to Madeleine's injuries. He'd refused to leave her behind, not wanting her out of his sight for a moment. He hadn't even wanted to return in a cart, knowing the bumps along the road from London would be too many to count.

Instead, he'd walked Ebony all the way home, never allowing the horse to break into a trot. He'd embraced Madeleine carefully, watching for every pothole in their path. He cherished every moment of her closeness—the subtle scent of lavender that rose as a cloud to tickle his nose, the feel of her new velvet tunic against his hands. He'd remembered how she had said she loved the feel of velvet. He certainly liked the feel of her in it.

He stopped Ebony and stared at his home. Madeleine turned slightly and faced him. Before she could speak, he gave her a reassuring smile and a slow, lingering kiss.

"How do you feel?" he asked. "Tired?"

Her deep, rich laugh bubbled up. "Breathless." She smiled at him with love and a warm glow filled Garrett.

"I love you," he whispered, stroking her hair. He felt complete in her presence and utterly lost without her. He thanked God in His heaven that Madeleine had come into his life.

"Our journey was a bit different from the last one we took on this road," she said, her eyes misty with tears.

"Yes." He took her hand in his and brought it to his lips for a tender kiss. "You know if it were possible, I would have made you Lady Montayne back in London." He grinned. "Then I could have traveled with her both ways on the road to and from London."

"You are impossible." Her smile melted his heart.

"Are you ready for what lies ahead?" he asked.

She nodded. "Are you?"

In response, he flicked Ebony's reins and they began the last few miles of their long journey.

Cheers greeted them as they entered the lower bailey just after midday. He'd written Ashby and his mother more than once while he and Madeleine remained in London. Both waited for them now, along with Lyssa.

Ashby reached up and gently removed Madeleine from the saddle. "It's good to see you home," he told her, a smile lighting his face. "We've missed you."

Garrett dismounted and tossed his reins to a groom. "Enough of that, Ash." He slapped his friend on the back.

Lyssa ran toward them, Edith following closely behind. "Papa! Papa!" She captured his waist and hugged him tightly.

Garrett kissed her soundly. "I'm very happy to see you, Lyssa."

He leaned over and kissed his mother's cheek. "Hello, Mother."

His letters to her told that Madeleine would be coming home with him. He'd not given his mother all of the details but he made it clear that, as soon as possible, he planned to wed Madeleine. He didn't know if what he learned this day would impact that decision or if he'd still need to wait for the bishop to act on his petition. Still, he wanted his mother to know that Madeleine was in his life to stay. He wondered briefly how accepting Edith would be because she had been very close to Lynnette.

He needn't have worried. She embraced Madeleine carefully but warmly. "My dear, it's so good to have you return to Stanbury."

Madeleine blushed. "I'm afraid I left rather

hurriedly."

Before she could continue, Edith stopped her. "No harm in that." She smiled at her son. "It's rather romantic how Garrett raced off after you. I wish I had known such love." Her expression grew wistful for a moment then she brightened. "Mayhap you could turn it into a ballad."

Ashby laughed. "That, I'd like to hear. Garrett, the love-struck fool, pining away. Madeleine, the heartbreaker, who makes him dance to her tune."

"Enough!" Garrett cried, laughter in his voice. "Let us adjourn inside and remove ourselves from this cold wind."

He draped an arm about Madeleine's shoulders and found Lyssa between them, clinging to Madeleine's skirts.

"You look funny, Madeleine. Your face has all different colors on it. Ashby said you fell. Did it hurt? I fell one time. Annie told me I was black and blue. I don't think I turned any colors at all."

"I did have a bad fall, but your papa took special care of me." Madeleine glanced at him. "He's made me better in every way."

Garrett squeezed her lightly and they went up the steps and entered the great hall. Lyssa prattled on about her kitten. He let his daughter spend some time with them, chattering on about all the things that had happened while they'd been gone before he signaled Annie.

"Time for yer nap, Lyssa," the nursemaid said.

"But Annie . . . Papa . . ." She looked around for support.

"But no," he said firmly. "Madeleine is weary from our journey and she also needs to rest. You won't miss out on anything."

His daughter opened her mouth to speak but his stern look led her to close it again. Instead, she kissed both Madeleine and him and scooped up Luke before she went with Annie up the stairs.

Edith asked, "Would you like something to eat now, Garrett? Madeleine?"

Madeleine shook her head. "No, I am too tired, my lady. I want simply to lie down."

"I've had a chamber prepared for you. Would you like me to take you to it?"

Madeleine looked to him.

"Go ahead, sweetheart. I've much to do before we settle the other matter."

"You'll wait for me?" she asked anxiously.

"Of course. Go ahead."

Edith took Madeleine's arm and they exited the great hall. Garrett's eyes followed them the entire length.

When they'd gone, Ashby whistled low. "My God, Garrett. If this is what she looks like after three weeks, I shudder to think what went before."

"I thought I'd lose her, Ash. He'd beaten her

so badly. When I think . . ." His voice broke and he swallowed hard. "God's teeth! When I think I could have lost her . . ."

Ashby placed a steady hand on his shoulder. "But you didn't, Garrett."

"Thank the angels for that." He met his friend's intent gaze. "I love her, Ash. I love her with every bone in my body. I love every inch of her, down to her smallest toe."

"She is rather tall, Garrett. There's a lot to love."

Garrett broke into a smile. "I've missed you, Ash." He grew solemn. "Barth?"

"He suspects nothing. When do you confront him?"

"Tonight. I'm exhausted from our ride. I'd like to have all my wits about me. I think I'll sleep for a few hours and then attack one of Cook's pheasants. Then," he said, his eyes growing dark, "it will be time for the truth."

CHAPTER TWENTY-FIVE

MADELEINE AWOKE TO find her hand in Garrett's, their fingers entwined. His chair was pulled as close to the bed as possible. He seemed very uncomfortable, all rumpled and slumped, but how handsome he was. Her heart turned twice over just looking at him.

She thought about what it meant to return to Stanbury with him and how different her world had become. She had longed for sanctuary from her physical and emotional abuse in the confines of a nunnery. Instead, she had found salvation in the arms of this fierce, honorable man. Garrett had become her King Arthur, the hero from the stories Cadena had told her in her youth. He'd come to slay Henri-the-Dragon. She'd been rescued from her cruel captor and now she viewed all of creation through such different eyes.

She was safe—but not free from worry. What

Garrett would learn from Barth weighed on her mind. He had pinned such hopes on what this one serf could tell him. She hated to see him hurt or disappointed if he hit a stone wall. He had delivered her from her worst nightmare; she wished she could do the same for him in return. All she could offer now were her love and support.

Madeleine marveled at that. The notion of romantic love, the dream of her youth, had disappeared during her time with Henri. All her emotions had, in truth. Henri had always been ready to pounce upon any weakness, any display of sentimentality or caring. She had hardened her heart to everything that surrounded her. The wall she'd erected had kept her strong, helped her maintain her sanity, and eventually allowed her the courage to flee.

How she thanked her Dear Lord that she'd run into the arms of her love. For months, she'd fought her growing attraction to Garrett, the need for his touch and the simple craving for his company. He was witty and intelligent, caring and passionate, everything her heart had ever desired.

His cold, grim exterior hid a gentle and loving spirit within. Garrett was a man like no other. She was certain God had led her to him. She prayed desperately that He would guide Garrett now as he searched for the answers concerning

Lynnette. God created the love between them. Surely He would not have put them through so much only to keep them apart? He couldn't possibly be the angry God the priests were so fond of portraying. No, God created this beautiful world and all in it. She must place her faith in Him.

Madeleine drank in the sight of Garrett a bit longer, happy to be in his presence. Finally, she wiggled her fingers slightly and he practically leaped to his feet.

"You are a light sleeper, my lord." She grinned at him mischievously. "And very disheveled, I might add. Did you really have to sleep in that chair?"

He kissed her fingers. "Not for long, my sweet. I found it lonely in the solar, though. Now, if you'd rather me in your bed, I could—"

A loud rap at the door cut him off. Edith and Annie came bustling in with trays of food.

Garrett rose and helped Madeleine sit up against the pillows.

Edith smiled at them. "We thought you'd be hungry by now."

"I don't know about Garrett but I'm ravenous." Madeleine glanced at the trays. "Why, you've brought enough to feed a small army."

Edith laughed. "Garrett devours food much like an army." She passed him a cup of ale. "The evening meal is about to begin downstairs but I thought you'd like a bit of time to yourselves."

Garrett tore off a bite of the pheasant and chewed slowly, savoring its tenderness. "Actually, we both still bear the stains of travel, Mother. If we could have a bath drawn for each of us, it would be most welcomed."

"I'll take care of it now, my lord," Annie said.

Edith made a motion to follow her, but Garrett stopped her. "Mother?"

She turned. "Yes, Son?"

He went to the door and took her elbow, moving them out into the corridor. The torches flickered, lighting the hallway. "Would you stay and assist Madeleine with her bath? I don't want her left alone."

Edith nodded. "Of course." She started to enter the room again, but he stopped her.

"Mother." He hesitated. "It's bad what was done to her. I just wanted to prepare you."

She sighed. "Oh, Garrett. I know. One look at her as you rode up and my heart was in my throat." She faced him squarely. "I *was* married to Ryker, my son. I know from experience what a beating looks like."

He wrapped his mother into his arms and held her for longer than his usual quick hug. Then he stepped back and saw her eyes brimming with tears.

"It's over and done," she reassured him. "Those shadows were lifted from Stanbury long ago. Come, finish eating. I'll help your Madeleine. No prying servants' eyes. Just your mother helping care for the woman you love." She kissed his cheek.

⟫⟫⟪⟪

ONCE BATHED AND dressed, Garrett returned to Madeleine's chamber. He paused, surprised at the sound of laughter as he pushed open the door.

They obviously did not hear him come in and their conversation continued uninterrupted. Madeleine was seated upon a stool close by the fire, his mother braiding her hair.

Garrett watched Madeleine as the two women chatted, oblivious to their words. Despite the fading bruises, she appeared radiant. She had lost the harried look she'd worn in recent weeks, as if the weight of concealing her identity from everyone had been a physical one, pressing down upon her. With her so visibly relaxed, he knew her emotional scars, as well as the physical injuries, had begun to heal.

"Then Garrett tried to . . . oh, hello, Son," Edith said, noticing him for the first time.

Madeleine glanced up. As their eyes met, she burst out laughing.

Garrett frowned playfully. "What's so amusing?" He crossed to her and placed his hand on her shoulder.

Both women looked at each other and erupted into giggles. Edith finished her work by tying a ribbon of midnight blue on the end of Madeleine's braid.

"I'll tell you more later," his mother said mysteriously and left the room.

Garrett began kneading Madeleine's shoulders. She closed her eyes and sighed. "That feels wonderful. Don't ever stop."

"I'll keep on. As long as you tell me what I missed."

She opened her eyes. "Your mother was telling me the most amusing stories about you and Ashby." A smile tugged at the corners of her mouth. "I can't wait to tease you both."

His fingers slid up her neck. "I'm afraid I can't allow you to speak with Ash anymore."

She twisted around to look at him. "Why not?"

He stroked her neck as he said, "With all the lecherous looks he was giving you? I doubt I'll trust him to be within twenty paces of you ever again."

She cupped his face and gave him a light kiss. "You are so silly, Garrett. I should—"

"Kiss you again," he replied. He leaned down for a hard, fast kiss. He smiled at her as they parted.

"Now I'm fortified for whatever occurs." He

squeezed her hand. "I must take care of the business at hand, though. Ash is awaiting word from me. I need to see him but a moment and then I will return to you."

"Let me accompany you," she pleaded.

In answer, he put an arm about her waist and led her to the great hall, happy she didn't want to be parted from him for even a short length of time.

The evening meal was being cleared as they entered. Servants scurried along, clacking empty tankards and returning the trestle tables back against the walls. Many moved close to the hearth fire, which crackled and danced. Several called out greetings as they entered.

Cook rushed over to them. "Was the pheasant pleasing, my lord?"

"It surpassed your usual standard, Cook."

She beamed with pleasure. "Would it be possible for Madeleine to grace us with a song?"

Garrett spoke for her. "Tomorrow. Madeleine is still weary from our journey home."

Madeleine nodded at the woman. "I promise that the first song will be for you, Cook."

Cook chuckled, rubbing her gnarled hands together. "Can't wait to tell that stinking Coster. He thought the first song 'twould be for him. Hmmph!" She waddled off in triumph.

"Oh, dear," Madeleine said. "I hope I haven't caused any problems."

Ashby approached and bowed low to Madeleine. He took her hand, brushing a kiss lightly across her knuckles.

"If you're interested in keeping your hand attached to your wrist, Ash, I'd suggest you release Madeleine's."

Ashby's eyes lit with mischief. He gave Madeleine's hand a squeeze before letting it go. "If I must," he said, then quipped, "I have become rather attached to it." Then his expression grew serious. "Barth has finished his meal. He's over in the corner playing dice."

Garrett glanced casually in that direction. "I don't want this turned into a public spectacle. Give me a few minutes and then tell him he's to come to the solar. Have a guard of six waiting outside the hall to escort him. Mayhap he'll have plenty to think of on his way to see us."

He led Madeleine back up the stairs. He took her warm hand in his cold one. She pressed it reassuringly and he squeezed hers in return, drawing strength from her calm.

They entered the solar. The fire's warmth enveloped the room, its shadows dancing along the wall.

He seated Madeleine on a stool and took the chair next to it. "I know you want to be here but this will be an ugly matter we address. I'll not play gentleman to this cur."

"As long as we find the truth, Garrett. That's

what we must come away with."

"We shall," he said with determination.

THEY WAITED IN silence until Madeleine heard footsteps in the distance. She tensed in anticipation as the noise of booted feet grew closer. A heavy knock sounded at the door. Garrett did not respond to it immediately. She looked at him as he stared at the door, his jaw clenched. Her own heart raced as he finally called, "Enter."

Barth was brought in, led by Ashby and surrounded by the six guards. All were armed with swords by their sides. Next to their height and width, the serf seemed dwarfed.

Madeleine instantly recognized Barth from the jeweler's description of him. She did not recall ever having seen the man during her time at Stanbury but he was memorable. His thick hair and beard were bright red. That, along with the massive patch he wore over his right eye, would make him stand apart in a crowd. Edith had told Madeleine that years ago Barth had been kicked in the face by a horse and lost the eye.

She remembered how Evan had complained about Barth's short temper when he'd worked in the stables briefly before he left Stanbury. Evan, with his sunny nature and love for life, had nothing good to say about the stableman. Madeleine realized that mayhap children were the best judges of character, after all.

Madeleine glanced over as Edith slipped into the room and took a seat near the window. Garrett signaled the men and they moved a few steps away from their prisoner. Ashby went to stand close to Edith.

Now that the knights had moved aside, Madeleine had a better view and could see the utter terror on Barth's face. He was not a large man, shorter than she was, but he seemed to shrink within himself with each passing moment, thanks to Garrett's silence.

Madeleine gained a new respect for Garrett as she watched his control. She realized how eager he was to find out what this man knew and yet he sat calmly, leisurely studying his servant. He leaned an elbow upon the arm of his chair, his chin resting atop his fist as he inspected the man before him.

Barth wiggled and squirmed under such scrutiny, but Garrett's gaze was unrelenting.

Suddenly, Garrett asked, "Do you know why you were brought here, Barth?" His voice was low, but no one present had trouble hearing what he said.

Barth licked his lips nervously. His eyes flicked about the room before he met Garrett's penetrating gaze. "No, my lord." He attempted a casual air but his voice wavered slightly. "Can't say I do."

"No?" Garrett shifted in his seat and ran a hand through his dark hair. "I thought you might have some idea."

Barth started to answer but no sound came out. He cleared his throat noisily and tugged at the collar of his tunic. Finally, he answered, "No, my lord. Haven't got a clue."

Madeleine saw that the stable hand's legs began to tremble. His lips quivered as he tried to form his words. "Well, it could have to do with, and I'm not saying I'm at fault, but it could be the drinking."

Garrett looked almost amused. "The drinking?" he questioned innocently.

"Well, my lord, I know you warned me about it but every now and then I do like to take a nip." He paused a moment and then nodded furiously. "Yes, I do believe I'm here about my drinking."

"No."

The one word was all Garrett uttered. He sat motionless in his chair.

Barth began fidgeting again. He scratched his head and then a surprised look appeared upon his face. "Oh, of course. I know now. You want to talk to me about the fight."

"Fight?" Again, Madeleine thought Garrett look almost bored as he sat facing Barth.

"Not the fight?" Barth asked weakly.

"You mean the fight with John? The one where you fought dirty and almost blinded him in one eye?" Garrett shook his head. "No, I don't think that's it either."

Barth's face began to reflect his rising panic and flushed dark red above his beard. Nervously, he bit a nail, then another, as the room remained silent. He finally realized what he was doing and quickly lowered his hand from his mouth. He swallowed hard and then muttered, "Must be about the girl." His eyes were downcast and his shoulders slumped.

Garrett sat forward, his elbows propped on his knees, his hands clasped together. "I know about no girl, Barth."

Barth winced.

"Do you want to tell me about this girl? Who is she? What do I need to hear about the matter?"

Barth blurted out, "'Tis Sarah. She's going to have a babe and she says it's mine!" He shook his head back and forth vigorously. "But it cannot be, my lord."

Garrett sighed. "Why would I have expected better from you, Barth?"

The man trembled in both legs and hands now. "Oh, I'll do better, my lord. I promise you that. Yes, old Barth will do much better in the future. You can count on me."

Garrett did not mince words. "As I counted

on you to take care of Lady Montayne?"

The sudden switch in subject startled Madeleine, although she had known it would come. As for Barth, his previously flushed face whitened immediately. He tried to speak but his words didn't form beyond a wheeze.

"What can you tell me about Lady Montayne's disappearance four years ago, Barth?" When the serf didn't answer, he snapped, "I want the truth. Now. *All of it.*"

As he spoke, Garrett stood and moved closer to the bearded man. He leisurely reached into his purse and removed Lynnette's necklace. He dangled it in front of him, letting it rock back and forth as a pendulum, just inches from the serf's face.

"No," Barth whispered. "It cannot be." He turned to run but the guards surrounded him, leaving his only way of escape through Garrett. He shrank back and turned in circles, trapped as a rat by an army of large cats.

Garrett's features were now hard as stone. "I want answers. *Truthful* answers."

The servant fell to his knees. "You're a hard man, my lord. You expect too much of us. 'Twas fear that kept me from coming to you. Everyone around Stanbury way knows how . . ." His voice trailed off.

"Knows what, Barth?" Garrett glared at Barth in anger, his fists balled at his sides. "That I kept you on, despite your drinking and carelessness, because of your family? Or that I demand things be done right? A fair day's work for a fair day's wage?"

"Fair?" Barth hissed. "You're as wicked as Satan Himself. You should suffer as long and hard as I have."

Garrett remained remarkably cool. Only his eyes were ablaze. As Barth's eyes met his master's, Madeleine saw the dawning moment of defeat in them.

Silence blanketed the room. All that could be heard was Barth's labored breathing. At last he blurted out, "I might as well tell you the truth. Though it weren't my fault at all, no, not at all. It was an accident."

Garrett moved away.

Barth seemed to relax a bit with the distance Garrett placed between them. He rubbed his one good eye and sighed.

"Tell me about the day Lady Montayne disappeared," Garrett demanded calmly.

"I'd been having a nip behind the barn, just to tide me over, when Lady Montayne came for her horse." He squinted, as if he could see it in his mind's eye. "'Twas the new one, the filly with the temper. She was a bit hard for the countess to handle but Lady Montayne was determined to ride her."

"I remember. Go on."

"She was in such a hurry. She always was. Rushing me here and there, distracting me with all sorts of foolish questions. How's a man to concentrate with all that female prattling going on? Can't do my work properly at all, if'n you know what I mean."

A spasm of coughs interrupted Barth's tale for a minute. When he recovered he said, "Then our reeve, Stephen, showed up, hurrying me. Said he had important things to do and would I please get the saddles on? He didn't have time to be riding around with Lady Montayne anyhow." Barth cleared his throat with a miserable sound. "Nobody appreciates me. They never did. Not Mrs. Barth, not my little ones, not no one. At least until that day. Then our reeve done owe me. He appreciated me for all my help in the matter."

Madeleine shuddered involuntarily. She had never liked Stephen. He'd seemed efficient in his work but she had never forgotten the pleasure he'd taken talking about the typhus running rampant through London when he'd returned from one of his trips there.

Barth scanned his audience, seemingly pleased he had all their attention now. "Stephen told me when they began to ride hard, the girth suddenly came undone. If'n she just hadn't rushed me, I could've saddled the horse properly. But, no, my lady fell from the horse when the saddle did. The horse spooked and trampled her. Crushed her skull."

The silent horror on the faces of those present was deafening. All had been led to believe that Lynnette had run away with some secret lover—when all along, Stanbury's reeve had been present at her death. He'd lied to Garrett all these years, forcing his liege lord into limbo.

She observed the tension surge through Garrett from head to toe. Madeleine wanted to call a halt to this sordid tale but she knew Garrett must hear it to the end before he could ever make peace with it.

Barth continued, more unsure of himself now as he took in the cold looks from those gathered in the solar.

"Stephen came and got me to help him. The countess was all broken and crumpled on the ground. He told me it was all my fault."

Barth's shoulders heaved and he began to weep. "We took her jewels and buried her in the forest."

He raised his head toward Garrett, his eyes glassy and unfocused. In a pleading tone, he said, "We knew your temper, Lord Montayne. You're Ryker's son, after all. We knew we'd both be blamed. That it'd be the end of us both."

He wiped his nose with his sleeve. "Stephen had me take my lady's horse and ride it to London. I was to sell it there and the jewels, too.

He said he'd cover for me. That I wasn't to worry about being missed. He said he'd fix things for us both."

Barth smiled satisfactorily. "He were right. Nobody suspected a thing at all." His mouth hung in a surly pose. "Until now."

"Do you remember where the grave is?" Garrett's voice rang hollowly in the room.

Barth nodded wearily.

Garrett motioned his men-at-arms. Once again they surrounded Barth, whose pitiful sobs filled the room.

"Ash? Take three men and find Stephen. We'll meet up in the outer bailey."

He paused a moment and then said quietly, "I must see the grave. I must see it for myself."

CHAPTER TWENTY-SIX

T HE HOUR GREW late. Much of the household had bedded down. Madeleine had comforted Edith as best as she could before the noblewoman excused herself and went to her room.

Madeleine left the solar and went downstairs, scanning the great hall for one of the guards that had accompanied Garrett.

Ashby came up quietly and took her elbow. He wore a weary expression across his usually jovial face.

"Where's Garrett?" she whispered as he drew her away from the hall and those sleeping.

He led her outside, where the air was briskly blowing. A full moon hung low in the sky, its golden tones bathing the inner bailey in soft light.

"Did you find Lynnette's grave?"

Ashby nodded. "Yes. It was just as Barth had described. Stephen put up quite a struggle and tried to break and run when we reached the site. Garrett sent him directly to the dungeon, even before we began to dig." He shrugged. "Barth was quite helpful. Maybe he thought Garrett would go more easily on him if he cooperated."

"What will Garrett do with them?"

"I wish I knew." He scanned the sky as if he could find the answers painted across the stars. "He's been so angry, so bitter, for so long. Now, it seems all the fight's gone out of him."

"Where is he, Ashby? I felt sure he'd come back to me."

He frowned. "I don't know. He supervised as the men dug up Lynnette's body. He had her wrapped in linens and brought back inside the gates. He mentioned visiting with the priest. He wants a memorial mass first thing tomorrow for her soul." Ashby wiped his hand across his brow, drawing her attention to the fatigue lines edging his eyes and mouth. "I thought after that he would come to you." He took her hand. "You have done him a world of good, Madeleine. The change in him is so great. If he didn't have you right now, I don't know how he'd make it through these next few days." He brushed his lips against her brow in a brotherly gesture. "Help him, Madeleine. Keep him sane." He turned to go back inside. "Coming?"

Madeleine shook her head. "No. I'll sit here on the steps and think a bit." She waited for

Ashby to depart. She now knew where Garrett was and intended to go to him.

She wrapped her arms around her for warmth, regretting that she hadn't thought to bring a cloak with her. The wind picked up as she made her way across the meadow, awash in bright moonlight. The field felt so strange now, empty of the stalls and tents that the mummer's troupe had brought. Summer solstice seemed so long ago.

She picked up her pace as best she could and crossed the length of the grassland. As she approached their rock, she saw Garrett's silhouette in the moonlight.

He must have sensed her presence because he lifted his head and met her gaze. Even in the dim light, she could tell his face was ravaged with grief.

Wordlessly, he slid from the rock's surface and met her, enveloping her in the warmth of his arms. He held her close for many minutes, no words necessary between them.

At last, he relaxed his embrace and cocked his head to one side and with a weary smile asked, "Will you never learn to put on a cloak?"

She half-laughed, half-sobbed. "I seem to have a knack of running into men with cloaks to spare."

Garrett lifted her upon the rock and climbed up beside her, opening his cloak and wrapping the comforting fabric around them both. He smelled of the outdoors, the woods, the cold, and that very masculine scent she'd come to love. She felt utterly safe within his arms.

They stared over the empty field, neither breaking the silence that surrounded them.

"You know," he finally said, "Lynnette was a gentle soul. Always kind to the servants. Always willing to please everyone." His mouth tightened. "She didn't deserve to die that way and lie in an unmarked grave all this time." He paused. "I'm consumed with guilt, having thought the worst of her all these years."

"I'm sorry, Garrett." She pressed his hand. "You know none of this was your fault." Madeleine wiped the single tear trailing down his cheek. "You've found her now. She'll be buried properly. That's got to be of some comfort."

"Yes." He sighed. "I must tell Lyssa. Mayhap you can help me with that. I want everyone at Stanbury to attend the mass tomorrow. We'll bury Lynnette in the family plot afterward."

"What of Barth? Stephen?"

"It's out of my hands." He shook his head. "The royal circuit court will decide their fates. They'll be held in the dungeon until the court comes around the end of next month." Garrett sighed in the darkness. "Thank God I have you, my love."

Madeleine snuggled close to him, his warmth

like a siren's call to her body.

He pressed his lips to hers tenderly. "I may have fallen in love with you at this very spot," he told her. "I remember that kiss as if it were yesterday."

She shivered. She had wanted him that night more than anything—but she'd run away instead. Taking his hand in hers, she pressed a kiss to each finger. "I doubt I'll run from you this time, my lord. You see, I love you with all my heart."

Garrett gazed deeply into her eyes. Even with the ache for Lynnette's passing in his heart, Madeleine had brought him complete happiness for the first time in his life.

"Before you, sweetheart, I was empty, but your music filled my soul with love. You are the song of my heart."

About the Author

Award-winning and international bestselling author Alexa Aston's historical romances use history as a backdrop to place her characters in extraordinary circumstances, where their intense desire for one another grows into the treasured gift of love.

She is the author of Medieval and Regency romance, including *The Knights of Honor*, *The King's Cousins*, *The St Clairs*, and *The de Wolfes of Esterley Castle*.

A native Texan, Alexa lives with her husband in a Dallas suburb, where she eats her fair share of dark chocolate and plots out stories while she walks every morning. She enjoys reading, Netflix binge-watching, and can't get enough of *Survivor*, *The Crown*, or *Game of Thrones*.